Uncommon Emotions

Lynn Galli

Outskirts Press, Inc.
Denver, Colorado

Outskirts Press, Inc.
http://www.outskirtspress.com

ISBN: 978-1-4327-1809-1

Outskirts Press and the "OP" logo are trademarks belonging to Outskirts Press, Inc.

PRINTED IN THE UNITED STATES OF AMERICA

Chapter 1

Everyone hates me. It's the nature of the job, but it still doesn't make it any easier. Really, it's only the people in this company that hate me. If I were an IRS agent, then everyone really would hate me. So, by comparison, only a relatively small number of people actually hate me. Not exactly comforting to think about, but it's enough to get me through this unremarkable Wednesday. Nothing extraordinary happens on Wednesdays.

Until you find yourself innocently walking down a hallway and someone reaches out to haul you into a dark supply room where the softest lips imaginable slap a languorous kiss on your mouth. Suddenly, Wednesdays become remarkable.

Since this had never happened to me before, several seconds elapsed before I realized that one, I didn't know the person kissing me; two, I was at work where I don't kiss people; and three, wow, soft, soft, expert lips. And sweet perfume, and silky hair falling over my fingers which had grabbed hold of shoulders to maintain balance. *Yowza, this is a woman! Kissing me, a woman.*

"You're not Raven." A husky voice spoke into the darkness after jerking back from our embrace.

My heart was hammering, and my breath came in gasps. God, that was the best kiss I'd ever had in thirty-seven years. And it happened in a dark supply room at work. On a Wednesday. *From a woman!*

"Oh God, you're definitely not Raven."

"Nope, not Raven," I managed, barely.

"I'm so sorry. I saw her walking down the hall, and I thought I timed it right. Forgive me." Her hands clamped down on my shoulders in urgency. One lifted off and flicked the light switch for the room. Blinding brightness forced my sensitive eyes to blink and shy away from the light. "Holy—! You're, you're, oh God! I didn't mean it, honest, I'm sorry. I didn't even see you. God, this is awkward. Are you going to fire me?"

Her fear brought my racing heartbeat to a screeching halt, reminding me where I was and what I'd been doing before I got yanked into a room and kissed senseless. "No," I started, wishing I could remember her name. I'd only been here three weeks, and there were too many people on staff to remember everyone's name. Long blond hair, washed out blue eyes, upturned nose, freckles even, but damn those still plump lips kept drawing my gaze. "I'd suggest you stop abducting innocents as they're walking down the hallway at work, though. In general that's not a good thing, but at work, HR would have a conniption."

"I'm really sorry, Ms. Simonini, I didn't—"

"Joslyn," I corrected her. After all, we'd been better acquainted just moments ago. "Let's forget it. I'm due in the CEO's office in two minutes, and you've got work to

do, I'm sure. Work that doesn't involve kidnapping, right?"
She laughed with what seemed like a lot of relief. I couldn't blame her. I did have the authority to fire her and telling human resources would probably necessitate me firing her. But it was an innocent mistake, a pulse pounding, toe curling kiss—I mean, mistake!

"Yes, and I'm sorry for the mix up. I won't try anything like that again."

"Since I'd like to keep the entire HR staff from having a collective heart attack, I think that's a wise decision."

She chuckled again, much easier this time, and her stare became more penetrating. I'd faced this stare in countless business meetings and knew she was trying to figure out what I was thinking. Since I was so off kilter about the whole capture and kiss thing, I decided to flee as quickly as possible. A hand on my forearm stopped my escape. "Um, Joslyn, if you're meeting with the CEO..." She turned me back to face her. My heart started to pound harder than after an hour doing cardio at the gym as I watched her hand float toward my face. "You're a little smudged." A thumb swiped across my lower lip, igniting the lingering sensation of tingles as she took off the last traces of our kiss.

Holy cow! I'd kissed a woman. A very pretty woman, but a woman. I'm hip, I could do this, no big deal, right? So, why did it feel like Wednesdays were suddenly my favorite day and maybe not everyone hates me?

In a daze, I made my way to the CEO's office. I existed by compartmentalizing my brain. Work is work, home is home, friends are friends, lovers are virtually nonexistent, but still, lovers are not at work. Kissing isn't done at work. Kissing a woman for someone who'd never kissed a woman really isn't done at work.

"Ms. Simonini?" The CEO's admin jerked me out of my haze. "Mr. Paul is ready for you."

"Thanks." I smiled, feeling the last of the tingles stop with the stretch of my lips.

"Joslyn, tell me you have good news?" Mr. Paul stood from his desk and gestured me inside. Balding, thin, elderly bordering on archaic, pale skin dappled with brown age spots clung to his person as he settled onto the edge of his desk far too close to my chair for my taste.

"I haven't finished all the evaluations, Mr. Paul."

"Archie," he barked because he was used to barking orders.

"Of course, Archie. I've yet to meet with finance and sales. It's still early to make any recommendations."

"I'm poised to fire everyone if you tell me. Ungrateful souls. No offense, Joslyn, but people of your generation have no work ethic. Present company excluded, of course."

"Of course," I agreed because he wouldn't give me any other choice. Plus, he was paying my fee.

"Don't know why you're different, young lady, but I know we're lucky to have you help us out with this unpleasantness."

Unpleasantness? As if his company's near bankrupt status was a minor skirmish over the last piece of pizza at a company luncheon. "It's what I do, sir." And have been doing for seven years. As a turnaround specialist, I was revered by CEOs but abhorred by the company masses because my recommendations often caused the demise of their positions. Not exactly my recommendations, more like the CEO's interpretation of my recommendations. I had a feeling that was how it would go here as well. Just once I'd like to find a company that was willing to put my recommendations to good use for the benefit of the whole company, not just its bottom line.

"Are you getting cooperation from everyone?"

His question brought back the twinge I'd felt in my shoulder as I was yanked into that supply room. The twinge had been replaced immediately by shooting surges of excitement as lips covered mine. "Yes, everyone's being very accommodating. I'm with finance after lunch."

"Fantastic. You let me know if you need me to knock some heads around."

Trying to keep my eyes from bugging out at his violent suggestion, I gave a tight-lipped smile. "That won't be necessary, I'm sure." I took leave before he got mired in more clichés.

Lunch, the first one I'd taken since arriving at this company, awaited me. I ignored the undisguised glares I received as I made my way to the elevator. If I did my job correctly, at least some of these people would lose theirs, and they knew it. Add to that the fact that I start every consultation by working undercover in one of the departments and they feel I've not only betrayed their trust but also deserved to die. Yep, everyone hates me. Give that woman in the supply room a few minutes and even she'll start hating me again.

"Hey, baby." A deep voice sounded from behind me as I stood in line at the café in the building's lobby. Arms swung me around and forceful lips kissed me sloppily. I broke the contact immediately, never one for public displays of affection and certainly not at my place of business. What was it with the kissing today? Were Wednesdays some official kissing holiday or something?

"Don't call me baby," I stated sternly.

Chase McCovey, my lunch date, looked affronted in his own smug way. He'd been asking me to lunch every day since I'd taken this assignment so close to his office. I knew I'd have to give in at least once, but I didn't think he'd try to make a claim on me at my client's home base. "Sorry, snookums, I know you hate that." He grinned, showing enough teeth to make me wonder if he had werewolves in his family tree. His thick blond hair flopped bangs onto his forehead as his head tipped toward me again.

I pressed my palms against his chest to keep him in place. "Don't call me that either." I glanced around the café, praying that no one from work would be witness to this. No such luck, I recognized a dozen people from my last department meeting. At least they had the class to snap their heads around when I looked in their direction.

"Jeez, bad day, I guess," Chase muttered and took my spot in line, ordering first.

I shook my head at his increasingly annoying behavior but turned away to hide the eye roll. The blonde from the supply room was staring unabashedly at me and gave a quick grin when she caught my eye roll. Her raised eyebrows indicated she'd figured out what she wanted to know in that moment I'd tried to escape the room. Great. So much for professional detachment.

God, her kiss. Now that was how you kissed someone. Not possessively, sloppily, with no effort or forethought. Raven, whoever she may be, was damn lucky.

Chapter 2

*T*ablet PC in hand, I wandered through the finance division's maze of cubicles. Not quite one o'clock, so a lot of them were empty, thankfully. Normally, the hate-filled stares wouldn't faze me, but I wasn't feeling completely myself quite yet.

The door to the CFO's office was open, but no one occupied the admin's desk. I didn't want to intrude, yet I didn't want to be late either. Through the opening, I caught a glimpse of a trim, dark haired woman with her back turned. Her well-defined arms easily slipped two heavy binders from the top shelf of a bookcase. She was wearing a sleeveless shell in deep burgundy and black slacks that looked beyond tailored, almost sewn especially for her.

I knocked on the open door, causing her to flinch and whirl toward me. Jet black hair flipped away from her oval face and elegant neck in a chic trend that, if I had to guess, happened naturally for her. "I didn't mean to startle you," I said, catching what looked like an appraising glance as she noticed me in the doorway.

"Kelly usually makes a little noise when she's on her way in. You, on the other hand, downright stealthy." She blessed me with a genuine smile, the first I'd seen since revealing my true purpose for being at this company. The smile enlivened her face. Before it had been serious and focused; now it was graceful and engaging. So caught up in not having someone immediately scowl at me, I barely noticed that my heartbeat sped up a couple of cranks. I attributed it to the fact that my professionalism was suffering today, what with being surprise attacked by a stranger and, later, practically molested by my not-so-significant other at lunch.

"Special training," I replied easily. It was nice to have a conversation that didn't start with the words: *you're not going to fire me, are you?*

"Really? I don't remember a class like that at my school." She set the binders on her desk and reached over to grab her suit jacket from the back of her chair.

I watched those enviable arms disappear into the sleeves before she faced me again. "Special school."

She smiled at my joke, allowing me a peek at her perfect teeth. "Ms. Simonini?"

"Ms. Malvolio?"

"Coupla Italians, no?" A glint showed in her whiskey brown eyes. The color perfectly complimented her subtle olive skin tone, a shade lighter than my own.

"Looks like. It's nice to meet you." I moved forward to shake her hand.

"And you as well. I hope everyone's been treating you kindly during your time with us." It was issued as a statement, but her expression told me she was asking a question.

"Yes, thank you." They hadn't been, but no one else

needed to know that.

A long glance from her told me she didn't quite believe me, but she pulled out a chair at the table to her left and gestured for me to sit. The first of the chief officers to do so. Most of them used their desk and deep executive chairs to exert the aura of power over their guests. If I had to see another executive lean back and lace his fingers behind his head, I was going to scream or put a can of deodorant in their offices so I wouldn't be distracted by the sweat stains.

"What was it like working for my cousin?" Her question shocked me into abandoning the task of booting up my laptop.

"Your cousin?"

"Robert." A slow grin inched across her face.

Heat touched my cheeks. I'd chosen to work in his department when I first started with this consultation. Being part of the staff was the best way to get an inside glimpse of any corporation. If you walked in as a turnaround specialist, everyone kisses your ass but wants to stab you as you walk past. Things hadn't gone well in Robert's department. In fact, in the two weeks I'd worked there, I was certain most of the company's woes were stacked up inside that division.

"You're a member of the family?" I shouldn't find that surprising seeing as it was a family business. Two of the three Paul brothers acted as CEO and president, and several offspring managed on the chief and directorial levels. "Your last name," I started then wised up quickly and shook off my stupid assumption. "Oh, of course."

Her eyebrows shot up into stylish bangs. "Of course?"

"I'm a little slow. I forgot that most women change their names when they get married." I glanced down at her ring finger, surprised to find it bare. Great, she was probably divorced and I'd just made an insensitive remark. What a perfect way to warm up to someone. Batting a thousand for my Wednesday so far.

A soft chuckled sounded, interrupting my self-condemnation. "Actually, I took my mother's unmarried name when I joined the company. I didn't want anyone thinking I was getting special treatment because of a relation. Of course, everyone now knows the connection, but it served my purpose for over a year. Now, I won't change it back." The flash of grin held a wicked tint to it this time, daring me to delve further into her story.

"Well, you're the CFO, so clearly it's worked out."

She cocked her head. "What makes you think I wasn't given this position right off the bat?"

"I learned that in my special school, too," I joked. Truthfully, I was a research fiend. Career paths of executives and managing directors always told me a lot about what I'd expect to find prior to taking an assignment, especially in a family business. Often, that was the root of the company's problems.

Ms. Malvolio had a MBA, spent several years at two other firms before joining Paul Industries, and worked her way up from financial analyst in the firm. She'd earned her position, working harder than all of the other directors, family relation or not. Every other Paul had started out as an assistant chief first.

She laughed at my deflection. "You're good at that, and you never answered my question about Robert."

I joined her laughter. It felt good to ease up on my defenses in what I'd usually consider a guarded environment. "He has an interesting technique for motivation." I grasped for the only thing I could construe as positive about her cousin's management style.

That wicked grin flared broadly on her face this time. "Yes, it's very used car lot, wouldn't you agree?" Then, as if she just realized who her audience was, the grin dropped out of her expression, and she straightened up in her seat. "I mean, it seems to work over there, just not something I'd try with my division."

I resisted the urge to squeeze her forearm in comfort. I wouldn't give this kind of conversation weight under any circumstance, especially after we'd been joking around. "It serves him well, yes," I agreed, easing the tension a bit. "If I'd stayed another week, though, I'm sure I would have been fired. I don't function well within the accolades-on-the-board operation style. Just as well, I guess."

She gave a grateful smile then reached for the binders. As she opened them, we heard a heavy sigh and thump outside her door. A short exclamation followed before a voice interrupted us. "Hey, boss, I'm back, just wanted to—oh!"

We turned in unison at the interruption. Only my trained stony façade kept me from blushing when I recognized the owner of the voice. Ms. Supply Room stood in the doorway. Her blush, however, was in full bloom.

"Kelly, have you met Ms. Simonini, yet?"

"Um, ah, er," she hemmed, shifting her weight from one foot to the other.

"We ran into each other earlier today," I cut in, trying not to let the sensation of her lips trace across mine again. "Nice to see you again, Kelly."

"Same here." She sounded far less confident than the last time she'd spoken to me.

"We're just getting started, but if you could make sure that Sara adjusts those balance sheets before this afternoon's meeting, I'd appreciate it."

"Sure thing," she accepted the order easily. Unlike with several of the other chief officers and their AAs, clearly no tension existed between these two. "You remember I'm leaving early today, right? Just say the word and I'll be glad to postpone the appointment if you need me."

"Nice try, Kel. You've been putting off this root canal for months. The pain is killing you. Get in there and get it over with, okay?"

Kelly flicked her gaze at me then pinned an awe-inspired glance at her boss. "Thanks, Raven, I will."

Raven? No, no, no! The one person I could relate to in this company; the one person I was going to have to spend a ton of time with pouring over financials; the one person who seemed to treat me as anything other than a leper was having an affair with her administrative assistant? So not right, and if their employee manual was as good as it should be, she might have to be my first recommended termination. Crap, Wednesdays blow.

Chapter 3

"What?" The black haired temptress asked with wide innocent eyes.

I shook my head of the thoughts and tried to focus on the meeting. Maybe Kelly'd been talking about a different Raven. Not that I've ever met anyone with that name before, nor did I believe it was likely that, even if it was a common name, two would be working for this company. I realized I'd been staring and silent for longer than would be polite. "Ah, that's a nice name. The contact list only shows first initials. It goes well with your chosen last name."

A faint pink spotted the crest of her cheekbones. "Thank you."

I wondered how long I could keep from saying something to her. How disappointing that she'd been this careless with her position. For a while there, I thought she might be a confidante; someone who could help me get her uncle to utilize my recommendations to their fullest advantage. Instead, I was trying to keep from being embarrassed for her.

"Is something bothering you?" she asked just as innocently.

Yes. How can you be so reckless when you seem so together? I wanted to shout in judgment. "Not at all." My business training managed to beat my inner voice into submission. "I'm Joslyn, by the way."

She smiled and nodded her head. "Should we get to work, Joslyn?"

"Good idea, Raven." Anything to keep from imagining an encounter between Kelly and Raven in a darkened supply room.

An hour later, she closed her binders and I shut down my computer. The meeting had been the most productive and informative of all the others combined. Just as I suspected it would be, but her lack of judgment with her subordinate still rankled my mind. Too bad. Not that I could blame Kelly. Raven was hot.

Whoa! Now, that's a new one. I'd never thought of women that way, never imagined how soft their lips would feel, never contemplated how graceful their bodies were or how dexterous their fingers might be. For an hour, in between concentrating on the various financials, I couldn't stop these thoughts from entering my head. Not about Kelly, who'd surprised me with the kiss, but about Raven, the beguiling creature beside me.

In an effort to get my focus back, I offered politely, "Thank you for your time, Raven."

"You're welcome, Joslyn. I know you're going to be able to help us turn things around."

"That's my assignment."

She grinned again as I brushed off her unnecessary gratitude. "Well, I'm at your service while you're here."

"You may live to regret that offer; I usually need to

spend the most time in finance." I stood to leave and extended my hand for a parting handshake. She gripped it with the perfect amount of pressure. Obviously, her business school had taught their students how to properly shake hands as mine had. I'd always thought it was a waste of class time until I went out into the corporate world and discovered just how many people lacked that simple skill. I drew back reluctantly and exited with a goodbye.

"Um, thanks," a soft voice called out from my left. I glanced over and saw Kelly standing by the file cabinets next to her desk. "For not saying anything about earlier."

"It's forgotten, a case of mistaken identity." I brushed a hand through the air, not that I believed what I said.

"That doesn't make it any less embarrassing."

"Well, as long as you can refrain from seizing others from the hallways, we'll overlook this one time."

"Thanks, Joslyn, and I'm sorry, again. Tell your boyfriend it was an honest mistake."

My mouth popped open at the mention of Chase. I wanted to protest the classification as my boyfriend, but that would bring something personal into my client's workplace. Very unprofessional. "Don't worry about it." I nodded brusquely before I left.

On to the meeting I'd been dreading for days. Robert's sales department. I hadn't been exaggerating when I said he'd have fired me in another week if I'd really been working for him. A clash of personalities would be a polite description for how we functioned together.

"Hey, Jos," Robert's admin, Zina, called out cheerily. She'd actually liked me, which meant that she hated her boss. After any blowup with Robert, she'd be the first person at my desk offering support or encouragement. I suspected that Robert had afforded her many opportunities to perfect her empathy with his staff.

The brilliant white of her teeth broke through her dark complexion with a bright smile. Even though I'd deceived her for two weeks while working in Robert's department, she didn't hold it against me. "How's things, Zina?"

"Peachy. You ready for your meeting? Boss-man's been griping about it all day."

"Not sure you should be telling me that," I kidded.

"Like you're gonna fire me for it." She stood, towering over my five-four frame at close to six feet and walked me to the door. "Boss, Joslyn's here."

"Christ!" he growled before he looked up to see us both standing in the doorway. I turned my head away from Zina before we both broke into hysterics. This guy was such an idiot.

"Robert." I acted as if I hadn't heard his expletive. Apparently, I wasn't the only one dreading this meeting.

"I don't have much time for this." He couldn't meet my eyes. The straw blond shade to his hair looked darker today, almost as if he hadn't washed it this morning. No doubt his way of flying in the face of this meeting by not caring enough to feign personal hygiene. Other than his unkempt hair, he was quite good looking. Usually, he wore the hair perfectly coiffed, a crisp line an inch above his collar, sideburns trimmed to look like he didn't work on them, and fabricated five o'clock shadow that stayed with him always. The women in his department lusted after him, which is why they let him treat them like dirt.

"We can schedule this for another day if it's more convenient." If my tone got any sweeter, I'd have to check for cavities.

"No, I just can't give you the full hour you requested. You can get whatever you need from Zina."

"Robert," I started in a tone that bordered on condescending, not that he'd recognize it. "I asked for an hour, we scheduled an hour, we're going to take an hour today, or we'll take an hour some other day. I'll already be working with Zina on everything else, but there are some things that only you know about your department, wouldn't you agree?"

He looked momentarily stunned by my apparent compliment, which I would label more as manipulation. "Uhh, yeah, I guess."

"Great, let's start with your budget."

He shot out of his chair. "Oh, no you don't. You're not taking a damn thing from my budget."

"May we sit, please?" Why was it necessary to pull teeth during these meetings? As a member of the family, he should be invested in pulling this business back from the brink. Instead, his pride and wounded ego fought me every step of the way. "I merely want to review your budget, particularly your travel budget. Every department's budget is being examined.

"But mine's the most important." Spoken like a true sales schmuck.

"I'm sure everyone feels that way."

"They can feel it all they want, but this company doesn't exist without sales, and that's my department."

"Some might say that you wouldn't have anything to sell without the products and services provided by everyone else in the company."

"That's bull."

Here we go again, degrading ourselves with a schoolyard back and forth I-know-you-are-but-what-am-I argument. "That's neither here nor there. I'm simply stating that everyone's budget needs to be reviewed, and yours is the most expensive."

"Obviously," he shot back.

I let his tone slide right off my back. You couldn't win by being defensive with guys like this. "Are you aware that more than half of your budgeted travel dollars are spent on lunches and dinners for your own staff, not on wooing buyers?"

"Hey, they need to eat, too."

"Not on the company's dime, they don't. I'm going to recommend instituting a pier diem allowance for travel expenses and a distance requirement before per diem kicks in."

"Wait a minute, you can't do that." Robert was the worst offender of the bunch, so his protest didn't come as a surprise.

"It's already written up." I used a tone that let him know he could whine all he wanted to no avail. "How much of your travel budget is spent on your own staff?"

"Umm, I don't think we have that kind of detail."

"Can you give me a guestimate?"

"You said half already, so half," he answered like I was an idiot.

"In dollars, Robert, any idea?" I knew he didn't, but I didn't like his attitude and felt like needling him. Call me petty, but I'd disliked working for this guy, and I didn't see anything wrong with giving him a taste of how insignificant he'd made me and several others on his staff feel. "Zina?" I called out through the open doorway.

She popped her head inside and raised her eyebrows. "What's up?"

"How much does this department spend on its travel expenses each year?"

"$850,000," she replied without hesitation.

"How much of that is consumed by the salespeople on their own?"

"About 520 K." Again, without any hesitation which is something I'd noticed from the first moment I started working here. His AA was more qualified and more adept at running this department than he was, and I wanted him to know it.

"How much by the local reps? And of that, what percent would you say is spent on entertaining the client?"

"125 and we budget thirty percent for entertainment, but the local reps run closer to twenty."

"Thank you, Zina." She flashed a quick grin before returning to her desk. "That's roughly 100 grand that can be shaved from the expenses for the local reps, and with per diem limits, your overall budget can easily be slashed by thirty-five percent."

"Dad won't go for that."

"Mr. Paul will take my recommendations and speak with each department head about those he wants to implement. Since this one has already been approved by finance, I believe it will be instituted first."

His eyes narrowed. "What do you mean, it's already been approved by finance? Who the hell in finance would stab me in the back?"

"It's not stabbing you in the back, Robert." I suppressed a sigh. "It's good business sense. Why should the people who work in every other department have to bring or pay for their lunches and dinners, when you and your staff get to charge it to the company under the guise of a sales call?"

"We have to eat on the road," he whined.

"Everyone who works here is away from their homes, and they don't get their meals reimbursed. Your company is operating at a one point six million dollar loss. We have to cut costs significantly. This is one of the easier measures that doesn't involve reduction in work force."

"Dad and Raven will back me up on this. I don't know who you spoke with over in finance about these figures, but it's crap."

"I met with Ms. Malvolio earlier, and she agreed with me. I'll present this to Mr. Paul when I give my executive summary."

"Goddammit!" he roared at me again. "I knew you were going to be trouble the second my dad recommended you for my department. You were totally worthless while you were here, and now you're talking about slapping handcuffs on my staff because you hate me."

"I don't hate you," I tried to assure him. "I have a difference of opinion about your management style, but you've had some success. With a few controls, your department could be more efficient and productive."

"Whatever." His expression closed off completely, a sign that he wouldn't be listening to anything else I had to say, rendering this meeting over.

"We're done." I felt the tension in my shoulders ease as soon as I let us both off the hook. "I'll get what I need from Zina and your staff. If you like, I can bullet point my recommendations for you prior to giving them to your father?"

"Yeah, do that!" he barked very much like his dad.

When I passed by Zina's desk she looked up with an encouraging smile. "Let me guess, it didn't go well?"

I laughed at her assessment. "Not really. Thanks for playing along, though."

"Sure, hey, heard you met with Raven earlier. How'd that go? Isn't she great?"

I cocked my head at her fond tone. Didn't take a genius to realize she respected Raven. "She was very helpful."

A wide smile broke up that dark chocolate skin tone again. "I knew you'd like her." She leaned in to whisper, "She's nothing like the rest of her family."

"Is that so?" I gave an innocent look like I didn't know what she was talking about, but one moment in Raven's presence, and I knew she was nothing like all these other Pauls.

"Shut up, you saw it, too. She'll be your best resource, Jos. If you need anything from me, just ask. Oh, and you're taking my beautiful black self to lunch soon."

"Am I?" I laughed.

"Hell yes. I was the only one nice to your sales challenged ass while you were here. I deserve a lunch." This was why I liked her so much. She'd made me feel welcome while I was working in the department, and she still made me feel welcome when nearly everyone else wanted to shoot poisonous darts into my neck as I wandered the corridors.

"Hey, I brought in some clients, you'll recall."

"Yeah." She eyed me suspiciously. "I've been wondering how you joined us pretending to be a salesperson yet managed to land the two largest clients we now have."

"I have my ways." Or former clients that would buy anything I told them to buy. I waved in parting. The clock on her desk told me that only a half hour remained on this rollercoaster of a Wednesday. At this point, I didn't know if I should consider that a blessing or not.

Chapter 4

Holed up in my little conference room, I thought about putting in earplugs to block out the comments of people walking by the door. If they only knew I wouldn't be recommending significant reductions in workforce, maybe then they'd like me. Although with many of the other changes I'd been planning, probably not.

"Heard things didn't go so smoothly with Robert." A confident voice sounded from the doorway. Raven leaned against the open door, her slender body sheathed in dark blue today. Her confidence had nothing to do with cockiness, more like complete and total comfort with herself.

"You must have a bad informant. The meeting went just as I expected." As a general rule, I never let my clients know when people rattled me, and I certainly wasn't going to insult her by belittling her cousin.

She laughed in soft rhythmic spurts. I wondered if that melodious tone was her knee slapping laugh then found myself hoping it wasn't. It was a nice enough laugh, just completely controlled. "That's the kindest way anyone's ever told me that Robert is difficult."

I waved my hands defensively. "No, I wasn't trying to imply..."

"I know you weren't. I was just giving you a hard time. Don't imagine many people try that with you." She grinned with an eyebrow flutter. She looked even more beautiful today than she had yesterday. Listen to me: beautiful? I get kissed and, all of a sudden, I'm noticing how attractive women are?

"Can't say as many do. And really, Robert was fine."

"You'll let me know if you need help with him? He's used to taking orders from me."

I could almost picture them as kids together, Raven bossing him around with threat of torture probably. That might explain his problem with women. "Family dynamics?"

"We all have them. So, how's it going?" Dropping into a chair facing me, she waited for me to reply rather than steal a peek at the printouts scattered on the table.

"You can tell Archie that he'll have my preliminary summary next week."

The controlled laugh sounded again. "He wanted me to make sure you were getting all the info you needed."

"I am, thanks."

"There you are, Raven." Kelly appeared in the doorway, nodded shyly at me and smiled at her boss.

"Oh, hey, you're in. How's the tooth? Rootless?" Raven grinned up at her.

"Don't remind me. Sanctioned torture, that's what a trip to the dentist is these days."

"Poor thing," Raven sympathized, raising a hand to stroke Kelly's upper back. "It's over now, but I thought you were taking today off, too?"

"I felt a lot better than I thought I would, and I knew you had that meeting with Mr. Paul later."

"Thanks, Kel, you're a dream." Raven squeezed her shoulder, and I bit down on my tongue so I wouldn't scream at how stupid she was being by carrying on with her subordinate.

"I'll get started on everyone's quarterly inserts, but I wanted to see if by some miracle I'd made it into the office before you. I should have known better," she scoffed. "See you soon. Bye, Joslyn."

I tipped my head as she left then caught a quizzical expression on Raven's face. "I know Zina calls you Joslyn, but I thought everyone else was keeping it pretty formal with you."

"Because I'm the evil dragon lady who's going to take their jobs from them?" I couldn't help but tease.

She smiled at my description. "You don't get tired of being the scapegoat for their anger? Why don't they see that it's whoever hired you that's to blame?"

"Because I'm Lizzie Borden, or are they not calling me that here?"

This time her laughter wasn't controlled, and the sound tickled up my spine. "Lizzie Borden? They actually call you that to your face?"

"Oh, no, the phraseology is usually much more colorful by the time I leave a company." I joined her laughter, glad to have someone else make light of what is often a tense situation.

"Creative. Well, I hope no one's giving you that kind of a hard time around here. You've won over Kelly, so you're probably a real softy." The mention of Kelly shuttered my expression. This woman was so smart, and she was screwing her underling who not only directly reported to her but looked about fifteen years her junior. What was she thinking? "I'm sorry. I didn't mean any offense by that," she backtracked, noticing the air had changed between us.

"No offense taken." I decided then that I should give her some notice about what I planned to discuss with Archie at our summary meeting. Just because she was reckless didn't mean I didn't like her. She deserved a little warning before I annihilated her personal life. "I should let you know that I've noticed some pretty big gaps in the employee manual regarding code of conduct. I'll be recommending some changes that will alleviate a number of potential employee lawsuits."

She frowned for a moment, probably trying to figure out how to handle my statement. "Taking away ambiguity in what is considered unacceptable behavior is always a good thing."

Her complete acceptance of my suggestion baffled me. "I think so."

"Did you want me to look at your recommendations; is that why you told me? HR isn't within my purview, but as a manager, I can certainly offer another opinion."

"No." I waved off her offer. Perhaps she thought she'd be immune as a member of the family. "It's just that some of the recommendations might be hard to comply with for certain people."

"Give me an example, and I'll let you know how I think people will receive it." She seemed not at all concerned that any suggestions might affect her.

I could have chosen any of the other recommendations I'd planned to make, but instead I decided to go for it. She'd been decent to me, and I should give her some notice that her ill-advised affair would have to be even more illicit or risk getting fired. "I'm going to recommend instituting a restrictive policy on workplace relationships among coworkers in the same department."

She contemplated that for a moment then nodded her head thoughtfully. "That's a good idea, and it may cut down on the few awkward situations that have transpired in the past. What about if they're in different departments?"

My turn for a frown. Kelly not only worked in her department but directly reported to her. How did she think she could get around that? "Honestly I think it's best to eliminate all fraternization unless they sign a waiver on sexual harassment claims, but that's a draconian principle."

"Draconian? Great word. Just how smart are you?" She pinned me with an inquisitive stare that lit off a blush. "Never mind, you'll probably downplay it. You're right, though, cross departments would be a little hard to push through, but I think you're on the right track with putting something in the manual about office relationships. Always good to cover your bases. I can't believe HR didn't think of it."

I shook my head, still perplexed by her approval. "You mean you're all for limiting office romances?"

"Sure, I think it's a huge distraction, and when it doesn't work out, there's always a lot of awkwardness."

Okay, about a million things didn't add up in her statement. All right, only three. One, she's having an office affair. Two, if Kelly's actions yesterday were typical, clearly it was a distraction. And three, "when it doesn't work out"? Interesting that she thinks office romances were doomed from the start. Maybe Kelly was only a casual fling for her.

Because I wanted to make sure she got it, I clarified, "My recommendation will include all supervisor-subordinate relationships, regardless of department."

Her frown came with an interested lean this time, depositing her face only a foot from mine across the table. "Is there something you're trying to tell me? Some good gossip that I'm missing out on? I don't usually seek out gossip, but you've got me wondering now."

"Well, no. I just meant that if HR accepts this policy change, it might make it a little more difficult for..." I motioned with my hand for her to fill in the blank.

She tilted back in her chair, studying me intently. "For what?"

"Well, for one to have, that is to say, for anyone to conduct a..."

"Now, you've really got me curious. Oh God! It's not one of my relatives, is it? If it is, I don't want to hear about it. I'll let HR deal with it." So, she was going to continue to deny that she was having an affair with her assistant. She probably thought she covered it up well, but wouldn't Kelly have told her that she'd blown their cover? Although, maybe not. If my significant other snatched and kissed some other woman by mistake, I wouldn't want to know about it.

"Probably the best course of action, yes. Sorry I brought it up."

"All right. I'd better get back to my office if I don't want to be on your list of recommendations." She winked at me, actually winked at me, and it looked incredibly sexy when she did it. *Sexy?* Wow, that kiss really did a number on me.

"Wise, yes." I watched her get up and leave, torn between wanting to admire her intuitiveness and scold her for exploiting a gap in HR policy. Either way, the view she offered as she walked away twisted my gut into more confusion than it had endured in probably all of my years.

Chapter 5

*O*pening night. I just loved opening night. It meant three, possibly four months of nonstop thrills whenever the team was in town. Still, opening night was always special. They had another sell out, but dammit, they were playing Los Angeles again. Why did the schedulers always put these two together on opening night? Half our team just got here a week ago; they weren't prepared to play L.A. yet.

As I made my way into Key Arena with the rest of the crowd, I felt the excitement burn through my veins. How sad was it that I considered basketball one of my vices? Thankfully, this wasn't the type of vice I'd need to give up. The worst that happened with this vice is that I neglected the friends who wouldn't go to the games with me over the summer. Too bad, they didn't know what they were missing.

"Slyn!" My favorite seatmate, Trinity, strode toward

me with her girlfriend. A Storm bandana covered most of her reddish blond hair and her bright green eyes sparkled with rowdy excitement. Until I'd met Trinity, I didn't think anyone else got as much enjoyment from these games as I did.

"Hey, Trin, hi there, Kayla," I greeted them. "Opening day!" Trinity and I chanted together and high-fived because we became wholly unlike ourselves at these games. Kayla resisted rolling her eyes, but I knew she was happy for her girlfriend's excitement.

"Are they ready?" I asked Trinity, knowing she'd been in her seat early enough to see the pre-game warm ups with the team.

"They look great. LJ's not hurt, Birdy isn't wearing a mask, and they actually seem to have a bench this year. Did you read this week's articles?"

"Haven't had a chance to surf the site yet, been a little negligent."

"Loafer. You are damn lucky you sit next to me." Three years ago, Trinity showed up in the seats next to mine, and we've been making sure our seats remain together each year. Most games we're yammering away about team stats, league history, play by play or sitting quietly tense until LJ decides to take over the game and get the win for her team.

"Joslyn?" a voice called out from behind me.

"Raven?" I questioned when I turned to find the normally pristinely pressed woman standing in threadbare jeans and a fitted Storm t-shirt.

"Hey, I didn't know you were a Storm fan." She stepped toward me as if wanting to hug me hello but stopped when she realized that we barely knew each other and she was technically a client of mine.

"From the start," I stated proudly then introduced Trinity and Kayla. She in turn introduced me to the three women with her. If I hadn't known about Kelly already, I'd wonder if one of these women was her girlfriend. All were pretty enough and certainly looked at her with enough fondness.

"A founding Storm fan, really?" she asked as her friends and mine took up places in the coffee line behind us.

"Truthfully, I got tickets because I wanted to support the only professional women's sports league in the country. But, damn, that first year was tough to watch. It took two first round draft picks before we finally had ourselves a team. Now, I'm hooked. What about you?"

"You're putting me to shame. I started going the first year they made the playoffs. Very exciting." She grinned widely, her brown eyes dancing with some sort of secret. She probably had a crush on one of the two stars like half the arena. "How are you handling the possibility of the team moving out of state?"

My hands flew to my ears without conscious thought. "We do not speak of it!"

She laughed at my succinct declaration. "Ahh, denial, always a good way to deal with things." I joined her laughter because dwelling on the likelihood that Seattle wouldn't always have this team was too depressing.

"Hey, baby." Strong arms circled my waist from behind and a kiss dropped onto the back of my head.

I fought the sure blush at Chase's affectionate display in front of someone he didn't know. "Don't call me that." Annoyance slipped into my tone, but I dropped it to make introductions. "Raven Malvolio, this is Chase McCovey. Chase, Raven's working at the company I'm evaluating right now."

"Nice to meet you, Raven." Chase shook her hand.

She gave him a penetrating look, somewhere between surprised and appraising. Her eyes dropped to his hand wrapped around my waist before a kind smile graced her mouth. "Likewise, Chase. Where do you sit, Joslyn?"

"Jos has courtside," Chase said with exasperation. He

was insanely jealous of my tickets, which cost one-tenth the amount they charged for his beloved Sonics.

"Oh really? Jos does, eh?" Raven smiled at me. "I've been trying for courtside for a couple of years now, but nothing's ever open."

Inexplicably, the sound of the familiar version of my name from her lips sent a ribbon of heat through me. "You'll have to sit with me at one of the games."

Her eyebrows rose in anticipation but Chase stepped over any reply. "Yes, please. God knows I don't want to go to all these games."

"I went to enough of your Sonics games, mister, so pipe down," I admonished. He shook his head and pointed toward the Pyramid Ale stand, calling out a goodbye.

"Looks like you have a pseudo fan on your hands." She stared after him.

"His first game. I hadn't planned to bring him, but my usual Storm buddy had to attend his daughter's play tonight instead."

"Is he a true fan?"

"Converted and very loyal, yes, but his daughter has to come first."

"Understandable." Raven nodded approvingly.

"He usually has to miss four or five games every season because of stuff with his kids. Maybe next time you can sit with us? You can't beat the view."

"Thanks, Joslyn. I'll look forward to it." She glanced back at her friends. "I'd better get over there or we'll never make it to our seats before intros."

I was dying to ask where Kelly was, but her affairs were her business. "Yeah, I'll see you tomorrow." I watched her disappear into the crowd and felt the excitement ratchet up a notch at the prospect of sitting with her at a game.

* * *

"Where are you going?" Chase twisted back to glare at me in his darkened driveway.

Seeing as I'd just given him what I thought was a goodnight kiss, I assumed the question was unnecessary. But now he stood on his porch with an expectant look, wondering why I was headed back to my car. "Home. The dogs need to be fed, and I've got a ton of work to look over."

"You're kidding, right?" A brief snort escaped as he worked through whether or not I was putting one over on him.

"No, I told you I could only make the game tonight."

"You can do your work here." He walked over and pulled me into his arms again. "You've got auto feeders for the dogs; they'll be fine. Come on, baby, stay the night."

Having only ever stayed the entire night with him once, I was a little surprised by his request. Up to this point, we had an understanding: dinner or something out once a week then maybe some horizontal activities back at his place. Informal, just the way I liked it. "Not tonight. The game was my break; I really can't take any more time away from work."

"Why do you always do this? Every other woman would want to spend the night with her boyfriend."

I bit back what would have been a rude sigh, but damn I was tired of this argument. "You know I don't sleep well. Even if I didn't have all this work to do, I wouldn't want to keep you up."

"I can sleep through anything, baby." He smirked and leaned down to slant his mouth over mine for a possessive kiss. "Let's head inside, you can do some work, then we can get some real business done. I promise it'll be worth your while. I'll make you come so hard you'll be screaming my name tomorrow at work just from the memory." He wiggled his eyebrows.

Considering I'd never once screamed his name in the

throes of sex, I doubted he'd get his wish. Not to mention he'd never once made me orgasm. I imagine that piece of information alone would crush this newly evident, oversized ego. "Unlike you, I can't sleep through anything. I've got a big day tomorrow, and I can't risk not getting any sleep. I had a great time tonight. Thanks for going to the game with me."

His lips started in on my neck, ignoring my attempt to say goodnight. Hands drifted from my shoulders to squeeze my breasts like he was working out his aggression on a stress ball. It didn't matter how much I coached him, he never got it right. After a few moments, he finally recognized that I wouldn't be swayed. "You know, when we're married, you'll have to spend the night. Oh, and no more condoms either. In fact, let's not wait to get married on that one. There's lots of other birth control we can be using."

The off the wall topic would have warranted a long discussion on birth control not being the only necessary protection if I hadn't been so shocked by what he said. "M-married?" I stammered.

"Well, yeah. Isn't that where we're headed here?" He dropped his hands to my waist and leaned back to search my eyes. "I'm not on bended knee right now, but we're in love and that's where couples in love end up."

Christ! I knew there was a chance he might get there eventually, but usually, guys move more slowly than this. I'd never once returned Chase's declarations of love. So far, he hadn't noticed. Now, he was boosting the pressure level, and I didn't think I could deflect this one.

"We haven't discussed marriage, Chase. I didn't realize you were ready for that."

"I wasn't until I met you, baby, but these past six months have been the best of my life. You're the last thing I think about before I go to sleep at night and the first thing I think of when I wake up. That's true love."

Actually, that's an overused cliché, but I didn't think it would be a good idea to mention that right now. Even I'm not that insensitive. "That's sweet. I just thought it would be a while before we started talking about marriage. I'm not really ready for that. I'm not sure if I ever will be."

"What?" He seized my hips; the motion shaking me in place. "You don't want to marry me?"

I placed my hands on his forearms to keep him from crowding me. His tall, semi annoyed form looked a little daunting. "It's not just you, Chase. I've never really thought of myself as the marrying kind." I tried for a lighter tone. "I thought we had a good thing here. It's been a lot of fun. Why get so serious so quickly?"

"Because I want to. You've become important to me. I wasn't going to ask so soon, but now that we're discussing it, I have to know. Are you going to marry me or not?"

My jaw dropped open. Didn't he see that I was trying to dissuade him from the idea of marriage? Who the hell proposes to someone when she's trying to flee the scene? Not to mention his slightly desperate and miffed state. *Oh yeah, I was living a best selling romance right here.* "Can't we talk about this some other time? We haven't given any thought to combining households, lifestyles, finances, or anything else. Marriage takes planning and consideration, we haven't done either."

"I know that I love you and you love me. That's all we need. We're practically married already. Let's make it official."

"No, we're not, Chase." I began to wonder if I was in the same relationship he was in. We saw each other once a week, and I never stayed the night. That was hardly the equivalent of being married. "We've only known each other for a short time. I don't want to hurt you. I do care about you, but I'm not ready for marriage and neither are you."

"Don't tell me I'm not ready for marriage. I want an answer." He gripped my arms emphatically. "Throw caution to the wind for once. Say yes, baby."

I blew out an audible breath. "This is exactly what I mean. I've asked you not to call me baby at least once every time we get together because it's degradingly infantile. I've tried to tell you that I'm not at the marrying point yet and I might never be, but you're not listening. I can't marry someone who doesn't hear me."

He looked like I'd slapped him. "God, you're not even considering my feelings. I'm throwing my heart out here and you're stomping all over it."

"Chase, please, I don't mean to." I lifted a hand to touch his cheek. "You're the one pushing here. I have great affection for you."

"Great affection? Damn, that's cold. Fine, you don't want to marry me?" His expression hardened immediately. "Forget that. There's no coming back from that, and I don't want to be involved with such a cold bitch. We're through."

The sound I made was somewhere between a cough and a laugh, surprised by his absolute change of manner. He'd forced this and now I'm the bad guy? It's not like I didn't wish I could fall in love with him, or feel something stronger for him, or climax when we had sex, but I couldn't force those things. I was willing to keep trying with him, but he pushed the issue right off a cliff.

"Goodbye, Chase." I knew my voice sounded emotionless, but I couldn't muster the hurt or scorn someone in my position would probably feel. Maybe he was right. Only a cold bitch would date a guy for six months, let him constantly declare his love without reciprocation, and listen to a spontaneous proposal then turn him down flat. I'm thinking cold bitch might actually be too kind a portrayal for me.

Chapter 6

The bothered sigh, issued for the fourth time in ten minutes, ripped through my eardrums like a drill bit. It probably didn't help that we were in the tiny conference room that magnified the sound, but I really wanted to reach across the table and slap the offender's mouth to keep him from continuing his dramatic wisps.

"Let me give you a helpful tip in conducting these interrogations," he informed me with a smirk. "Throw the girl into a river and if she floats, she's not a witch."

Now I wanted to do more than just slap the sigh from him. What a moron. How had he managed to land a job in the finance department? "Not only is your attempt at an historical reference inaccurate, it's inapplicable," I responded coolly.

This was my eighth interview today. As part of my consultations, I spent a couple of weeks interviewing everyone about their positions. Most of the time, I get nervous responses to questions, fumbling attempts to answer intelligently, giddy false exclamations, but sometimes I get these guys. The ones who are pissed at me for trying to make any changes to the company. The ones who feel they can give smart ass replies to my questions because they don't think I'm going to help.

"Huh?" He stared dumbly at me, having stopped snickering at his own declaration.

"If she drowns, she's not a witch. That particular form of torture was known as swimming. Tie them up, weight them down, and throw them in a lake, river, or pond. The Inquisitors believed witches would use magic to release their binds and float. Once accused, the best way a woman could prove she wasn't a witch was by drowning. That's what I meant by your statement being inaccurate. It's also inapplicable because this isn't a witch hunt, Kurt. I'm not jealous or fearful of anyone's abilities or intelligence, nor do I want anyone to be jailed, tortured, or killed as a result of any deficiencies I might find."

He snorted, a real snort, before he erupted into an ugly sounding laugh. At least one of us was amused. Through the window behind him, I saw other members of Paul Industries walking to and fro, going about their business day. What I wouldn't do to be out there among them.

"Get off it!" he shouted after he'd finished his cackle. "This is a witch hunt if I've ever seen one."

"Considering you didn't live in the Middle Ages, you never have," I informed him. "And unlike me, you don't have a history degree, so why not take me at my word? We could spend hours talking about the various other forms of heinous torture that were given innocuous names like pinching, scratching, strappado and perhaps the most grueling, pricking, but we don't have that kind of time." He looked like he was about to continue with his asinine analogy, so I cut him off. "I've asked a fairly straightforward question. Describe your typical day."

"I told you, I don't have a typical day," he threw back at me.

"You're in finance, Kurt, not customer service or sales. Numbers are fairly consistent from day to day. The sooner you answer my question, the sooner you're out of here."

"Oh, please, who are you kidding? We all know you're going to can most of us. Why should I cooperate? Robert was right about you, and I've got nothing to lose."

"Yes, you do, Kurt." Raven stood in the now open doorway, her tone and glance stern enough to make both of us sit up. Apparently, the walls weren't that thick around here because she looked like she'd heard more than Kurt's last dismissal.

"Relax, chief, I'm just kidding around." He blanched in her presence.

Raven strode around the table to stand beside my chair. I felt honored that she'd taken a figurative and literal stance on my side. Her linen colored pant suit accentuated her frame perfectly. A lavender vest added just the right amount of color under the single button jacket and set off her amethyst earrings and pendant. She stood ramrod straight beside me, glaring at her senior financial analyst. "It didn't sound like you were kidding. I know my uncle wouldn't appreciate you wasting Ms. Simonini's time, and I don't appreciate you treating her with such disrespect."

"Sorry, but this is a joke, boss." He flicked his hands off the table. "Our department is better equipped to turn this company around than a cut and run con artist."

Raven placed her hands on the table and leaned forward. She looked like she was going to tear his throat out, and the protective stance she'd taken brought about an unexpected swirl of feelings for me. No one ever stood up for me when I was doing my job correctly, not even the owners who hired me. They'd make me fend for myself.

"I'll only cut what's necessary, Kurt. Like if a person

can't tell me the importance of the job he's had for," I checked his résumé, "three years. Now, if you'll just answer my question, we can get you out of here and back to that work."

"I run financial projections and review ratios all day," he grudgingly admitted.

I hoped he did a lot more than that, but with our lack of rapport and his boss glaring at him, I doubted I'd get much out of him now. "Thank you, Kurt, I appreciate your time." He probably wouldn't recognize my sarcastic tone. Not only was I good at hiding it, but he wasn't the sharpest tooth on the shark either. He shot out of his seat and didn't bother to glance back before escaping with another sigh. Only one hundred and thirteen more to go.

"I'm sorry about that." Raven perched on the table beside me. "I've had trouble with his attitude in the past, but he does mostly good work."

"No need to apologize. People get threatened when they feel their job security is at risk."

She squeezed my forearm and a zing of surprise traveled up to my brain. People didn't unnecessarily touch me. The whole Lizzie Borden reputation usually kept them at a distance. "You're very gracious. He was incredibly rude to you, and you're excusing his behavior to his boss."

"I had a feeling if I let him keep talking, you might be down one senior financial analyst, am I right? If I let you do the firing around here, it would ruin my reputation."

She laughed conspiratorially. "I never thought there was such a thing, but you might be too good at your job, Ms. Simonini." Another squeeze of my forearm before she declared, "You shouldn't have had to put up with that. Let me take you to lunch as a reprieve."

Yes! was my immediate reaction, but usually my sensible, detached, professional head prevailed in these matters. I waited several moments for my brain to speak aloud as it normally does to keep things entirely professional. My mind didn't seem to want to disappoint her hopeful expression.

"C'mon, I've always wanted to have lunch with an expert on medieval witch trials," she coaxed with a wide smile.

Enchanting. I didn't need to be into women to recognize this woman was definitely enchanting. "Just how much of that interview did you hear?"

She pushed up from the table and pulled on my arm to join her. "I'll tell you over lunch."

* * *

Tucked around a table in an off the beaten path restaurant, Raven and I leaned back and moaned at the same time. "Oh my God," I voiced the sensation we were both feeling.

"I know, right?" Raven agreed after she'd finished her mouthful of the best tasting rigatoni outside of Italy.

"How did you find this place?" I looked around the cozy bistro expecting to see the Italian countryside through the front windows.

"The owner taught a cooking class years ago, and I was one of the lucky attendees."

"You know how to cook like this?" I couldn't stop shock from seeping into my expression.

She shook her head. "No one cooks as well as Amalia, except maybe Giovanni, her husband."

"*Ciao, bellissima!*" An elderly, squat man in a sauce stained apron approached the table. He reached out and pulled Raven out of her seat for a hug.

"*Buongiorno, Giovanni, come stai?*" Raven responded to his greeting in flawlessly accented Italian. Now, that's beyond enchanting, bordering on sexy.

"*Molto bene, grazie.*" He pronounced "grazie" with an "ah" sound at the end instead of the traditional pronunciation. That meant he came from somewhere in southern Italy if I had my dialects correct. *"Sono felice di vederti."*

"Anch'io." Raven's Italian sounded as delicious as the meal we'd been enjoying. She gestured toward me. "Giovanni, please say hello to Joslyn. She was just experiencing Amalia's cuisine for the first time."

"Ah, sì, sì. My Amalia is like a goddess, no?"

"I think that might be an understatement, and I've only tasted the rigatoni so far."

He beamed at my compliment and bellowed back toward the kitchen, "Amalia!" Other restaurant patrons turned to stare at us as we waited for his wife to join us.

"Raven! You beautiful girl. You sneak in here and do not say a thing?" A shorter, stouter woman with a wild red dye job crowded Raven and her husband until they all bungled into a group hug.

"I know better than to bother you at lunch. Besides, I'm in here so often you must be sick of me."

"Dici sciocchezze!" Giovanni exclaimed just as vehemently as when he bellowed for his wife. *"Ti vogliamo bene,* Raven."

She kissed his cheek in response and turned to his wife. "Amalia, this is Joslyn."

"Hello." I reached out to shake her hand and found myself encircled by her arms. Basil, garlic, tomatoes, and parmesan caressed my sense of smell while soft pillowy curves enveloped my sense of touch. Raven turned a stifled grin to the side at my surprised expression.

"Did you eat, Joslyn?" Amalia's accent added an extra syllable to my name, Jos-a-lyn, but it sounded singsong coming from this native Italian. She'd pulled back from the hug, anxious for my response.

"We were just enjoying your fare, Amalia. So far, it's been a taste extravaganza."

Giovanni's frame swelled at my compliment while

Amalia placed a hand to her heart. "My, how wonderful you are." She gave a pointed look at Raven who was biting her lip to hide the grin now.

"La tua nuova ragazza è bella, dentro e fuori. Siete una coppia bella."

Raven's eyes widened at his words. She grasped his shoulder before shaking her head hurriedly. *"No, no. Lavoriamo soltanto insieme."*

The older couple's expressions fell immediately as they turned in unison to look at me. Amalia smiled kindly and asked, "Joslyn, you are not full yet, *si*? I have special just for you and our beautiful Raven."

"I understand you share your talents with some lucky students, Amalia. You'll have to tell me when you have your next class. This food is too good not to attempt to replicate."

"You are very kind. I gave up the teaching. Not enough students put the good energy into it." Her hand slid around Raven's waist and tugged her closer. "I met our Raven; that is enough for me. My work is done."

A bit disappointed, I offered, "If you ever decide to take on students again, I'd promise to be very attentive and clean the kitchen afterward."

Giovanni gave a satisfied grunt with a nod, elbowing Raven and gesturing to me. She shook her head with an exasperated smile. "Sit, sit, you must save energy for eating." He pulled out Raven's chair first then rushed over to pull out mine as well. Once we were seated, he and Amalia headed back to the kitchen, promising to fill us with every Italian delicacy ever invented.

I chuckled, feeling their happiness settle over me. "Wow, they're something."

"They sure are. They make you feel like family, only better, you know?" Raven watched them disappear through the swinging door then shook her head as if disagreeing with herself. "No, of course not, that made no sense."

"Actually, it made perfect sense. They are all the good parts of a family without any of the destruction."

She turned a curious stare my way, the look softened by kindness. "We must have similar family experiences."

Unable to resist, I added cryptically, "Well, that would make things easier."

Her brow furrowed. "Easier for what?"

"If we have similar family experiences, I'll know how to handle yours when you introduce me as your girlfriend." I tried for a dry delivery, but my undeterred grin blew the joke.

"You speak Italian!" she accused in a delighted voice, realizing I'd understood Giovanni's words about me being her new girlfriend and how we made a nice couple. An endearing red suffused her cheeks. "I can't believe you just stood there and didn't say anything."

"It's more fun that way. I get a lot of mileage out of the invariably embarrassing things people offer up when they think you can't understand."

She shook her head and chuckled. When she glanced at me, her face held hopeful concern. "I hope they didn't make you uncomfortable."

"Not at all," I rushed to eliminate her unease. I wondered if all gay people went through that moment of panic just after disclosing their sexuality. Although I barely knew her, I had an overwhelming wish that Raven had never had reason to worry about that. "It's obvious how much they love you, even without the ability to translate."

"I feel very lucky to have met them." She gave a wistful smile and glanced over at the kitchen door where we could hear Giovanni serenading Amalia.

"Well, thank you for sharing the place with me."

"I figured after putting up with Kurt you deserved a little treat. Of course, once Giovanni and Amalia find out you speak Italian, they'll never let you leave."

"Since I'm working on something that will benefit your

company, perhaps we shouldn't tell them right away? I've got twelve interviews scheduled after lunch, and I have a feeling I might have to wade through more medieval references before the day is through."

She laughed that rhythmic half-chuckle half-laugh again. "I'll tell them next time."

I managed to stop the surprised double-take before it happened. Next time? There would be a next time? The idea pleased me more than I could put into coherent words. I was glad for the diversion that Giovanni and Amalia provided with the shouting announcement of the second course. The food would be a nice distraction from these confusing thoughts.

Chapter 7

*P*layful snuffling sounds echoed through the garage as I worked on my prized possession. My dogs were having a wrestling slash jousting match somewhere near the open garage door, amusing themselves while keeping me in sight. As soon as I surfaced from under the car, they'd no doubt have their snouts wetting my face. I lived for days like this.

In a few more minutes, my 1965 Stingray Corvette would have a new transmission and I'd get to drive it again. I'd missed driving this lovely piece of machinery, but the winter rain and a shoddy transmission kept me from partaking in a favorite pastime. I could hardly contain my excitement.

Task completed, I slid my dolly along the sunken groove I'd had put into one of the garage bays so I could more easily engage in my hobby of restoring cars. As suspected, the dogs, all five of them, attacked me the second I was free of the undercarriage. Wet tongues, dusty paws, and furry coats assaulted whatever piece of me they could find. By their reaction, you'd think I'd been neglecting them. Sure, I'd been busy with Paul Industries, but since it was a local company, I came home to them every night.

"All right, all right, crazy puppies," I assured them, crouching over their now prone bodies. None were actually puppies, but you couldn't tell by the way they acted sometimes.

I started toward the house to take a shower and they fell into step with me. I'd never meant to have this many dogs, but I couldn't say that it bothered me anymore. They were great companions and wise teachers when it came to love. I'd learned a lot from them over the years we'd been together.

After settling the dogs onto their favorite pieces of furniture in the sunroom, I checked my work voicemail as I passed by my home office. "Joslyn, Archie here. I got that comparative data you were looking for. I'll messenger it over to you. Thought I'd give you a head start on this information before our meeting on Tuesday. See you then."

"Great! I'm not supposed to be working this weekend, and now, not only will I be working, but you're sending someone to my house?" I have this annoying habit of talking to voicemail as if it were a live conversation. Thankfully, no one could hear my end of the conversation, or I might find myself fired from this and many other clients.

Now rushing to get my shower done, I stubbed a toe on the way into the bathroom, swearing and starting the water at the same time. If my clients could see what a dufus I actually was, I guessed I might never get another one again.

The hot water soothed my toe, my aching muscles, and the irritation that my client assumed I'd be working on his project this weekend. With a messenger on the way, I didn't have much time, especially if I wanted to meet him out at the gate. Even though my office was in my house, a box at a postal facility for mail and deliveries allowed me to maintain a professional distance.

Pulling on some jeans, I was just throwing my arms through a cotton blouse when the gate chime rang. So much for hoping to meet the guy at the gate, now he'd have to drive up to the house. I pressed the intercom button to greet the messenger. The sound was barely good enough to distinguish the voice as female. It reminded me that I needed to get the failing communication device replaced before the winter rain this year. I stepped into some leather sandals, tangled my lighter-for-the-summer-months brown hair into a ponytail that reached past my collar, and headed outside to accept the package from the messenger.

A green Beemer crunched its way around the bend in the drive and headed toward the front porch. Okay, I'd now be checking the financials to find out how much Archie paid his messengers. "Hello," I spoke to the opening door, unable to see inside the car through the tinted glass. "I'm Jos—" The rest of my name died in my throat as Raven emerged from the vehicle.

She broke into a wide smile. "Howdy, Jos."

"Raven?" I hadn't meant it to be a question, but she was a complete shocker.

"Uncle Archie didn't mention I'd be coming by, did he? I guess that makes us even because he didn't mention that he'd be sending me to your house." Her eyes bounced around my property before returning to mine. "I expected to drop this by your office where I hoped I wouldn't find you working on such a beautiful day."

Still a little stunned to find her in my driveway, I barely managed to put together something coherent to say. "So, not only are you the CFO, but your uncle uses you as a messenger, too?"

She chuckled, erasing the tension from the surprise visit. "Family business, what can I say? Actually, I live close by. I figured you must have an office around here, and I'd get to say hello on my way home if you were working. This place is magnificent, Joslyn. Tell me it's yours, that you're not just house-sitting?"

Pride stretched my smile wide. "All mine. Took a year to build, but it's my dream house."

"I'm just looking at the front of it and it's mine, too. Are you saying you built it yourself?"

"With a contractor, but I spent every weekend and two or three nights a week out here getting in his way, helping out where I could. Mostly it takes being able to make decisions, sticking to them, and being organized. If you can't make decisions, add five months, if you can't stick to them, double the budget, and if you're unorganized, scrap the whole project."

She let that uncontrolled laugh loose, and I found myself staring at her mouth, looking for the delightful tone that escaped it. "I've been dying to start from scratch on my lot, but it's a daunting task. Now that I know the secrets, maybe I'll stop dreaming about it and go for it."

"Jump head first; believe me, it's worth it." Because she'd been so enthusiastic and I realized I didn't want her to leave right away, I invited her inside. "Come take a look around."

"Would you mind?" she asked even though her legs were already moving toward the house with me. Once we hit the front porch, she made appropriate sounds of awe as we looked around the rustic façade and entered the sunlight foyer. Miles of hardwood led in two directions, down a long hallway toward the sunroom at the back and into the living room, kitchen, and dining room off to the side.

"It's exquisite, Joslyn. Honestly, I'd never go outside." She fingered the mix of antiques and modern furniture of the living room as we walked through.

"I'm often guilty of taking a couple weeks off in between assignments."

From the sunroom I heard the excited scuffles of nails on tile and questioning soft barks from the dogs. I knew they were contemplating vaulting the security gate I had up between their room and the rest of the house. I wasn't a very good disciplinarian. Raven must have heard something as well because she turned an expectant look my way. "What kind of dog do you have?"

Before I could respond, they made their presence known. All five of them, and like the perfect puppies they were, they dropped anxiously at Raven's feet, waiting for introductions. This part I'd worked on with them so they wouldn't overwhelm any guests.

"Five! You've got five dogs?" She looked from them to me and back to them. She extended a hand without trepidation, allowing each to sniff her scent and accept a welcome pat before they decided if she was going to be a future playmate.

"I used to have eight."

Her head swung up to stare at me. "You're pulling my leg."

I laughed and ran my hands over each dog to calm them a smidge. "Nope."

"Give it up." She beckoned with her fingers. For a second, I didn't know what she was talking about. As I was trying to figure it out, an image flickered through my mind that was so quick all I got from it was the sensation of something indescribably electric.

After what seemed like months just standing there, I finally landed on what she was asking. "Oh, when I decided I wanted a dog, I went by the only shelter in the small town where I lived at the time. It didn't have a no-kill policy, and without thinking, I went to the pen with the two dogs that were slated to be put down that month." I stooped to pat Eras, one of those first two dogs. The other had passed away last year. I was still getting over it.

"Four months go by and I get a call from the woman running the shelter. She's got another dog that they'll have to put down the next day if he isn't adopted. I show up to take that one off her hands, and that's when she knew she had me."

Raven's eyes sparkled. "I was right, you are a softy."

"More like a sucker," I snickered. "Anyway, five more dogs and two years later, I decide there has to be a better way to deal with this. So, I organized a fundraising shindig and got the businesses in town to donate everything. We did well enough the first year to keep the shelter from ever having to euthanize another pet and now local businesses bid for the chance to host the event each year. They raise enough for operating expenses and expansion as well as donations to other shelters."

"That's not only a great idea, it's impressive as hell."

"Purely selfish, I assure you," I brushed aside her compliment. "I love these guys, but I couldn't handle taking in every dog that didn't get adopted. When I got a call about several cats that needed a home, something had to be done."

"Heaven forbid you take in cats," she teased, placing a hand on my shoulder and leaning toward me. I caught a whiff of rosewater and, for a moment, my knees felt like they would give out. Being an entirely new sensation, I didn't know if I should step back to distance myself from the source and risk crumpling to the floor or simply continue to stand here being assaulted by the unfamiliar feelings. Fortunately, Augustus, my foxhound mix, chose that moment to whip his body around and stumble into me for a rub. The motion forced me back a step, and I used the excuse to grasp him to regain my figurative balance.

"Whoa, somebody needs a little attention." I rubbed his hindquarters.

"Jealous boys, I see." She looked down at the two

males, who doubled as the biggest attention seekers in the bunch.

"They're hams, these guys. My ladies are perfect angels." I indicated the others.

"I can see that. They must be fun to have around."

"They are that. Any pets?" I swept everybody into motion toward the kitchen for a continued tour.

"Two horses. It's why I live out this way," she referenced the remote by Seattle standards part of the eastside where we were. "I bought my place for the land, the barn, and the corral. Now, if I could just get my house to look like this, I'd never leave."

"Oh, thank you. I've been thinking about adding a corral for horses, but I figured I've got enough with these guys."

"Do you ride?" She faced me, excitement animating her features.

"Not regularly, but I love to ride when I get the chance."

"Say you'll join me sometime? I don't know many people who like to ride, and if I take one horse out without the other, talk about jealousy when I get back to the barn."

Another acceptance screamed inside my head, but something kept me from blurting it out. She was my client, well, the niece of my client, and I should keep things professional. There's a difference between possibly sitting together at a basketball game for which we both have tickets and going to her home to spend several hours exploring the countryside on unpredictable beasts.

She seemed to sense my reluctance. "I'm about ten minutes away, and it would be great to get your input on remodeling or starting from scratch with my place."

I stared at her for a moment longer, unconsciously making my decision. "That sounds fun. We'll definitely have to take a ride."

"Something tells me that I'd better pin down a specific

day or it will always be a someday sort of thing with you."

Any second I expected to start feeling defensive about how easily she'd read me, deny her guess, and shut down her attempt at becoming friends, but miraculously the self-preservation didn't occur. "You might be right."

She smiled like she'd just discovered a secret about me. "Next weekend? Not only will we get to ride, but we'll keep you from working. Don't think I haven't noticed that you're in the office most weekends. I'm amazed to see you here now."

I couldn't help but laugh at how well she seemed to know me. "You must be just as guilty if you're noticing that I'm in the office on the weekends."

"Definitely guilty. Kelly always gives me a hard time about it. She claims that my working weekends makes me crankier every day of the week, not just on Monday mornings. But now that it's summer, I make it a point to take as much of my weekend off as I can manage."

The mention of Kelly felt like she just snapped her fingers in front of my face. *That's right. Raven's not entirely the incredibly sophisticated, amazingly smart, uniquely together woman she appears to be.* I wanted to slap myself for being so critical of her, but the affair with Kelly went completely against type for her. Not that I knew her that well, but it was such an anomaly from the rest of the character traits she presented every time we were together.

I took a step to the side, nearly stumbling over Dria who liked to keep her little terrier body close to my feet. The movement broke the cycle of verdicts running through my head about this woman. Raven clasped my arm to make sure I didn't fall but dropped her hand when I made a show of righting myself. She studied me cautiously, obviously confused by my sudden change in demeanor. I tried to hide it under the guise of continuing our tour.

When we'd looked through the rest of the house, I took

her out back to the extra building that could serve as a barn if I ever got livestock, or a guest house if I ever had guests, but currently acted as a combo gymnasium and game room. "Oh, wow!" Raven exclaimed on the walk over. I thought she was talking about the three bold yet temporary splashes of color on the side wall of the building, but she wasn't facing that direction anymore. She'd started toward my open garage. "That's a '63?" She reverently ran a hand over the hood of my car.

A chuckle escaped before I could answer her. "'65, I liked the back end better."

She moved to the rear to get a look. "It's a beauty."

"You like old cars?"

"It's kind of a thing with me. My first car was a '64 Mustang, then I upgraded to a '68 Camero SS. I don't know why I got rid of either."

"Yeah, I'd have to agree. You're crazy for letting those classics get away," I joked.

"Go ahead, give me grief. I berate myself daily. This is a true classic right here, topped only by the '57 Thunderbird, maybe."

"Please!" I argued playfully. "Nothing beats a Stingray, especially when you get your hands dirty doing most of the work."

Her appraising eyes turned back to me. "You're a modern marvel, aren't ya? General contractor, auto mechanic, dog rescuer—"

"Corporate raider, thief of jobs—"

"All right, I can see I won't win this one." She waved a hand, pushing aside the argument.

I looked down at the car and made a decision. "I haven't been able to drive it for a while, but I finished putting in a transmission earlier. I'd planned to meet the messenger, you, at the gate, and get back here to enjoy the work. Now that I actually know the messenger, you, want to go for a spin?"

What sounded like a blissful moan left her mouth, causing a swimming sensation to flood my senses. I must not have gotten enough to eat today because these reactions were so unlike me. "Even more than I wanted to look at your house. Are you sure you don't mind company for your test drive?"

"No, and I'd like it even better if you drove."

Her face registered excited shock. "Tell me you're just the nicest person on the planet and not letting me drive because you're about to recommend that Uncle Archie shut down the business?"

"You'll find out when I present to the board, I guess," I quipped.

She took the proffered keys and slipped behind the wheel. Her hands ran over the dash, along the steering wheel, around the gear shift, and across the immaculate interior. It seemed as if things weren't real to her until she touched them; this wasn't the first time I'd noticed. After kicking over the engine, she turned what amounted to an illegal grin my way. She could be jailed for the potency of that smile. I had no choice but to return the grin as we edged out of the garage.

My first full weekend away from work and, so far, nothing about it was going as planned. Looking over at Raven, I honestly couldn't care less.

Chapter 8

Mired in hour three of analysis, I wasn't all that bothered about it today. Especially when I felt that shoulder brush against me again. Raven was reaching for last year's financials and inadvertently tilted toward me.

"Sorry," she murmured, settling back upright in her seat.

Like I was going to protest. It wasn't just that we'd spent the better part of Saturday afternoon driving around and getting to know each other. No, it had started with Kelly's kiss. That kiss had more than surprised me, it had awakened my senses. I'd never been more aware of my personal space than I was right now. To distract my imaginings, I asked, "Are you seeing the same line item appear prior to 2002?"

She flipped through page after page of expenses. "Yes, but it's not nearly as large as what we've been questioning.

How did you pick up on this?"

"Number crunching is my life."

"Ahh, a person who really knows how to live." She bumped her shoulder against me on purpose this time.

"You're a little twisted, aren't you?" I risked that she'd understand my sense of humor and not get offended.

"Just a little?" *Okay, she definitely gets it.*

"Do I need to ask who your favorite Sesame Street character was?"

"Big Bird," she responded immediately.

"Liar." My accusation started a round of laughter, and I felt dismayed by how much I already liked her. It wouldn't be the first time I got along with one of my clients, but definitely the first time I'd consider extending the friendship past the contract period.

"Hey, Auntie R," a cheery voice called out just before a young woman sailed through the doorway. "Oh, excuse me. Kelly wasn't at her desk, so I didn't realize you were busy. Hi, I'm Ray." She waved and brushed her long brown hair back over her shoulder in the same motion. The wide smile she wore reminded me of someone else in the room.

Raven and I stood from the table together as she introduced me. "Joslyn Simonini, meet my favorite niece."

Ray chortled at the introduction but accepted her aunt's warm embrace. "She means her only niece."

"Doesn't mean you're not my favorite, kid."

"Hi, Ray, nice to meet you." I shook her hand in greeting.

"Nice to meet you, too." She responded before turning her flashing brown eyes to her aunt. "Quick question since you're busy. Can I steal you for dinner sometime this week?"

"Is that code for take me out to dinner before I kill my parents while I'm on summer break?" Raven touched her forehead to her niece's. The simple display of affection spoke volumes about their closeness.

"They're driving me crazy." Her statement didn't come with the usual petulant exasperation of youth. "I want to be an actor, so what? Can't you talk to my dad at least?"

"Hon, they're parents; it's their job to worry. You could appease them with a fallback major, you know." Raven managed not to sound authoritative or condescending when giving this advice.

"Like this company isn't my fallback? Come on, it's everyone's fallback." The young woman sighed dramatically before her eyes snapped back to her aunt's. "Not yours, I mean, but everyone else in this family. I already spend my summers here. Uncle Nathan tries to make me commit to an employment contract every year before I go back to college. I think Dad's been bribing him."

"Well, you are a whiz with computer security, youngster."

Ray gave her an exasperated look that said she thought absolutely everyone was good with computers. "So, dinner? What do you say?"

"Sure, we can try that new Indian place over by your house. How's Thursday?"

"Cool for me. Thanks, Auntie R."

Kelly interrupted from the doorway with a message for Raven. "Dwayne Lightfoot is on line one for the third time today."

"Excuse me a moment." She looked tempted to roll her eyes but went to pick up the phone instead.

Kelly joined us and squeezed Ray's shoulder in greeting. She turned to me and asked in a hushed voice, "Did Raven find the cash flow statements from 2000-2002?"

"She did, thanks. I think we're going to need '95-'99 as well."

"Oh sure, I can get those out of storage on my way back from lunch."

"That would be great."

"Are you new to Aunt Raven's staff?" Ray asked me.

Kelly snickered and jutted an elbow into Ray's side. Ray glanced down at her arm before shooting her a questioning stare. "She's the, umm…"

Ray stared expectantly at her before her eyes widened. She faced me again with surprised amusement and an accusing finger. "Oh, oh! You're the slasher?"

"Raven!" The admonishing tone came from behind us. We turned at the sound. Raven was just setting down the phone. I didn't have time to make sense of what she said before she continued, "Joslyn's here to help this company. Please don't refer to her that way."

"Sorry," Ray apologized easily to her. Then, with even more sincerity, she turned to me and repeated, "Sorry. It's just that by the way everyone else is talking I expected some huge East German mama who cleans her fingernails with a buck knife."

The funny image she painted helped to jar me out of my bewilderment. "Hate to disappoint, but I'm short, Italian, and I don't even own a pocketknife." Even the responding chuckle couldn't deflect my confusion from earlier. "Did she just call you Raven?"

"She's my namesake." Raven grasped the back of her niece's neck. "She likes to butcher her father's gesture by referring to herself as Ray."

"Raven sounds like I'm trying to sound Hollywood. Ray is believable and unique," Ray reported like she'd done a ton of research on the subject.

One look at Kelly's affectionate expression, and I realized that this was the Raven she'd meant to rendezvous with in the supply room. My heart started pounding so loudly I was afraid everyone else would hear it. What a huge relief. All those awful judgments I'd been torquing myself over just rinsed out of my mind. It was so nice to realize that Raven wasn't irresponsible.

"I love trying to sound Hollywood," she joked. "Anything else, kid, or can Joslyn and I get back to work?"

"Nope, hop to it. Things to slash after all."

"No one better to do it," I kidded.

When Kelly and Ray left, I didn't realize I was staring at Raven until she glanced back at me with a penetrating look. "What?"

I shook my head to get back into a professional mode rather than revel in the feeling of extreme relief. "Nothing. She favors you."

Her face broke into a proud smile. "I know, it's weird. My brother and I look nothing alike. Whenever we go out, people think she's my daughter."

I laughed at the silly notion. "C'mon, what, they think you had her when you were five?"

"Flatterer!" she accused with delight. "Fifteen, thank you very much."

Automatically, I ran through the math in my head; a fifteen year difference put her at or near my age. She definitely looked younger than mid-thirties, but if I believed what others told me, so did I. "You're close, obviously?"

"No way I could hide it. She was the first baby I'd held, the first diapers I'd changed, the first emergency room visit for a skateboarding accident, and the first confidante I had in the family. We're it for the female Pauls, so I needed her to grow up quickly."

"And now she wants to be an actor and she thinks your name is too Hollywood? That's pretty funny."

"Actually, she insisted on being called Ray from the time she was twelve. People used to tease her that Raven wasn't a fitting name for a brunette. They'd ask if her parents were colorblind."

"Well, that's ignorant." I couldn't help offering my opinion.

"And insensitive, yes."

"Especially since Raven means dark haired or wise, either of which would make it fitting. Not that parents are always concerned with the origin of a name before choosing one."

Her interest turned into amazement. "You are a smart cookie, aren't you? What, pray tell, does Joslyn mean?"

"Lots o' resources out there for you to find out, my dear." Once the words slipped out, I felt immediately uncomfortable. I'd let the relief of finding out that Raven wasn't sleeping with her assistant push our banter to a more familiar footing. She'd laughed at my suggestion, but I wanted to move away from that friendly term of endearment and into something safer. "Where is she going to college?"

"USC. I tried to talk her out of it, but it's got a great drama department with lots of support from the movie studios. She's very hopeful."

"She's certainly gorgeous enough to be a movie star. I hope it works out for her."

"Thank you, so do I." She gave me a grateful smile. "What about you? Did you always want to be a business consultant or were movies in your future, too?"

"God no, to both questions actually. I definitely couldn't handle the attention that comes with fame, and no one grows up wanting to be a business consultant." She chuckled at my certainty. "No, from the time I was five, I always wanted to be an accountant."

Her chuckle turned into another laugh, and I let the sound settle in with the relief I felt. So, she wasn't reckless or unethical, but she couldn't possibly be as great as she seemed. I'd find a flaw somewhere to prove that she was human at some point.

Chapter 9

When I turned onto the gravel driveway, I double checked the address before allowing my pickup to crunch farther up the pathway. Evergreens, birch trees, maples, and various shrubs shrouded the property within. Like mine, the length of the driveway indicated multiple acres to Raven's home.

I'd been both looking forward to and dreading today since she issued the invitation last weekend. The scales tipped toward excitement after realizing that she wasn't having an imprudent affair with her assistant, but I still couldn't forgive my usual guarded nature crumbling whenever I spent time with her.

The driveway switched back and again before her house came into view. The barn and corral were off to the right and in immaculate order as if the prior owner planned to live there instead of the ranch house. Neither building matched in style or era. The barn looked like a timber ski lodge and far more modern than the fifties style ranch house.

Pulling in behind her BMW, I shut off the engine. My dogs made excited sounds from the truck bed. They'd been my idea to bring, both for their exercise and for the extra buffer. They could hardly wait for me to step out of the truck and bring down the gate before bounding onto the ground beside me.

"Oh, wow!" Raven's voice boomed out from the barn door.

Her words echoed inside my head when I caught sight of her. She wore dark jeans, a pale yellow shirt open but for two buttons over a white tank. Well used cowboy boots looked like slippers on her feet and an Aussie style cowboy hat dangled halfway down her back from the thin leather strap at the base of her throat. She looked like she'd been working a ranch her entire life.

With purposeful strides, she made it over to me in a flash. The look in her eyes intent and, for a moment, I thought perhaps bringing the dogs had startled her. "A '56 Chevy? How many more of these beauties do you have?" Keeping her eyes on the truck, she reached out to greet the dogs swirling around both of our legs.

"I have a thing for classic cars."

"We're like kindred spirits." She touched the side panel of the truck bed then whipped around with a panicked look and struggled with something to say. She didn't have time to find the right words before my dogs darted in between her legs, causing her to lose her footing and grip the truck to stay upright.

"V, Stus, Eras!" I snapped my fingers to get them to heal. "I'm sorry, are you all right?"

"I'm fine. I wasn't paying attention to them." She knelt to give each dog another pat. "Let's hear their names again?"

On cue, the pointer stood for her introduction. "V, here,

is short for Octavia, then we've got Augustus, better known as Stus, and finally, Eras, short for—"

"Erasmus," she finished for me, spotting my historical trend.

"I thought they'd enjoy a walk with the horses."

"And your other two?"

"Alexandria and Medici, both too small to keep up so I left them with the run of the house. I'm not sure they'll let us back in when we get home."

"They're that clever, eh? Well, these three will have a grand time. Come meet my horses." She reached out as if to take my hand but changed the motion to gesture toward the barn. Two magnificent animals waited inside tied to the stalls and already saddled. Both Paints, one black and white the other brown and white. One female, one male, both gentle and eager.

"They're beautiful." I patted the neck of the closest horse. Black swirled evenly among the white on his coat, whereas white splotches showed through on the other mostly brown horse.

"That's Fate," she indicated the one I was petting, "and this is Calamity."

A laugh escaped before I commented, "Ironic, that's great."

"Why do you say that?" She stared quizzically at me.

"I assume they're mates, and you've given them names that most would consider antonyms."

"Most? But not you?"

"Or you. They have vastly different connotations but are still synonyms."

"I didn't think anyone would ever get that." Amazement took over her expression.

I flushed with pride. "You need to hang out with more nerds."

She gave me a wide smile, allowing my self-deprecating description. From her earlier statement, she clearly thought we were alike in many ways. Maybe she thought of herself as a nerd, too. Although, the way she looked now went against nerd type. "Ready to ride?" She didn't bother to contain her excitement.

Swinging my backpack onto my shoulders, I nodded, matching her excitement. "Whom do I get?"

"Calamity loves making new friends." Raven moved with me to the brown horse. She kept a hand on the mare's neck as I swung up into the saddle. "No hat?"

I shook my hatless head, ponytail swishing back and forth. "I've got sunglasses and sun block. Do you need any?"

"I'm all set." With practiced ease, she swung up into the saddle and had Fate in motion simultaneously.

Calamity started forward a couple of steps behind. One whistle and my dogs were trotting along with us. Raven slowed Fate so that we could ride side by side. She tugged on the leather strap to grab her hat and set it on her head. Ranch hand look complete, she took us toward the far fence along her property.

The scent of fresh pine and majestic scenery kept us silent for quite a while. I didn't realize it until Raven pointed off toward one of the foothills. A doe with two fawns stepped away from the sheltering shrubbery to extend long necks down to the babbling brook at their feet.

"Marvelous," I breathed, astounded by how delicate the deer seemed despite knowing how large they actually were.

When I didn't offer anything else, Raven smiled wistfully. She seemed glad that I recognized the majesty in wildlife. "We get a lot of animals around here. My neighbor told me he's seen black bears roaming the hills."

"Oh my." A small part of me wished we could be treated to that sight, but my practical side knew it would be troublesome for our little gathering.

We rode on with only the sounds of the horses' snorts, hooves scuffing, and playful nips that my dogs took at each other accompanying us. Normally, I would have filled the silence with small talk or polite queries, but I didn't feel that urgency with Raven. She was really easy to be around.

When we'd gone a ways longer, she turned us toward the large foothills edging her property. Leaning forward, Calamity and I hiked our way up the trail behind Raven and Fate. The dogs took their time scampering along behind. At the crest of the ridge, we high-stepped over some boulders and made our way to a clearing.

"Feel like some lunch?" She stopped Fate and dismounted with a proficiency that made me think she'd been born on a horse.

"Sure." I realized how hungry I felt now that the suggestion had been offered. I slid from Calamity with much less grace and found my legs slightly bowed when I hit ground. Oh, goody, it wouldn't just be my butt that hurt tomorrow.

Tying Calamity's lead to the nearest tree, I reached for Fate's to do the same. Raven dug into the saddle bags from each horse while I took out a plastic bowl and water bottle from my backpack and filled the container. The dogs made sloppy work of gulping down water, thirsty from their trek. When they'd finished, I refilled the bowl and took it to the horses.

"Oh, thanks, I usually let them stop by the creek on the way down." She laid out a blanket on the soft grass and placed some plastic containers and water bottles on top.

"You thought of everything. I didn't know if we'd go this long, but I packed some pasta salad and coffeecake just in case." I brought out the food from my backpack.

"Now, we definitely have everything." She sat cross-legged on the tartan blanket, pulling off the covers of the plastic containers.

As I took a seat, I plucked out three chew bone treats and tossed them to the dogs. When they were met with doggie glee, we laughed. Hers sounded throatier than I remembered, and I found myself searching for the source again. Realizing that I'd been staring at her mouth, I dropped my gaze and took a bite of the sandwich she'd given me. A burst of flavor met my tongue, forcing me to sift through the various ingredients to tackle the taste mystery. "Honey mustard, but there's something else," I guessed.

"Bourbon."

"Bourbon chicken with honey mustard, delicious combo."

"Thanks. I don't dare bring your pasta salad near Amalia; she'll want to serve it at her restaurant."

I laughed at her exaggeration. "My dad's recipe."

"Your dad was the cook in the family, eh?"

"It was him or me, and he didn't like to do dishes." That was the deal we'd struck as soon as I could wash more dishes than I broke.

"Your mom?" Her brown eyes showed great concern.

For once I didn't feel awkward with the question, nor did I feel like giving my standard brush-off reply. "She fell in love with a guy when I was eleven, followed him to New York, and didn't fight my dad for custody."

Unlike others who'd heard some version of this story, Raven didn't respond with pity. She gave it due consideration before offering, "That must have been tough."

"Actually, I know this may sound cold, but it's the best thing that ever happened to me. For the next three years I had to spend summers with her in New York where I didn't know anyone, couldn't earn any money like I did working for my dad, and had to deal with diapers of the twins she had a year after leaving my dad. I learned to adapt, learned to be independent, and learned that parenting is the hardest job anyone can have. Not all kids get to see that."

"That's an upbeat way of looking at what must have been a painful time for a young girl." She didn't have to know me well to guess that those first few years after my mom had left were incredibly difficult, dealing with missing her and with my dad's sadness. After a couple of years, it became easier and my dad and I built a great life based on trust and love.

"Are your parents still together?" My curiosity helped move us off the sometimes prickly subject.

"Yep, I'm very lucky. With most of us working for the family business, you can probably tell that we had an 'it takes a village' attitude about raising the kids in the family. I spent almost as much time at my uncles' houses growing up as I did at my own."

"Hence the bossing Robert around comment?" I teased.

"He's the youngest of the cousins. He had to take crap from everyone, but only because he deserved it." Her eyes twinkled.

"I'm twelve years older than my sisters, but they've been bossing me around from the moment they were born."

She laughed with me as we tore into the coffeecake. "What does your dad do?"

"Contractor."

"Ahh, the true secret to the success of your beautiful home."

"He's actually retired, but I'd worked alongside his apprentice at sites since we were kids. He was more than happy to build my place as long as I helped out." I put the rest of my coffeecake back in a plastic bag, too full to eat any more. "Why is your dad the only brother not working for Paul Industries?"

"He's a surgeon, so the family let him off the hook. My mom and brother are doctors, too. Pediatricians. They share a practice that my brother will take over once she retires next year."

"That's great. No medical calling for you?"

"Hell no, I got queasy dissecting the frog in biology."

"Me, too," I agreed. "The smell, the rubbery guts, so disgusting."

We chuckled, lost in the memory of seventh grade bio lab. She looked relaxed and happy, reclining back on her arms with legs stretched out in front of her. Sunlight touched off purple highlights in her black hair as her face turned up to the sun. My eyes were drawn to her tilted neck. A slight tremor pulsed at the base of her throat from her steady heartbeat. The sight mesmerized, pulling a ragged breath from my lungs. I shook my head at the sudden flush of heat in my belly.

"Can I ask you a personal question?" Her hesitance pierced my moment of insanity.

"Because these others haven't been personal?" I joked.

The stylish cowboy hat bobbed up her back when she ducked her head at my tease. "How long have you and Chase been together?"

Surprised by the sudden change of topic and somewhat embarrassed at the mention of Chase, I took a few moments to respond. "We're actually not seeing each other anymore."

Brown eyes flared at my revelation. "Oh, I'm sorry to hear that. When did you break up?"

"It's been a long time coming."

She considered her reply. "So, it wasn't just one thing?"

"Not really." The interest in her expression made me want to confide the rest. "Although, the assumption that we were getting married before we'd even discussed any kind of future together kinda tipped me over the edge."

"Hmm, that would be annoying," she mimicked my lighthearted tone.

"Ever had anything like that happen to you?"

"Can't say that I have." She studied me with an amused expression. "I must admit I was a little surprised to meet him."

Surprised? Was the idea of me in a relationship so surprising even to an acquaintance? "Why?"

Raven took time to choose her words carefully. She

looked back at the dogs who'd made fast friends with the horses, snoozing at their hooves. "I don't mean to embarrass you, but I heard something about a dark supply room a few weeks back."

I coughed in surprise. Kelly hadn't seemed like she wanted to tell her boss about that. "Oh really, you heard about my abduction, did you?"

"Sure did, and by the way you reacted so nonchalantly, I wouldn't have guessed that you had a boyfriend."

"Oh?" Now, I was really curious.

"Not that I like blanket statements," she chanced a look at me before continuing, "but most straight women don't handle being kissed by another woman with such a 'no biggie' attitude."

"She told you a lot," I said with cautious amusement. "Did Ms. Supply Room Kissy Face spill that she thought I was someone named Raven?"

She sat up straight, eyes widening again. "Actually, Ray was the one who told me about it." She tilted her head toward me with a piercing look. "Is that why you brought up the no fraternization policy? You thought I was having an affair with my assistant?"

"How many Ravens do you know? And what's the likelihood that two of them work in the same company?"

"You honestly thought I would be that stupid?" Her tone sounded incredulous. Not disbelief that I might have thought that, more like astonishment at the idea of entering into a relationship with her subordinate. Like it was the most absurd notion she'd ever heard.

"Stupid is a little harsh, and I didn't want to believe it." I tried not to sound defensive. "You can't help who you fall in love with, right?"

"No, I guess you can't," she agreed so easily I thought she'd moved past my misperception about her. Her mouth slid into a wicked grin as she kidded, "Might explain you and Chase."

I was so shocked by her instant camaraderie that I blurted, "I wasn't in love with Chase."

"Really?" Her shock didn't contain itself to her tone of voice. Wide eyes, raised brow, and intent lean accompanied her surprised retort. "He's talking about marriage and you're not even in love with him? Either he's clueless or you're a damn good actor."

"Now, that's a personal question," I kidded to cover my embarrassment at admitting something so private.

She smiled at my attempt to move off the subject. "You're right. We should start back anyway."

"Sure, and it's a nice way to dodge any personal questions aimed at you." I stood to help her gather up the blanket and start packing up the saddle bags.

She laughed and slid a smirk my way. "Ask away."

"Ahh, umm…" Her easy response was so unexpected I couldn't formulate a more original question. "No one special in your life that I can tease you about?"

A spark flashed in her eyes when she turned toward me. It made me abandon the task of fastening the saddlebag. She stepped closer to finish the job for me. "Not in a while."

The statement, issued at a lower than normal register, kicked my heartbeat into a higher gear. Could I really be thrilled that she wasn't dating anyone? Thrilled may be too strong a word, but I was definitely gladdened by her response. Maybe I realized that, since we were both single, days like this could be repeated more often than if she was in a relationship. Yeah, that sounded right.

Chapter 10

The descent down the backside of the hill helped refocus my attention away from rare feelings of close friendship to our beautiful surroundings. When we reached the foot of the slope, we rode along the creek for a while, slipping back into silence. Raccoons, squirrels, more deer, and a beaver dam kept my mind occupied so I wouldn't have to contemplate the confusing emotions tangling up my thoughts.

Just before the trail turned inward away from the creek, Raven halted Fate and stepped down from her saddle. "They usually take a drink here."

"All right." I dismounted beside her and led Calamity over to the creek.

We watched the dogs splash through the brook as the horses leaned their long necks to taste the water. Raven stretched toward the sun, providing a glimpse of her flat stomach beneath the now hiked up tank top. I found the sight riveting and confounding all at once.

"Is all this land yours?" I turned back toward the horses because I couldn't handle the thoughts my brain was entertaining.

"I've got ten acres. We're on my neighbor's land right now. He's got another ten acres and the one over there," she pointed to the left, "has five. We all ride horses and agreed to allow each other access to the natural trail that runs up the hill on my property, down the hill on his property and across this creek over to the other neighbor's. None of the overlapping trail runs near our houses, so it's nice and private. Although, I have bumped into them both on the trail before."

"Guess we were lucky to have it to ourselves today." I silently thanked both neighbors for staying off their horses for the day.

Calamity declared her thirst quenched with a quiet whinny. I moved her back from the creek and stepped one foot into the stirrup. A movement caught my eye, and I saw the snake as it shot toward us from the tall grass. My leg was mid swing over the saddle when Calamity reared at the advancing snake, and I found myself falling back to the ground. The fall seemed to take forever. I had plenty of time to hope I didn't land on my dogs and to realize this was going to hurt. What made the fall interminable was the panic that Raven might be bucked off as well. I managed to slip my foot out of the stirrup to try to break my fall. A stab of pain shot through my foot into my ankle when my weight joined in, and I hit the ground with a thud. My head felt like it dribbled several times against the ground as the air rushed from my lungs.

I'd heard the start of Raven's shout when my foot touched down, but my head bounce dimmed all other sound. Having my wind knocked out stunned me enough that I didn't immediately register any other pain. Raven's face loomed over me, her eyes frightened and her lips moving, but I couldn't make out the words. When I felt her fingers press against my forehead, my hearing started to become clearer. "...kay? Oh God! Joslyn?" She gently touched the planes of my face. "Don't move. Please, God, please be okay."

"Snake," I rasped when my wind came back. "Look out."

"Shh, Jos, honey, it's okay. It took off when Calamity reared." Her face showed only a hint of relief that I'd responded to her.

"Is she okay? Fate and the dogs?"

An anxious breath leapt from her mouth as she dropped her forehead to where it touched my shoulder. "They're fine. I can't believe you get bucked and you're worried about the horses and dogs." When she swung her head back up, her eyes looked shiny like she was fighting tears.

"Are you okay?" *Why would she be crying? And did she call me "honey" before? Maybe I really was hurt.*

She blinked several times. "You're the one that's flat on your back. Are you hurt?"

Panic assuaged, I took stock of my faculties. My head hurt, my back ached, my butt was sore, and my ankle felt like someone was repeatedly stabbing it with a hot poker. "Ugh."

She let go of a nervous laugh. "Ugh? I take it that's a yes. Please tell me you can move your hands and feet?"

"My neck's fine." I eliminated the fear of paralysis. "Everything else, not so much." I kept my tone light and moved to get up.

She reached out to pin me to the ground. "Jos, wait! You could have broken something." Her hands moved down to check my ribcage, tenderly probing along my torso.

"Ribs are good. Nothing's broken, but I think I twisted my ankle. I'll know when I try to put weight on it."

"But you hit your head."

"Are you saying I'm loopy?" I kidded, making another move to sit up. This time her hands slid around my back and easily pulled me up. The throbbing that was in my ankle spread quickly to my head. "Whoa!"

"Oh God, you've probably got a concussion. I'm so stupid. I shouldn't have brought us all the way out here."

I placed a hand on her shoulder to calm her and my dizziness. "Raven, stop. I'm fine. Now, if you'll just stop wavering, I can stand up."

"You're joking. You're hurt, you've been thrown from a horse, and you're joking?" The concern in her eyes turned to disbelief.

"You're not the only twisted one." I sucked in several breaths through my nose and out my mouth to regain some equilibrium. When I could twist my head back and forth without any dizziness, I told her, "Okay, up and at 'em."

Raven stood and reached down to help me up. The strength of her arms made me think she probably could have picked me up and set me on my feet without any help from me. I let her haul me up and stood clasping her forearms as I attempted to step down on my hurt ankle. *Ow! Yep, sprained for sure.*

"Jos!" she shrieked when I winced and pulled back the weight from that foot. Her arms came around to steady me and hold some of my weight. I felt the dizziness return. If I'd been able to think clearly, I might have realized that some of the dizziness wasn't only from the pounding in my head.

"Ankle's twisted, too." I reported, laughing at my own joke. Now, I was getting downright silly.

Warm breath swept across the base of my throat as she bent to examine my ankle. My head fell back on its own, the dizziness making me feel weightless. "You're not okay. I'm so sorry. Calamity is usually so gentle. I've never seen her rear up before."

"It wasn't her fault. Snakes wig me out, too."

Raven's relief came in the form of breathy laughter, but two tears escaped her eyes. Without thinking, I reached up and brushed the tears from her face, saddened that she felt responsibility for a freak accident. She watched my fingers leave her face before her eyes snapped back to mine. The emotion in them was so raw it stole my breath. She stepped back, moving her hands from my waist to my arms to keep me steady.

"Here's what we'll do." Her voice cracked when she spoke until she cleared her throat. "As soon as you feel up to it, we'll get you into the saddle, and I'll ride with you. Calamity and the dogs can follow us."

"I'm sure I can ride, Raven." I knew it sounded like I was trying to convince myself, but only because I was.

Her brown eyes, so like fine whiskey, stared sternly at me. "Humor me, Joslyn."

The process of loading me into the saddle convinced me that I wouldn't be able to keep my balance right away. I was glad when she eased onto Fate behind me. Her arms shot forward on either side of me, keeping me poised in the saddle as she grabbed the reins and got our convoy moving.

Fate's first step brought my back against Raven. I tried to move forward, but that spinning thing happened again. All I could do was close my eyes and let her act as my backrest. She didn't seem to mind, her sinewy body strong in her seat, arms resting against mine. Every so often I had to close my eyes to block out a falling sensation and fight to refocus my vision. Clearly, I was a little worse off than I thought. After a long trek, my ankle swelled painfully which kept me from succumbing to the drowsiness I felt.

"Hey, stay with me," Raven ordered softly into my ear. I'd slumped against her left arm and rocked back into my seat after she spoke. "Good, we're almost there."

On cue, Fate broke through the last of the evergreen trees and her house came into view. My dogs tore ahead, racing each other to the truck. When we made it to the barn, Raven dropped Calamity's lead and slid off Fate. She walked around to help me dismount the wrong side of the horse because it would be easier with my injured ankle.

"Perfect." She kept a steadying hand on me. "Let me tie the horses up, and we'll get you inside."

"We've got to get the saddles off and rub them down," the obsessive compulsive in me spoke up.

"I'll do that once I get you settled with an ice pack on my couch." She held up her free hand to stop any reply. "You're hobbled, Jos. Don't argue 'cause you won't win."

I laughed and felt her arm slip around my waist as we limped toward her place. Once we reached the door, I snapped my fingers and the dogs dropped into a squat.

"They can come inside," Raven said.

"They're fine on your porch." We moved through the door awkwardly, but soon, she had me sitting on her leather couch in a sprawling living room.

"Don't move." She dashed up the two steps into the kitchen and banged around her freezer for an ice pack and a towel.

Pulling a pillow off the easy chair next to the couch, she set it beside her thigh when she returned. She gingerly grasped my calf to bring my leg up. I tried to stop the motion, not wanting to put my boot on her couch, but one stern look from her told me I wouldn't win that argument either.

"Oh good, they're ropers." She noticed the laces on my boots. Perching my boot on her thigh, she began untying the laces. With more tenderness than was necessary, she pulled off my boot and sock so we could look at my ankle for the first time. "That's an attractive shade of blue you have going there, Jos."

"Goes with my eyes."

Hers snapped up to study mine intently. "For a second there, you made me doubt my observation skills."

Mine were technically hazel but rather than shifting between blues and greens like most hazels, they moved from grey to amber depending on what I wore. With my red shirt, I guessed they were more amber today than grey. "How's it look, doc?"

"Like we should get you to a hospital for an x-ray."

"No way. I've sprained these ankles enough to know that nothing's broken. Some ice, some rest, I'll be good to go."

She tested my resolve with a long agonizing stare. "Fine, for now." She moved her knees and put the pillow directly under my ankle before draping a towel and ice pack over it. "You're taking some Ibuprofen for those aches and going to rest here until I'm sure you don't have a concussion. I'll go get the horses put away."

When she returned with a glass of water and two tablets, I downed both, feeling much better now that I wasn't moving. "Thanks, Raven. I appreciate your help."

Three fingertips brushed against my temple and onto my cheek before she spoke. "You're welcome, Joslyn. Thank you for being concerned about the horse that bucked you off. You're an amazing person."

Before I could respond, she stood quickly and darted out of the room. I heard the screen door slam shut and measured the thumping in my head against the curious pounding of my heart.

Chapter 11

"That's my girl!" Trinity declared after watching the Storm's power forward, in her classic spin and shoot move, hit the winning jumper to bring the team to six and one for the season.

"She's *my* girl," Stuart, my usual Storm buddy, asserted forcefully. He and Trinity operated under the delusion that each could win the affection of the famous and highly skilled forward. In fact, Stuart referred to her as his girlfriend, much to the dismay of Trinity and, well, the object of his affection if she ever found out.

"Don't start, Stu. I will fight you for her." Trinity, who stood an inch taller than me at five-five, rose off the couch to threaten the towering figure of my buddy. Stuart had a center's body, tall and muscular, yet his teddy bear attitude made him raise his hands in defeat.

Kayla and I watched with wide smiles from our seats.

They got into this argument during every televised away game. I hosted the away game broadcasts because Trinity and Kayla didn't have a television and Stuart's place was a pit. For today's game, I'd suffered the teasing from my friends as I hobbled to the door to greet them. As if that wasn't bad enough, they continued to razz me for not making my usual game snacks because I was trying to stay off my leg. After they'd pretend fed me grapes and fanned me as I reclined on the sofa with my foot elevated, they'd concentrated on the game.

The phone rang, interrupting Trinity and Stuart's face off for their favorite player's honor. Stuart trotted over and scooped up the receiver. "J's Leather Kitty Strip-o-grams, you've got a quip, we've got a whip."

"Stu!" I shouted, horrified by his greeting. Trinity and Kayla howled with laughter, drowning out most of what he was saying.

"She's here, playing the victim with Oscar potential. Hold on." Stuart sneered playfully at me as he handed over the phone.

"Hello?"

"Hi, Joslyn, it's Raven." My heart sped up and heat spread to my face at the embarrassment I felt over my accident yesterday. The replay of the events had wandered uninvited through my mind all day. I felt stupid enough for falling off the horse, but downright idiotic for needing Raven to keep me steady on the ride back. Oh, and mortified by my willingness to let her care for me. To top off the humiliating day, she'd had to drive me home because I couldn't work the truck's clutch with my injured ankle. "Jos?" Worry came through the line.

"Yes, hi. How are you?"

A mirthful huff sounded over the line. "I was calling to find out the same from you. How's your ankle?"

"Better, thanks, and thanks again for all your help yesterday."

"You're welcome. I was just on my way out with my niece, and I thought we'd bring your truck back to you?" The truck. With all those other embarrassing thoughts, I'd forgotten that we'd needed to use it because of my dogs, and she'd taken it back to her place after dropping us off.

"Oh, you don't need to do that. I've got some friends over; we could come pick it up."

"We'll be passing right by your place. Plus, it'll give me another chance to drive it."

I could hear the smile in her voice. Looking around at my friends, I thought they might help ease my humiliation over the reminder of yesterday when I saw her. "If it's no trouble, that would be great."

"Perfect. We'll be by soon," she signed off.

I turned back to a rapt audience. "What?"

"Who was that?" Stuart asked.

"The truck thief."

"The one whose horse bucked your skinny ass off yesterday?" Kayla teased.

"Hey!" I exclaimed in mock horror. Okay, I didn't have much of an ass, but there was enough there to keep me from hurting when I sat down at least.

"We get to meet the person with the sassy horses?" Stuart asked.

"Why don't I take you all over there and they can buck your no-riding asses off, too?" They laughed at my threat, and I couldn't help feeling more relaxed about seeing Raven in the glaring daylight of my humiliation. With a few clicks of the remote I had the other WNBA game started for the group. We settled in to watch with far less interest than the previous game.

Fifteen minutes and one more fight between Stuart and Trinity about another "smoking hot" player later, I heard the engine roar of my old truck heading toward the house. I jumped up and stifled the shriek of pain I felt in my ankle when I forgot about not putting all of my weight on it.

Limping ungracefully, I went to the door to greet my visitors.

"Hi." Raven's smile brightened the brown of her eyes to bourbon color. Since first noticing them, I started thinking I might have a little alcohol problem. At minimum, an obsession and maybe not just with alcohol.

"Hi there, welcome. How's it going, Ray?" I greeted the younger woman standing beside her aunt. I gestured for them to follow me inside where the dogs eagerly greeted them.

"You're up and moving, although, not very well I see," Raven indicated after making sure to give some love to each of my dogs.

"Better than yesterday when I couldn't ride a horse, or walk, or drive, or even think unassisted," I reminded her, setting off a shared smile.

"Ray? Hey, girl, how you doing?" Kayla jumped off the couch to greet Ray with a hello kiss and hug, surprising the rest of us. "Trin, remember Ray from my community theater group?"

"Sure. Hey there, Ray."

Ray turned to introduce her aunt, but Raven waved her off. "We've already met. Nice to see you both again."

I gestured to Stuart. "This is my good friend Stuart. Stu, this is Raven and her niece, Ray." He greeted both with handshakes. "Won't you stay for a while?" I invited, hobbling back toward the kitchen. "Can I get you something to drink?"

"Siddown," Stuart ordered with exasperation and took over getting beverages for the new arrivals.

Settled around the couch and easy chairs facing the television, we broke off into two conversations with intermittent overlap of commentary on the game that was on. Trinity and Kayla occupied Ray, while Stuart and I talked mostly to Raven. Without needing to ask, I knew Stuart was captivated by her. Who wouldn't be? She was beautiful and vivacious. If she stayed another hour, I was willing to bet a year's salary that Raven would rival his favorite Storm player as Stuart's imaginary girlfriend.

"Did you find out about Annabeth's game, Stu?" I asked of his daughter's all-star Little League tournament.

"It is next Saturday, so I'm out."

"They won't let the pitching coach off the hook for a Storm game?" I prodded.

"I tried to plead extenuating circumstances, but twelve-year-olds are so unforgiving." He flipped his hands in a helpless gesture. "Sorry to leave you hanging for the game."

"That's okay. I can usually find someone who wants to go," I assured him. I knew he felt bad now that I didn't have Chase as my automatic backup. Glancing at my visitor, I remembered our earlier discussion. "What about you, Raven? Would you like to sit with us next game?"

Her head whipped around from the television. "Absolutely. Thanks, I'd love to sit there."

"What's happening?" Ray spoke up from the other side of the sectional. "Where are you going?"

"Joslyn just invited me to sit courtside with her at the next Storm game."

"Oh cripes, you and that basketball team." She rolled her eyes at Kayla. Apparently, they both held the same take 'em or leave 'em attitude about our team.

"Wait a minute now, young lady," Stuart scolded. "Those games are the only social life I have outside of work and carting my kids around. Plus my girlfriend plays for the team."

"She. Is. NOT. Your. Girlfriend!" Trinity bellowed at him, starting another round of laughter from everyone in the room.

"Well, we better get moving, youngster," Raven spoke to Ray when the laughter died down. She turned to me. "This was fun, and thanks for the invite to the game. Are you sure you're doing okay?" Her concern felt like it physically touched me.

"I was planning to work from home tomorrow anyway, so I should be fine with another day off my feet."

"I remember when I spent all my work days off my feet." Stuart fluttered eyebrows suggestively.

"Man-Ho," Trinity accused.

"Gigolo, please. I was so high-end you would have had to take out a mortgage to even talk to me, girly," Stuart taunted, starting the laughter again. Sometimes it struck me how much those two acted like kids even though Stuart hit the big 4-0 last month and Trinity just cleared her twenty-ninth birthday.

"You wish," Trinity dismissed him.

When I turned my head back from watching their interaction, I noticed Raven's intent stare. She looked like she didn't believe me about my state of health. I gripped her arm and nodded my head. "I'm fine, really."

She reddened slightly, obviously embarrassed that I'd read her concern so easily. "Good. I guess I'll see you Tuesday in the office if you're not in meetings all day."

"Probably." I stood carefully this time and waited for Raven and Ray to say their goodbyes to the crowd. We moved slowly toward the door, hindered by my limp and the eager dogs. "Thanks for bringing back the truck. One less task."

"You're lucky you got it back," Ray said. "I've never seen Aunt Raven as happy to drive a car before."

"You should have seen her driving my Vette. I didn't think she'd ever get out from behind the wheel."

Ray's smile was almost as wide as her aunt's. "See you around, Joslyn," she tossed out before walking outside.

Raven touched the truck keys to my palm. I shivered when her fingers brushed my upturned wrist. "Until Tuesday." Raven's gaze moved downward briefly before colliding with mine again. With a nod, she joined her niece at her car.

I watched them drive off before returning to the living room. Stuart was making excuses about needing to leave, too. Trinity gave him a hard time about being a fair-weather fan, but she understood his usually jam packed schedule. After another journey to the door and fake sappy goodbyes exchanged all around, we resettled on the couch.

Trinity shot a meaningful glance at her girlfriend before she cleared her throat. "You know, um, I mean, ah, you're aware…"

I turned my attention away from the game over to the usually verbose Trinity. "What?"

She looked at Kayla again before rushing to say, "You know she's family, right?"

The first time she'd used this term, I'd thought she'd been talking about a sister that she'd never mentioned. After a few stupid questions that made them both laugh, they'd offered a translation. Now, I could stay afloat in nearly every one of their conversations. "Ray?"

"Her, too, but I meant Raven."

My eyes widened at her revelation. "I'm not completely versed in etiquette, but if she'd wanted me to know that, don't you think she ought to be the one to tell me instead of you spilling her business?"

Trinity blanched at my lighthearted reprimand. The realization of her statement crashed down on her. "Oh, crap, I'm a moron!"

"Take it easy," I let her off the hook. "I knew already, not that she told me."

"Who told you, other than moron here?" Kayla threw an arm around her girlfriend.

"Don't freak out," I started, knowing how they'd react to this story, "but a few weeks ago, someone hauled me into a dark room at work and kissed me thinking I was Raven."

"A woman someone?" Trinity couldn't hide her intense interest. "You kissed a woman?"

"More like she kissed me."

"So? How was it?" Trinity jutted her chin forward.

I laughed at their excitement and thought about my answer. "Soft ... unexpected."

"You kiss a woman for the first time and that's it?" Kayla bemoaned. "So, it's true, you're hopelessly straight."

I chuckled again at her disappointment, but something that felt like denial swam through my system. One more strange feeling that I'd experienced of late. "Honestly, the surprise at being abducted trumped any other emotions I might work through before it ended."

"Who kissed you? Was she hot?" Trinity raised her eyebrows.

"I'm not going to say, and she was pretty enough." I waved off their interest, intent on getting back to her original declaration. "What made you tell me about Raven?"

"Oh, um," Trinity hedged, shifting her green eyes from her girlfriend to me. "I thought you might need a heads up, that's all."

Now really confused, I asked, "About what? Why would it matter that she's a lesbian?"

"It doesn't, except that she has that whole please-God-don't-let-me-fall-for-a-straight-woman look of doom about her."

I stared at Trinity, not quite sure if I understood. "Are you ... do you mean ... straight woman ... me? Is that what you're saying?"

"Duh." *Ah, the eloquence of youth.*

"Oh, please, Trin," I brushed off her shortsightedness. "You think every woman is gay and hot for you."

"Yeah, but I know this one *is* gay and she's hot for *you.*"

"Cut it out," I disregarded her with a puff of breath.

Raven didn't act at all like a person interested in me. She acted like a woman making a new friend when making friends was no longer the easy endeavor that comes with youth. No, Trinity was reading this all wrong. But for a too brief moment, my ego inflated with the idea, however false, of someone as incredible as Raven liking me.

* * *

The dogs and I started pacing as soon as I'd finished fussing with my hair. I'm not usually a hair fusser, but tonight I was making an effort. Usually on the weekends, I strap my hair into a ponytail or twist it into a bun so that I always know what it looks like. The fifteen minutes I'd scrunched, moussed, and flipped the shoulder length into a manageable wavy do obviously meant that I didn't think the ponytail would suffice tonight. Miracle upon miracles, the normally medium brown showed sun bleached highlights in all the right places and, without any rain, stayed relatively frizz free. Just before I left the bathroom, I decided that I'd spent my quota of hair fussing time for the month on one night.

Checking my watch one more time, I switched back and nearly drop kicked Alexandria. "Oh, Dria, sorry, sweets. You guys look as anxious as I feel. C'mon, let's do something so we stop walking in circles, 'kay?"

Of course, the second we galloped into the living room, the front doorbell rang. The protectors of the bunch barked a soft warning while the others bounded to the door. Several deep breaths and calming orders were taken before I opened the door. The sight was worth all the fuss. Raven stood outside wearing cropped khaki pants and a sleeveless button up shirt over a silky cami. The stylish flip of her collar length hair looked like she'd fussed over it as well, but it was her excited smile that fit her best.

"Hi there, Jos. Hey, guys." She took a knee to greet each dog. They'd dropped and rolled to present their bellies for her attention.

"It's always all about them." I joined her in the doggie rub down.

"As it should be. You look nice. I like that blouse," she complimented easily. Then with a look of panic rushed, "I thought you'd be decked out in team gear."

"Oh, I don't bother, not sitting next to Trin. Not only is she usually head to toe in Storm gear, but she's been known to paint her face for important games. She's a walking team shop. I'd only pale by comparison with any effort."

"Now, I'm really glad my one team shirt is in the pile for laundry day tomorrow."

"Her apparel doesn't hold a candle to her enthusiasm for these games. I hope you don't embarrass easily because she goes a little nuts for this team," I warned.

She grinned and stood up from playing with the dogs. "Ready?"

I snapped twice and pointed to get the dogs moving off to their sunroom for the night. Every time it worked, I wanted to shout my thanks to the dog trainer who'd helped me with the whistle and snap conditioning rather than the choke chain yank and praise confusion that other trainers use. "All set," I responded when I closed the door of the sunroom.

Once in her car, I continued to regale her with Trinity the Superfan anecdotes. Partly to ready her for the experience she was about to go through, but also to ease my sudden nervousness. At the Key, we bounced out of the car, her excitement as apparent as mine. On our way down to my seats, we stopped by hers to greet her friends. A tall brunette was very happy that Raven gave her the extra ticket and therefore very grateful to me for making the extra seat available. By the time we reached my courtside seats, Raven was practically bursting at the seams with excitement.

"Hey, Trin, hi, Kay."

"Slyn," Trinity greeted barely looking away from the

court. "Oh, hey, Raven, I forgot Stu crapped out on us tonight. Glad you're here."

"Hi, Jos, Raven," Kayla called over from her seat beside Trinity.

Raven looked too dazed by the fact that no one separated us and the players on the court to say hello, but she managed a quiet greeting. Her intense concentration on all the up close action made her nearly miss her seat. I had to pull her closer to get her situated over the right chair before she completed her squat. She grinned so widely she didn't need to voice her thanks.

The game passed as if it were on fast forward all night. Trinity's usual exuberance was rivaled by Raven's complete awe at being so close to the court. When a ball came flying our way, I didn't expect the player to follow, falling onto Raven. Once the player had righted herself, Raven found the game ball sitting in her lap.

"You okay?" the player, one of the rookies on the other team, asked Raven.

"Yeah, thanks," Raven managed. She tossed the ball back to the ref to be inbounded and moved up the court. Turning to look at me, she wore the biggest smile I've ever seen.

"Pretty cool, huh?" I asked her.

She laughed, nodding enthusiastically. "So cool."

"Told ya you couldn't beat these seats."

"You were so right." She reined in her smile to speak her thanks for the fifth time tonight.

Teasingly, I asked, "How much are you digging me?"

"A lot." My mouth popped ajar when I looked over at the suddenly serious face next to me. She wasn't kidding anymore, and the dip in her voice made my heart jump. She really wasn't kidding.

Trinity's elbow jutted into me, jarring my stare. I swung around to see what she wanted and was met by raised eyebrows. "Told you," she whispered. "She's into you."

"Stop it," I automatically declined her assessment.

"Hey, just putting in my two cents."

"Keep them, please." When I turned back to Raven, her eyes were on the game. She gave a quick turn, locking eyes with me and her smile flashed brighter. After a long moment, she turned her attention back to the game. "Forget what I said," I whispered to Trinity. "I want a whole dollar's worth at the next game, okay?"

Trinity nudged my shoulder. "Should I dust off the membership application and toaster?"

"Shut up!" I said, but we both broke into giggles.

Chapter 12

*W*alking down the hallway on another Wednesday, I passed the infamous supply room and felt a lingering sensation from that day. The feeling was slightly different in my imagining this time, but before I could identify the source of the difference, a voice pierced the lunchtime silence of the deserted hallway. "...straight? Are you sure?"

Soft murmurs continued before I moved closer toward the corner office's ajar door. "...boyfriend. What more proof do you need?"

"But you like her?" The man's voice was deep and sure. No reply this time. "I'm sorry, Raven. I know how that feels."

At the mention of Raven's name, I stopped dead in the hallway. Luckily, no one was walking behind me or I would have caused a pile up. Raven's reply was too soft to hear, or maybe it was the voice screaming inside my head to keep moving that hampered my hearing abilities.

"...one time, Rave. This could turn out differently. I don't know." He sounded frustrated. "I don't want you hurt again, but damn, Rave, you can't keep restraining your feelings because you were hurt badly once."

"There's being hurt, Dax, and being hurt by the same entirely avoidable thing." Raven's voice sounded just as frustrated.

Leave, leave now! my head screamed and, thankfully, my legs responded by taking me past the office and around the corner. I guessed they had no idea that the door hadn't been latched shut. I wished I hadn't overheard such a private conversation. I didn't let my mind repeat the words, nor would I allow it to think about the subject of their conversation. Trinity didn't need to be elbowing me and whispering in my ear to plant the idea that I was certainly a possibility. *Please, how cocky could I be?* Trinity was wrong about her own relationships enough times; what made me think she could read Raven, a woman she barely knew?

"Oh, Joslyn, good." Kelly intercepted me on my way back to the conference room. She'd stopped blushing every time she saw me now, her mistake all but forgotten, which was a relief. "Raven was looking for you earlier. She thinks she isolated that line item you had a question about."

Her news pulled my thoughts into focus. "Great."

"She's over in Nick's office." Kelly pointed back down the hallway I'd just fled. She started us moving in that direction. I wanted to come up with some reason to delay our progress. The last thing I needed was to overhear more of that particular conversation. As we approached, a familiar looking man strode up to the office and walked inside. Kelly knocked on the now partially open door before pushing through. "Hey, Raven, I found her." She stepped aside to let me edge by.

Two men, the one we'd just followed inside and the other a thin reed of a man with white blond hair and light blue eyes, sat on the edge of the desk facing Raven. They were hunched over some files, but Raven straightened when I entered.

"Great, thanks, Kel." Kelly left after a quick hello and goodbye to the others. Raven beckoned me over. With a proud smile, she introduced me to the blond man. "Joslyn Simonini, this is my brother, Daxson Paul, and I think you've met my cousin Nick, right?"

"Yes, hello, Nick." He gave me a wary nod, eliciting a glare from Raven. "Dr. Paul, it's a pleasure to meet you." I turned to shake her brother's hand as surprise flared in his eyes.

"I see my sister's been bragging about her older, wiser, better looking brother again." He tried to sound bothered but wasn't pulling it off. Raven smacked him on the shoulder.

"I seem to remember her saying something about you studying to pass the South Pacific med boards while you were in prison, yeah." They laughed at my tease, exchanging a quick look.

"You don't want to know what I've heard about you, Ms. Simonini," Daxson joked back.

Raven smacked him again and shot an apologetic look my way. Nick, on the other hand, smirked satisfactorily. "Oh, I believe I've heard every possible description, Dr. Paul, and please call me Joslyn."

"All right, Joslyn, and I'm Dax. Give us your best." His blue eyes twinkled with amused interest, but his sister gasped at the request.

Without missing a beat, I deadpanned, "That I only recommend cutting jobs at companies to then tempt those now wandering souls with acceptance and tranquility in the cult I've created."

Three seconds passed before the siblings burst into

laughter. Nick looked on skeptically then attempted a half-hearted chuckle. "That *is* good. And the true calling of your cult?"

"Government overthrow, feminist upheaval, liberal occupation, abolishing reality television, you know, nothing too radical." They expected my deadpan this time, starting their laughter before I'd gotten through all of my objectives.

"I love *Survivor*," Nick grumbled, and I had to refrain from groaning at his choice of reality shows.

"Get a life, Nicholas, she was kidding." Daxson turned back to me with a piercing look. "Yeah, I like you." He said it simply, like the way kids make honest declarations without regard for how it might be interpreted. After another long look at his sister, he said, "Well, I'd better go see if I can coax my daughter out to the lunch she promised me. Nice meeting you, Joslyn. Take good care with this company."

"That's why I'm here."

"I'll walk you over to IT, cuz," Nick offered, probably to flee my presence before I fired him. Not that I could, but he hadn't warmed to me any more than the rest of the Pauls outside this room.

"Did Kelly let you know about my discovery?" Raven turned my attention back from Dax being herded away by Nick.

"Yes, that's good news. Can't wait to take a look."

A smile met my nerdy declaration. "I'll show you." We headed back to her office where she pulled up an old income statement on her screen. She twisted the monitor so I could see and pointed. "Principal and interest payments on an expansion loan from fifteen years ago. When the location closed, the former CFO mislabeled the payoff as bad debt. Mistakes like that were why Uncle Archie asked me to join the company. I never thought to question it because we had records for the bad debt."

I leaned forward to examine the statement and automatically reached for the mouse, pulling my hand back when I realized it was on the other side of the desk in Raven's hand. She motioned for me to join her. I walked around, sliding past her chair to grip the mouse on her right side. Clicking through each of the financial statements from that year, her explanation made sense but didn't sit right with me. It might have been because the line item had raised a red flag for me, and I never let them go easily. Normally, when I find a red flag in a company, it turns out to be the size of a tent by the time I've tracked it down.

"Do you have the original loan papers?" I tilted my head and found Raven inches from my face. She'd leaned toward the screen and finding her so close astonished me. Her expression was almost as hard to read as the emotion in her eyes, but I could eliminate repulsion. Neither of us moved right away until my usual aloof professionalism propelled me upright.

The movement caused Raven to blink harshly and stare up at me. "Not on the system, but I'm sure we've got them archived. I'll have Kelly check the file room when she gets back from lunch or call them over from file storage if necessary." She studied my reaction. "What is it?"

"It seems too pat."

"Ockham's razor."

"This may not be the simplest explanation, and it certainly wasn't easy to find, Raven. I've been staring at it for weeks and hadn't thought to look into any retired loans. Nicely done."

She smiled at my praise. "We'll know for sure when Kelly digs up the loan docs. For now, can I interest you in grabbing some lunch?"

Hell yes! Then my dispassionate head prevailed and kept me from immediately accepting her invitation. What if she and her brother *had* been talking about me? It would be wise to stay away from opportunities where I might send signals that could be misinterpreted. It wouldn't be fair to her, especially since my own feelings were a complete jumble at this point. "I don't think I can get away today, but thanks. I'm nearly ready to present to your uncles, and I want to go over everything again."

"And again, and again, I bet." She gave me a pointed look. "Okay, well, maybe once you present we can head back over to Amalia's."

"Sounds good," I said noncommittally.

"I'll get a firm lunch date once you make those presentations." She left no room for argument.

I breathed out a laugh and nodded. "Sure. I liked your brother, by the way."

"He's a good brother, not that I tell him that. Doctors have big enough heads as it is." She eyed my backpedaling and said, "I'll have Kelly bring the papers by when she finds them."

"Great, see ya." I escaped to her call of goodbye.

I needed to focus on getting the work done for this client. Distractions like my friendship with Raven, her possible feelings for me, and my suddenly uncertain sexuality wouldn't help me close out this client. And no way did I have time to ruminate on the dread that filled my gut knowing that she'd been burned by someone. Not to mention the complete lack of time and energy to entertain the surge of delight I felt every time I saw her and the equally enjoyable idea that she might like me in that way. No, I definitely didn't have the time for thoughts like that.

* * *

The voice reached me before Raven did. "Get your coat."

I looked up from my summary report as she walked through the conference room door. "What? Why?"

"Amalia's reopened her student kitchen, one night only."

"What? Why?" The news stunned me into echoing my earlier questions.

"We need to get over there before she changes her mind."

Because I couldn't help myself, I repeated, "What? Why?"

Raven laughed, and I basked in the sound. "Cannoli, spumoni, and tiramisu, need I say more?"

I vaulted out of my seat, sparking another laugh from her. Whipping my jacket off the back of my chair, I practically pushed her out the door. My favorites, and while I hadn't sampled Amalia's recipes, I had no doubt they would be like one hundred Italian grandmothers had gotten together to perfect the taste.

We drove over in her car, mostly in silence. I realized I hadn't seen her since declining her lunch invitation and hadn't really chatted with her since the basketball game. I also realized that I'd been carrying around an emptiness for days that suddenly seemed full in her presence. I so wasn't emotionally equipped to deal with that realization.

"How many people will be here?" I asked when we exited the car at the restaurant.

"No idea. Last time she taught out of a culinary classroom that was much bigger than her kitchen. Twelve people can probably fit in there, but it'll be a tight squeeze."

Giovanni greeted us both with hugs at the door and ushered us into the kitchen. Six others already stood at various counter spaces. "Everyone is here, Amalia."

She came over to kiss Raven on the cheek and hug her hello. She turned to me with a sparkling smile and those welcoming arms again. This was almost as good as the chance to learn how to cook like her. When she finished hugging me, she scooted me over to the only open station and smushed me in beside Raven. Guess we'd be working as a team, not that I minded.

For the next couple of hours everyone worked together like we'd been on Amalia's kitchen staff for years. She was that good of a teacher. The aromas of the individual ingredients couldn't compare to that of the finished products. Every student had a personal relationship with Giovanni and Amalia, but none garnered the same affection that they showed Raven. I felt lucky to get some overflow acclaim by standing next to her.

We all had so much fun together I felt like I would be walking away with six new friends. Once we'd packed up our bounty, the other students tossed out goodbyes and promises to report back on their first solo attempt at the recipes. I went back to my workspace and gathered up the bowls, utensils, baking dishes and sheets to take them to the dishwashing station. As I was clearing the other counters, I noticed that Raven, Amalia, and Giovanni tracked my actions from the kitchen doorway.

"What?" I reached over to turn on the tap. "I believe I promised I'd clean afterward if this night ever happened, didn't I?"

"No, no, you dear girl," Amalia protested.

Giovanni beamed at both of us and turned to Raven. *"Lei è realmente meravigliosa, Raven. Non lasciarla andare."*

"Sono soltanto sul mia condotta migliore attorno a te, Giovanni." I used Italian to tell him that I was on my best behavior around him so that he'd know I was fluent enough to understand his matchmaking attempts. While I liked that he thought I was wonderful and someone she shouldn't let go, I didn't need him planting the altogether pleasing thought in my own head.

"Dio mio! Parli italiano?" he asked of my capacity to understand Italian. He turned back to Raven. *"Devi sposarla,* Raven.*"*

"Giovanni," Raven admonished, nothing teasing about it. The lovely blush of her cheeks tipped her embarrassment at his command to marry me. I'm sure if I looked in a mirror, I'd see the same blush appearing on my cheeks.

"I cannot let you do dishes, Joslyn." Amalia stepped in to ease Raven's discomfort, gripping my forearm to get me to stop.

"Getting your hands dirty never hurt anyone, or so my dad always says. Your kitchen staff is gone, Amalia, please let me do this."

"But it is my kitchen."

"Yes, and I'm asking permission to let me earn the tuition for my lesson tonight."

"But I do not charge tonight."

"You should have. I appreciate you sharing your talent with us, so let me do something for you. Take that hunky husband of yours into the restaurant, put your feet up, and I'll have this place spic and span in no time."

"*We* will have this place spotless in no time," Raven interjected, moving forward to take a position at the sink with me.

"Such wonderful girls." Amalia let Giovanni pull her out of the kitchen with a grateful wink at us.

"Thank you for this," Raven said.

"You're welcome." I hadn't realized until Raven spoke that our entire conversation with Amalia and Giovanni had taken place in Italian. Guess I didn't have to worry about my Italian being rusty now that I hardly spent any time on my dad's construction sites with his mostly Italian crew.

An hour later, Raven pulled her car into the Paul Industries parking lot. Mine was the only vehicle left, so she didn't need to ask where I was parked. "Ahh, modern," she teased of my Lexus.

"Boring but functional and an automatic."

"Is your ankle still bothering you?" She couldn't hide the worry from her tone.

"No, but automatics are much easier with all the traffic around here."

We got out to load my share of the desserts into the back seat of my car. The process took a couple of trips, and we only bumped into each other once. When I surfaced from my last drop off of takeout boxes, Raven stood a foot away. The look in her eyes halted my sidestep.

She held my coat but made no move to give it to me. Her gaze didn't shutter the emotions this time. She took a step closer before glancing at my mouth. When her eyes returned to mine, I knew without doubt that she wanted to kiss me. This was so different from the men who'd dropped me off after a date in the past. They would look at me with determination; they were *going* to kiss me. Nothing in their gazes could be mistaken for this kind of wanting. No, the men let me know what they were going to do. This, this look was of a desire to kiss, a craving to kiss, a near Victorian yearning to kiss me. I felt my breath desert me as suddenly as when I'd fallen off her horse.

Unlike with the men on similar occasions, my heart thumped erratically and something of a ruckus roared through my ears. I felt hot and cold and trapped and free all at the same time. Never once had I experienced this strong of a reaction to anyone. Desire had always been an elusive emotion for me. If I were being totally honest, I'd have to admit that I'd never felt it. Until now.

I wanted this. I wanted her to kiss me like I've never wanted anything in my life. Not because I wanted another woman to kiss me for comparison. No, I wanted *this* woman to kiss me. This incredibly smart, sexy woman.

I should do something. Give her a signal to tell her that she could turn her desire into action. If I looked down at her lips, maybe that would be enough of an invitation. Instead, I stared at those eyes, feeling her breath barely touch my face from her spot inches away. Why couldn't I move my eyes from hers? Give her the simple go ahead, or better yet, tip my head forward and capture those sensuous lips to taste what I knew could become addictive? Perhaps it was my stupid sensibility stopping me; or maybe my concern for her that if we kissed and I felt nothing, as per usual, I'd hurt her desperately. God, I hate being sensible almost as much as I hate being emotionally bereft.

Before I could break the spell and reach for my jacket, Raven stepped back as suddenly as if she'd been yanked by some unseen force. She shook her head and offered my coat, not meeting my eyes. When I took the garment, she waved and hurried around to the driver's side of her car.

"Goodnight, Raven," I called out weakly as the door was closing. Her tires didn't exactly squeal as they left the parking lot, but the escape was no less dramatic.

Chapter 13

The rumblings started before I made it up to the front of the large conference room. Now, these people really hated me. I didn't need to be able to read their minds to know that they wanted me to spontaneously combust right before their eyes. Not that I could blame them. This department had every reason to hate me.

Normally, I only present to the executive committee and board of directors, but since it was a family business, Archie didn't want to be the one to present the changes to the staff. Despite his declaration to "fire every last one of them," he didn't want to be the bad guy. He'd extended my contract to present the changes and oversee the implementations of the changes.

Today was the sales department's turn. My last presentation. Zina had taken the seat directly to my right, and for that, I wanted to hug her. I faced the angry mob that made up the sales department. Robert looked both pissed and bothered, not an easy look to pull off.

"Good afternoon, everyone. I've been asked by Archie and Nathan Paul to present the accepted changes that I've recommended based on my analysis of your department." The crowd groaned at my announcement. Oh yeah, I really had no chance of being voted most popular after this meeting.

"Corporate-wide changes will be released in hard copy in a new employee handbook next week." I held up the printer mockup of the handbook I'd worked on with human resources and legal. "The first page is an acceptance and agreement form. You'll have one week to read through the new handbook, sign and date the form, then return it to HR. Your next paycheck won't be released until you do."

"You can't do that!" Robert growled from the back of the room.

"Of all the changes, Robert, this one is the easiest to comply with." I offered a bland look, hoping he'd get the hint that something this trivial wasn't worth his ire. "Additionally, the sales department will have its own policy and procedures manual with the same acceptance form requirement." I held up a copy of their smaller bound book and turned on the projector.

Flipping through the slides of my sales presentation, I outlined and explained all the changes to their department. By the last slide, I'd barely heard any arguments. In fact, most seemed thrilled that their achievements would be recognized and documented without the threat of being embarrassed by less than stellar individual performances.

"Finally, you'll be moving to a per diem expense accounting basis for sales calls. All travel arrangements will be made by your sales admin assistants who have been briefed on the new spending parameters. Overnight stays are limited to trips that take you two hours away from the office. Your per diem allotment includes three meals and is only in play on sales calls that qualify as overnight stays."

"What?!" several sales reps yelled out.

"Per diem won't be given for local trips."

"You can't take away our lunches and dinners," someone exclaimed from the left side of the room.

"Yeah, screw that!" another person yelled from the back.

"What about our local clients?" Janice, the woman who'd sat closest to me while I'd been with sales, asked.

"Entertaining a client at a restaurant can still be expensed, locally or otherwise. However, you won't be reimbursed for meals that you take on your own while visiting a client within the 120 mile radius."

"That's unfair for those of us with mostly local clients." This whine came from Peter, who'd whined daily about all sorts of things while I tried to work in the cubicle opposite him.

"Then I would suggest you speak with your manager about extending your territory," I retorted. Outside of Robert, Peter was the biggest offender of this policy. They could go to lunch on their own dimes and whine about the unfairness then.

"What the hell, Robert? You just gonna stand there and let her take away our perks?" Peter prodded.

"I'm talking to dad about this, but he seems to think we need some changes. Don't worry, I'll have this one rescinded."

"You shouldn't make promises to your staff that you can't keep, Robert." I risked that my speaking out against him would anger him further, but I knew Archie wouldn't change his mind about this.

"I think I know my dad and my staff better than you, Joslyn." The way he said my name made me shudder from the laced hatred.

"Of course you do," I tried placating him. "However, Archie has signed off on this recommendation. It's been put into print, and the five-year budget incorporates the new projections. These changes have already happened and telling your staff that they'll change back is not practical."

"Goddamn bitch," Robert muttered loud enough for the whole room to hear.

"Robert!" Raven exclaimed, her eyes blazing. She must have slipped inside while I was distracted with the growing anger in the room.

"I'm not happy with you either, cuz," Robert told her.

"I suggest you let Joslyn finish her presentation without argument or join me in your office where we can talk about the budgeting issues. Which would you prefer?" Hands on hips, she left no room for argument.

"Fine, she can finish, but this isn't over. Mark my words, guys."

"You're overextended on this one, Robert. These changes will save the company millions over the next five years. Uncle Archie wholeheartedly agrees," Raven spoke with the authority that comes with being CFO, not as his older cousin. "Please continue, Joslyn."

I tried to keep my expression neutral as I went on despite the happy dance I was doing inside. "You'll find that the per diem allowance is the average of the entire department's expenditures both locally and long distance. Very few of you will find the limitations a hardship from what you're used to spending when making a sales call." I held up the new sales booklet. "You all need to sign the acceptance form in your new policy manual to denote that you've read and accepted the changes for the department."

That announcement finished my presentation except for questions. Surprisingly, many of the staff asked questions that had nothing to do with the expense cuts or bonus calculations. The end of the meeting brought about a few parting handshakes from my former "colleagues" and nods from others. Overall, it hadn't been too bad a meeting.

"I'm sorry about that." Raven approached me after

she'd seen everyone out.

Preparing these presentations had taken up the better part of the last two days. I'd completed them from my home office, which meant I hadn't seen Raven since she'd dropped me off in the parking lot a few nights ago. No traces of the flour from that night showed on her charcoal grey suit or dark blue shell. Nor did I suspect that if she drew closer I'd catch a whiff of the delectable pastries that we'd made. But I didn't need those prompts to remember that we'd nearly kissed.

"I appreciate you standing up for me," I said.

"Of course."

"You say that like it's nothing." I turned to face her, feeling a swirl of heat flow through me. "It's not nothing, Raven. You took my side against your cousin in front of his staff. I'm not sure it was the wisest thing for you to do, but no one has ever done anything like that for me. I thank you."

Her eyes blinked several times before she nodded to accept my thanks. "You did a nice job. I'm glad you agreed to make these presentations for my uncles."

"I've done it before. I find it's easier for the staff to accept changes when they come from me rather than the owners. Everyone gets to keep their hands clean in the process."

"From the feedback I've received, the changes are going over very well. Even the voluntary layoffs."

"Layoffs can be difficult no matter what, but by asking for volunteers you generally get the people that have been thinking about leaving or the underperformers who know they're in jeopardy of losing their jobs anyway. It's a great way to get rid of burned out employees and dead weight."

"Brilliant." She gave me a tentative smile. "Completely off topic, I'm headed out to a charitable gala this evening that might interest you. They'll be auctioning off some mint condition classic cars."

"Over at Salish Lodge? Yeah, I'm headed up there myself. I doubt I'll be bidding on anything, but I always love seeing restored vehicles."

The smile she wore moved from tentative to forced. "Oh, you'll be there? Great, perhaps we'll run into each other."

"I'll make sure to look for you."

"All right, well, I've got some changes to implement. See you later." Again, she seemed to race from the room. This was becoming a habit with her, and I didn't understand why. She'd brought up the gala; why would she be so perplexed to find out that I was going, too?

"Ms. Simonini?" Archie's EA interrupted my musings. "Archie is ready for you." She walked me back to the CEO's office and ushered me inside.

"Joslyn, wonderful. I understand the meetings are going well. How'd that last one go? Can't imagine those sales folks were too happy to see anything change."

"It went surprisingly well, Archie. Reluctance to any change is natural, but they'll get used to it, especially since the end result will bring this company back into the black."

"So you and Raven have assured me. You both better be right. I can't fire her; she's my niece, you know." His blue eyes sparkled.

"I do, and you definitely should not fire Raven. She's the most competent CFO I've ever met. You're lucky to have her both in your company and your family." Not that I was jealous or anything.

"Don't I know it," he beamed. "She and that brother of hers have always been overachievers, smartest of the whole lot of 'em. But I love 'em all equally, you know."

"Of course." I'd seen the truth in his statement every time he interacted with his niece, nephews, and kids. "I asked for this time to talk to you about some of your executive level staff. I'm not sure you're going to like what I have to say, but I told you when I took this contract that I wouldn't pull any punches just because this is a family business."

"Okay, lemme have it."

"You've got four chiefs and assistant chiefs that I think are inappropriately titled. Two in HR, one in ops, and one in sales."

"I've never thought those touchy-feely types in HR were of any use. Operations hasn't been—did you say sales?" His eyes snapped back to mine.

"Yes, I'm referring to your son Robert." At his look of denial, I rushed ahead, "I think he's one of the best salespeople I've ever met, and I've met a lot. However, excellent technicians don't always make excellent managers."

"What are you saying?" Archie leaned forward with a raised brow.

"I think he might be in over his head with the CSO position. Robert would excel as a senior sales rep. He could focus on sales, which he loves, and mentor the newer sales reps in the department."

"You're saying I should fire my own son?"

"No, sir. I'm saying that his expertise isn't being properly utilized. He lacks the attention to detail that all chiefs need and his disregard for anything other than sales calls isn't conducive to the efficiency or accuracy of his department."

"Is that so?" Confusion moved to incredulity in his tone. "Who would you recommend I replace him with?"

I hadn't expected that question, but the answer was obvious to me. "Well, you'd want to post the position to see what type of applicants you could garner, but I believe you've got the best candidate already in that department. Zina Redding."

"His secretary?" he asked in disbelief.

I winced at his antiquated term. "His administrative assistant, yes."

Archie's brow smoothed out as he started laughing. "Oh, you're just joshing with me. That's a good one, young lady."

All right, now what? I could push the issue and watch him get angry or let him brush off the suggestion as a joke. Best to go with ambiguity. "I've made my recommendation, sir." Confusion reappeared, giving me hope that he'd mull over the idea later. "I'll be in tomorrow to finish up your new business plan."

"On a Saturday? You are dedicated. Are you certain I can't entice you to stay on here? We could make another chief position for you. Operations, perhaps?"

"Thank you, Archie. I'm honored, but I like being a consultant."

"I had to try." He stood up and shook my hand over his desk.

I hoped his glow about the job I'd done would help him through the huge check he'd have to write as my fee on this consultation. Despite being very aware of the contract's length and the consultation fees, I often received a follow up phone call to try to bargain down the fee. I'd hoped to avoid that with Archie Paul. Not only because it was embarrassing to deal with, but also because he'd more than likely task Raven to do it. I wasn't sure I was in a position to deny her any request at this point.

Chapter 14

O ne look around the ballroom and I wished I hadn't agreed to come to the charity gala. Glamorous people traipsed back and forth between silent auction items, delectable food, and equally elegant individuals. I'd done my best to fit in, but my comfort zone was among the financial statements and competency questionnaires I'd left behind at the office. Or maybe in an Italian restaurant's kitchen making delicacies I have no business making or being elbows deep in dishwater earning my keep.

The classic cars had been worth the trip and knowing my purpose here helped as well. I just wished I looked like I belonged. Like the group of women over by the buffet table, all decked out in dresses that looked torn from runway models. Or those gentlemen in their fine, expensive suits. Or that woman in her stark white suit that must have been custom made the way it fit her so well. I should have worn a suit instead of forcing myself into the unavoidable discomfort of my dress and heels. Any of my business suits would have sufficed, but I'd wanted to dress up for the special occasion. That woman sure looked comfortable in matching slacks and jacket that accentuated everything they were supposed to. How odd would it be if I went up to her to ask who her tailor was? Is that how you broke the ice with people at these kinds of events or would it be considered tactless?

Before I had a chance to complete my internal debate, the woman turned and I gasped. *Raven.* Her black hair even more midnight in color against the winter whiteness of her suit. Under the single button jacket, she wore a black lace halter top, tastefully cut and clinging to her chest. Gorgeous.

And so was the woman who was greeting her with a quick kiss and close hug. Actually more than gorgeous. She could be a model, the classy old fashion movie star kind, not the emaciated near freakish looking runway type. Every man's head in the place turned and checked her out, but she was with Raven. Did I mention that I hate being sensible? Even if I could figure out what to do with these new found feelings, I didn't stand a chance against her.

Well, time to be a grown up. I started toward them, cringing every time the supermodel and Raven shared an innocent touch. When Raven smiled gratefully then kissed the woman's cheek, I nearly changed my course. I didn't want to interrupt their date, but mostly I didn't think I could stand being near Raven when she was on a date. Yet, I couldn't stay away either.

"Turns out you weren't too hard to spot, Raven," I greeted in a miraculously steady voice.

"Joslyn, you made it." She sounded overjoyed to see me. Even her eyes seemed to dance with a mingle of elated emotions, but clearly I had no idea how to read her eyes.

A pleased smile crawled over her date's face as she

looked first at Raven then at me. I held out my hand in greeting. "Hi, I'm Joslyn Simonini."

Raven's mouth parted but Ms. Gorgeous stepped in with her own introduction. "Elise Bridie, nice to meet you, Joslyn."

"And you as well."

"You look," Raven started and seemed to search through an entire thesaurus of descriptive adjectives before settling on, "very nice. That's a beautiful dress."

"Thank you and I eyed your suit from across the room. I was contemplating coming over to shake you down for your tailor's name before I realized I actually knew you."

"How is it that you know Raven?" Elise tilted her head, causing dark brown hair to sweep over one shoulder.

"Joslyn is the consultant my uncles hired. She's done a terrific job." Pride slipped into Raven's tone.

"I've had lots of help," I added to displace the sudden tingle of embarrassment. "How did you and Raven meet?"

"We went to grad school together." Elise slipped an arm around Raven's waist. "Raven was the only business major in one of my law classes, which meant she didn't have an agenda for taking the class. It also meant we'd get along perfectly."

"That's great." I hoped my reply didn't sound forced. They looked amazing together. I should be happy for her; too bad I was a selfish bitch.

"There you are, Jos." A familiar deep voice ignited my smile. Arms went around my shoulders and smashed me against a solid wall of man.

"Hi, Dad." I turned into him for a proper hug. He placed a kiss on top of my head as I took in his familiar scent. "You're looking very dapper." In a dark blue suit, the white streaks in his brown hair became more evident. He'd only started going grey since he retired. Prior to that, his brown hair defied science.

"Had to look presentable for tonight." He leaned back

and smiled at everyone.

"Dad, this is Raven Malvolio and Elise Bridie. My father, Michael Simonini."

"Hello." He shook their hands as they exchanged greetings. "Raven? Of the wild horses fame?" He grasped my shoulder and pulled me against him again.

When she paled, I stepped in to save her. "He's kidding, Raven. He stopped by the day after we went riding and noticed my limp, but I told him it was my own fault, right, Dad?"

"You should see a ladder buck her off. Or a roof, or scaffolding, hell, even a porch gives her troub—"

"Okay, Dad, they get it."

He grinned conspiratorially at them as the worry eased from Raven's face. "Your daughter mentioned that you're recently retired. How are you enjoying it?"

"Love it, should have done it ten years ago. Let my daughter keep me in the lifestyle to which I've grown accustomed." We chuckled at his joke. I knew he loved retirement, almost as much as he'd loved working the jobsites. "I know Jos has been working with you, Raven, so tell me what you do, Elise?"

"Elise works for the FBI. She's one of the law enforcement officers being honored tonight." A more potent dose of pride slipped into Raven's tone with her proclamation.

"How wonderful," I offered. *Great. Gorgeous and superbly noble.*

"Congratulations," Dad said.

Pink shaded her cheeks as Raven slipped an arm around her. "No one is better at her job." Elise smiled modestly, tapping her head against Raven's for a second. Yeah, they looked good together. Too good, dammit.

"Hubba, hubba, outlaw dress, Jos," one of two other voices I'd know at this function teased.

"Marco, my boy!" Dad grabbed him up in a bear hug

that would have cracked my ribs. Marco, a solid guy, didn't have to worry about broken body parts.

"Hi, Michael." Marco pulled away and turned to me. "You keep looking like this, Jos, and I might start thinking that you don't fit in at my jobsites anymore." He kissed my cheek and hugged me tightly.

"Marco Ventano, meet Raven Malvolio and Elise Bridie." I left an arm around his waist to keep steady with his muscular arm draped around my shoulders. Any motion by him tended to teeter me from side to side without some anchoring on my part.

He shook their hands in greeting and swiveled his head from Raven to me. "She's the one that took the crowbar to your ankle, right?"

I couldn't stop the giggle this time. "You guys are killing me. Please, play nicely. Raven isn't used to what gigantic p—"

"Portions of delight we are to you, darlin'?" Marco cut off my less than complimentary description of him. It got everyone laughing again.

"Should we take a spin through the auction items, Jos?" Dad asked. "You can buy me a new car to enjoy in my retirement."

"How about I buy you a model of a car that you can build with all that retirement time?" He grinned at my tease. I turned back to Raven. "I'm glad I caught up with you tonight. Good to meet you, Elise. Congratulations on the honor."

"Thank you, Joslyn. Great meeting you all." Elise gave us a friendly wave before settling her arm around Raven again.

"Same here." Marco got us started in the direction of the bid items with a hand on my back. Not exactly how I'd envisioned or hoped my meeting with Raven would go tonight, but she looked happy and that's all that mattered. Or so I could kid myself until I no longer had to see her on a daily basis.

After prying my dad out of several cars, making sure Marco had plenty of food, and sitting through the first group of honorees, I'd managed to ditch them for a much needed timeout. Outside, I took one of the illuminated pathways along the falls in the balmy summer night air. The view brought in many tourists each year, but the gala attendees stayed inside now that it was dark out. I had the pathway to myself. Almost.

The brilliant white of her suit glowed like a sliver of moonlight on the deserted ledge up ahead. Raven was leaning against the railing, her head tilted up toward the ridge of the waterfalls. "Hi," I called out softly, not wanting to startle her.

She turned with a timid smile. "Hello."

"I needed a break," I admitted, coming to a stop beside her.

"Not your kind of crowd?"

"Hardly, but I can mix it up when there's a good reason."

"Same's true for me. If it weren't for Elise, I'd be out riding right now."

"She's stunning," I let slip without editing. Raven turned an interested glance my way. "Really, she could be a model."

"Probably because she was, not that she lets anyone know that."

"Wow, well, you two make a nice couple. She seems great."

Raven's jaw nudged open. "She is great, but we're not together. She's married actually."

"Oh, I assumed…"

"In fact, that's her partner right now." She pointed a long finger downward to the path outside the lodge doors. We watched a short, slim figure walk with purpose toward a solitary Elise and touch her back in greeting. When the former model turned around, excitement and joy exploded out from her in almost tangible form. The shorter woman fit herself into Elise's open arms and pulled her tight. When she tilted her face up, their lips met and I felt the effect from twenty feet away. "That's Austy, and they make a perfect couple."

"I see that," I managed in a rough voice. Watching the couple kiss twisted my insides like I was working the trapeze lines without a net. Heat seeped through my body as their kiss ended and they exchanged an envious look.

"Your date is very handsome and nice. As is your father."

At the sound of Raven's voice, my head snapped around to look at her. "They're both hams so don't let them hear you say that," I scoffed. "And Marco's not my date."

"Does he know that?"

I wanted to laugh, but she seemed entirely serious. Too serious. "Marco isn't legally my brother, but that's how my dad and I think of him." She cocked her head, turning to face me. "Our dads were best friends. They owned the contracting biz jointly. Marco and I spent every summer and school vacations working the jobsites from the time we were old enough to swing a hammer.

"He lost his parents in a car accident when he was fifteen, and his whole world changed. His relatives yanked him to California where he bounced from one household to another, getting into trouble while trying to deal with all his anger at being abandoned. Less than a year later, he hitched his way back, showed up on our doorstep and never left. He became my brother that day and my father's son.

"Dad took him on as an apprentice after he finished high school then gave him his father's half of the business. Now, he owns it outright. He's an extraordinary person, and I couldn't ask for a better big brother."

"I would have to agree." She nodded solemnly. "He's overcome a lot, and I bet he feels just as lucky to have you and your dad in his life."

"Thank you, Raven. That's very kind of you to say."

"So…"

"Yes."

We locked eyes and something electric crackled between us. The guarded veil lifted from her brown again and trapped me in place. If someone blew a trumpet right in my ear, I wouldn't even flinch. My awareness existed only on her, those delicate cheekbones, sparkling eyes, disappearing line over one side of her lip when she stopped smiling, raised mole on the side of her long neck, provocative earlobes. Beauty personified.

The faintness I'd felt in my stomach witnessing Elise and her partner's kiss plunged toward uncontrollable vertigo. I wanted to close my eyes against the unsteadiness, but then I'd lose sight of her and that thought made me even more lightheaded. I silently screamed at my brain to make me move, but paralysis beleaguered me.

Raven's eyes took in every feature on my face, dropping to my mouth countless times. That same look of yearning crept into her eyes, but something held her back from kissing me. Something that was powerful enough to make her ignore her longing. Could I rival that powerful entity?

I forced my eyes to look at her mouth with those slightly parted, full lips. It was the only movement my body could manage under the weight of my desire. I'd gone my whole life without ever once feeling this, and when I finally do, I couldn't move.

Her eyes flicked back to mine with pleading. *Oh no!* She wasn't going to act on this. Something kept her from taking that step. I guess I had the answer to my earlier question. I wasn't enough for her to take a chance. She blinked harshly with a tight smile and nodded once. Swiveling abruptly, she took a step back toward the lodge.

My hand reached out on its own and grasped her forearm, turning her back. "Raven, please."

She cocked her head at the pleading tone in my voice, but she had to know what I meant. She halved the distance between us, studying my eyes intently. Her gaze dropped to take in my entire length before landing back on my mouth.

"Do something," I whispered, unable to voice anything more specific. Whatever she did would feel right.

Her eyes clenched shut. When they popped open, she leaned forward, placing a whisper of a kiss on my cheek. As her lips left my face, I felt her hands grasp my hips and pull me closer. Another feathery kiss landed on my forehead. I shivered when the night air touched the damp imprint after her lips moved on to my other cheek. Something like lightening singed along my body at the first press of her lithe frame to mine.

I found her eyes when she tilted back from the tender adoration of my face. No one had ever done that before. The gesture told me that she got just as much, if not more, from giving pleasure as from taking it. The realization nearly made me topple forward from displaced weightiness.

One of her hands moved from my hip up to cup my face. Delicate fingers slinked along my jaw to rest fingertips in my hair and a palm on my cheek. The motion spurred mine to slide around her shoulders. As her soft lips first pressed to mine, my head pitched backward at the unfamiliar burst of passion that blasted through me. She followed the motion, tightening her grip. I shot a hand up to her nape, pulling her into me. Supple lips moved over mine with a combined tenderness and fervor that I'd thought could only exist in dreams. Her kiss cherished and pleasured, nothing about it demanded.

A faint sound poured into my mouth, igniting a flood of lava that went straight to my center. I needed more of her. My tongue reached inside and her moan repeated at a more insistent volume. Our tongues tangled together as our lips tested every surface. Gently, I tugged on her bottom lip with my teeth before losing myself again in her kiss. Her hands moved around me to embrace my body as expertly as her mouth caressed mine.

When I shifted a leg between hers to keep from falling to my knees from the heady desire, she yelped into my mouth and jerked back. The sudden loss of her heat and softness made me stumble forward. I sucked in a deep breath, trying to gain some balance. A step away, Raven's chest heaved rapidly, a look of shock on her face.

"What's wrong?" I spoke between gulping breaths. "Raven?"

"This isn't a good idea," she said in a rough whisper.

The words shocked me. That was the most potent, blistering, heart-stopping kiss of my life, and she didn't think it was a good idea? She'd been right there with me, hearts pounding, hands grasping, tongues stroking, lips searching. I started toward her, but she stepped back like we were in a ballroom dance competition. Not a good sign.

Before I could say anything else, I heard Marco's voice call out. "Hey, Jos, there you are." My head whipped around to find him stepping onto the pathway to our ledge. "Phoebe's up in the next group. We should get seated."

My eyes went back to Raven. The whole reason I was here tonight was to show support for Marco's wife who was being honored for her work as a hostage negotiator for the police. She hated attention, but having us here would make the notice easier to take. "I'm sorry, I have to get inside. His wife gets anxious about the spotlight. We have to be there for her."

"Sure," Raven blurted out. "Go. This is her moment, right?"

"Jos? They'll be starting any minute, now," Marco insisted.

"Yeah." I moved forward, and Raven made a concerted sidestep to avoid brushing up against me. How could I have read that kiss so wrong? "Goodnight, Raven."

"Night," she spoke as her glance touched my face. A

repeat of the searing heat from her kiss accompanied the glance. She turned back toward the lodge and waved at my brother. "Goodnight, Marco."

"Bye, Raven." He reached a hand out and clasped my elbow to usher us inside. If he'd seen what happened, he didn't say anything. For that I was grateful, because I didn't know what to think myself.

Chapter 15

The sigh sounded content, echoing through the small conference room. When it bounced back to me, I snapped alert, realizing I'd been the one to issue the sound. Terrific. How many times had I done that this morning? At least no one was around to witness this complete lack of concentration and near dreamy state of being.

Those silky lips, tormenting fingers, smooth hair, taut but supple body touched peripherally at first then reached inside to caress all that I was. Her fragrance, a fusion of rosewater and citrus, jumbled with the pounding water from the falls and the sharp scent of evergreen pine surrounding us. The taste of her so savory, I was certain I'd never get enough.

Then it had stopped so suddenly it took my breath like a blow to the midsection. Even hours and hours later, I couldn't say which would cause more pain.

The rest of the night passed in a haze. I'd watched Phoebe receive her accommodation and provided a buffer between her and the many people who approached to offer congratulations. Marco, Dad, and I had perfected our Great Wall impression as soon as we realized Phoebe was the shy type. Afterward, I searched for Raven, hoping to speak with her, but she'd disappeared.

On the drive home, Marco, who'd needed a ride when his wife was asked to stay behind for a photo op, was strangely quiet. Usually, he'd be telling me all about whatever his homeowner's latest demands were at his current contracting project. He had a million great stories. When he spoke, it wasn't to say that his client wanted something horribly tacky like fuchsia carpet. No, when he spoke, he asked about me. "Anything you want to tell me, Jos?"

I glanced over at him in the passenger seat. The dark interior didn't allow me to see his expression clearly. I could make out that some of his brown curls, usually tamed to the top of his head, had loosened onto his forehead. "Don't think so. You okay?"

"Maybe I should have asked that a different way. Why don't you tell me about her?"

My mouth popped open, calming breaths pushed in and out. The pounding in my heart moved directly to my ears, and I found it hard to keep my bearings. "Her?"

"I saw you, Jos. I didn't mean to, but when I went looking for you, you were..."

"Kissing a woman," I finished for him.

"At first that's what went through my mind. Joslyn's kissing a woman. But after watching you for a second, I thought, no, she's kissing Raven."

I shook my head, trying to split my concentration between the road and what he'd just said. "What do you mean?"

"I mean that I went from being shocked to see you, who

as far as I know is straight, kissing a woman to being shocked that you were *kissing* that woman."

"I don't get your meaning."

He laughed in that comforting way of his that always made me feel safe and loved. "From the first time I caught that fumbling idiot in high school kissing you behind the gymnasium to the many boyfriends I've tried to intimidate because they weren't good enough for you, all the way up to that putz, Chase. I mean really, Jos, what the hell were you doing with him?"

I coughed at his bluntness. "Where are you going with this? And there haven't been that many boyfriends. You make me sound like a hussy."

"You're right, not many, but none of them were good enough." He shifted in his seat to face me with those dark brown eyes that always seemed serious even when he was joking. "You'd introduce us to someone you were seeing, and within minutes, I'd know if he was right for you. It wasn't just my impression of him. You'd tell me by the way you'd stand together, or react to his touch, or the tone of your voice. I'd always be relieved that you wouldn't be falling for the guy, but then I'd be sad, too, because you're so great, Jos. You deserve someone amazing."

"Marco," I managed through the wash of pride I felt because I had this incredible man to care for me.

"You do, but I didn't know if you'd ever realize it."

"Thank you, but not everyone can be as lucky as you."

"Damn right, Phoebe's the best. I want the same for you. From what I saw tonight, I think you might have found it."

"It was just a kiss." I purposefully played down the event, more for myself than for him. That denial reared up again, but this time I wasn't kidding myself about it.

"You're in the habit of kissing gorgeous women all of a sudden?" he teased but grew serious again. "I shouldn't make light, but you're insane if you think that was just a kiss." He paused, probably waiting for me to object. Not that I could.

"You're not freaked?"

"I should be asking you that question, unless you are in the habit of kissing women? Seeing as you broke up with Chase not long ago, I assume not."

"I don't know what to think, honestly," I admitted, pulling into his driveway. His house was a masterpiece like mine, as it should be since he'd built both.

"At the risk of you smacking me," he started and I tensed. Generally when he said that, I always felt like smacking him. "Could it be that you don't know what to think not because you find yourself attracted to a woman, but because you find yourself falling in love for the first time?" He reached for the latch, waiting until the shock left my face. "That wasn't just a kiss, Joslyn. Stop trying to think your way out of it. She's good enough. I didn't need to see the way she kissed you to know that."

I shook my head stunned by his observation and blessing. After he left the stillness of the car, I managed to drive myself home without getting into a wreck. Ever since, I'd apparently been sighing and daydreaming while reliving every sensation. What a hopeless loser.

Two clicks on the laptop and I saved then closed out the revised business plan. As soon as Archie arrived, I'd make my final report.

"Hi." Her voice worked like a sheepskin coat blanketing out the painful cold of dead winter.

"Hi," I replied softly, glad I was sitting when I glanced up. Raven wore casual clothes but they were no less striking than her immaculate suit last night.

"Final report?" Her hand gestured toward the bound report on the table next to my laptop.

"Yes." I kept from voicing the unnecessary. We both knew that, with this report and Archie's acceptance, today would be my last day at Paul Industries. I hadn't been worried about never seeing her again, but by her expression, maybe I should be. "I looked for you after the ceremony last night."

"I left early." She glanced away.

"That's what Elise said when I caught up with her. Everything okay?" I didn't know how to go about asking what I wanted to ask.

She brought her glance back to mine and nodded once. "How are you?"

The question wasn't an innocent follow-up greeting, and I chose my response carefully. "That depends on whether you're free for dinner tonight?"

"Joslyn," she started, but nothing else came.

"Just dinner, Raven. We should talk." I watched her defensive posture slacken. "I'll pick you up at seven?"

"I can meet you there." She sounded as if my suggestion was the scariest thing she'd ever heard. "Which restaurant?"

Before I could object, Archie pushed through the open door. "Ah, good, my beautiful niece."

"Hi, Uncle Archie." Raven smiled without any consternation for him.

"How are you, Joslyn?" His was a greeting.

"Fine, Archie. I've just finished the final business plan if you have some time?"

"That's what I was hoping you'd say when I waltzed in here. Shall we take this back to my office? Raven, join us?" He turned back to the doorway.

"I've got to get the quarterlies done. I'll leave you in good hands." She patted his arm as he started off toward his office.

I gathered up my report and laptop and went to follow Archie. When I reached Raven, she shifted slightly to allow me to pass through the open door. "Seven? I'll come by your place, and we'll decide where to eat then."

Her eyes flicked back and forth between mine as if

searching for her answer. She nodded twice, a brief smile pulling at the corners of those talented lips. With her acceptance, I had to keep myself from skipping off after Archie.

* * *

The guilty looks that intermittently peeked through troubled me the most. What did Raven feel she had to be guilty about? I could understand the looks of hesitation, wariness, even fear, but guilt didn't make sense. If those worrisome glances hadn't been broken by glimpses of desire and attraction, I'd have called an end to my determination to "talk" at this dinner.

Our ride over had been comfortable. When I'd shown up at Raven's, she looked as nervous as I felt, but I tossed her the keys to my Vette and delight took over her whole demeanor. She drove us to a restaurant that was farther away than I'd planned just so I could prolong her enjoyment.

Settling around the secluded table, I struggled to keep from confronting her while we ordered. When her conflicting gazes continued to sift through more and more disquieting emotions, I decided frankness wouldn't be the best course of action. We'd fallen into our usual easy conversation, moving from topic to topic without notice of the time slipping by. It was only during the lulls when a course was cleared or served that she'd flash those awkward emotion-filled glances.

Forcing myself to take a bite of the dessert I didn't want but had ordered to draw out our time together, I barely registered that her expression had moved from guilt to sorrow to determination. "I shouldn't have kissed you," she admitted softly.

I set down my fork and swallowed the suddenly bitter tasting cheesecake. "I asked you to. I wanted you to."

"You're straight," she accused without malice and so

quietly I had to lean forward to hear. "We shouldn't—I shouldn't have."

"You think you took advantage? I was the one who stopped you from leaving."

"I can't do this." Her gaze turned steely.

"Again," I added what I assumed she'd left out.

"Pardon?"

"You meant to say that you can't do this again, didn't you?" A look of surprise then confusion came over her face. Before it went all the way to denial, I continued, "You've shown reluctance to act before, which tells me that you've had experience with this and the result made you want to ensure that it never happens again."

Deep breaths pumped through her torso as she glanced around the deserted restaurant patio. "You're right."

"And you're certain that I'm like this person or persons who made you swear off potential relationships?"

She shook her head, looking down. "You're not like anyone I've ever met."

I waited until her head came up and locked eyes with her. "Thank you. You're not like anyone I've ever met either."

We held the stare a moment longer before she reached for her water glass. She took her time sipping from the glass, as if the liquid would provide her with the indisputable argument she'd need to end this topic. "I won't let myself be some test of curiosity; I'm too old for a fling; and I'm uninterested in a one-night stand."

"I wouldn't use anyone like that, much less you; I've had my limit of flings; and I never saw the appeal of a one-night stand."

"You don't know what you're saying." Her voice carried a heaviness that comes from deep hurt.

"I know that when you pulled away from our kiss last night I felt like you took my balance from me. I can't concentrate, and for someone who compartmentalizes nearly everything, losing concentration is more than off-putting."

"This isn't like what you're used to."

"I should hope not."

The waiter interrupted us with the check. I quickly handed over my credit card to limit his interruptions. Unfortunately, his appearance quieted Raven. We didn't speak again until we were back in the car with me behind the wheel. She hadn't even been tempted to drive this time.

"There are no guarantees at the start of any relationship," I said after making a series of turns to get back on the two lane highway toward her house.

"I know that, but there are more things for you to consider with this one," Raven retorted gravely. "This wouldn't be like entering a relationship with a man where if it doesn't work out, you haven't shocked your family and friends."

"I can't worry about that." The idea hadn't even entered my mind until she'd mentioned it. Would something like this shock my family and friends? Marco hadn't cared. Well, he'd cared that Raven obviously meant a great deal to me. So much, that I wasn't worried about anything other than her.

"You should," she came back immediately. After a long silence, she added, "Right now, this is only an attraction. One we can both fight. One that doesn't have to change your whole world."

Slowing to pull into her driveway, I thought of a dozen different arguments. With every switchback in her drive, a new direction presented itself for my response. As I shut off the engine in front of her house, I realized nothing but the truth would work. "It already has," I admitted.

A faint moan left with her breath. She turned to face me with that expression of desire, asking for me to touch her. My fingers brushed the back of her hand and onto her forearm. Goose bumps rose in their wake. That sound escaped again, and she twisted to open the door. She was out so quickly I barely remembered opening my door and darting around the car to meet her.

"Raven, wait."

"You have no idea what you're doing to me." Raven spoke in a voice laced with anguish.

"I know that when I'm around you I feel things that I've only ever heard about." In fact, those pesky feelings were making it difficult to speak right now. My throat felt dry and swollen. "I never understood what friends were talking about when they'd tell me they couldn't control themselves around someone they were attracted to. Not until you. I thought I was going to burn from the inside out if you didn't kiss me last night. Not just smoldering warmth or a brief hot flash, but actually char with a blaze that could reduce me to ashes. I've waited my whole life to feel desire like this. I hope that's what I'm doing to you."

Her eyes widened at my admission, breath pumping faster through her chest. Slowly she brought her hands up, reaching and retreating in a silent battle until, finally, they landed on my shoulders. "God help me, but I can't stop," she whispered, pulling me into her.

When her lips met mine, I fell against her. My car stopped us from tumbling to the ground. Our hands and tongues and mouths caressed and embraced and worshiped until the sensations threatened to inundate my sensibilities.

"I can't—"

She wrenched her lips from mine at the start of my plea. Tears threatened to escape her eyes. "We need to stop this."

"No," I denied firmly, capturing her face in my hands. "I was going to say that I can't stay upright much longer. I don't want to stop." One of the tears made a break for her cheek. At the look of relief on her face, I swiped my fingers across the tear. "Take me to bed, Raven," I implored in a husky voice that I now possessed because of my desire.

Those expressive eyes showed a flash of fear before the passion took over. Her right hand slid to my left and laced our fingers together. With a gentle tug, we were moving toward her house.

Chapter 16

*I*t wasn't until she'd guided me to her bedroom that the apprehension hit me. I'd never been nervous about sex before. I'd never had reason to be because I'd never cared enough about the person to be nervous. That realization alone caused borderline panic.

"You're incredibly beautiful when you're nervous." Raven's tentative smile eased some of my apprehension.

The breath I'd been holding let out as I grabbed her waist. "It's not because…"

"I'm a woman?"

No, that's definitely not it. I'd had plenty of practice with what a woman likes sexually, or at least what I liked. No, my nervousness centered on my own responses which, up until now, had always been lackluster when it came to sex. Her hesitant look grew fearful with my silence, so I rushed to assure her. "That doesn't worry me. You're so beautiful and amazing, Raven. I want to please you."

Her face glowed with soft surprise and delight from my admission. "You please me by wanting to be here, Joslyn. You don't have anything to be nervous about." She leaned forward and pressed her lips to mine. Tenderly she told me with her confident exploration how much she was already pleased. The blaze of heat from her kiss scorched all remaining hesitation.

My fingers started working the buttons of her shirt, following orders my mind had never issued before. I'd always let my partner take the lead, but now I finally understood frantic need. "And sexy. Did I mention how sexy you are?"

Brown eyes brushed shut when my fingertips slid across her skin. She moaned softly, and the temperature in the room rose dramatically. I wanted out of these clothes, I wanted to feel myself against her, I wanted to feel her touch. I couldn't ever remembering feeling anything as desperately as I wanted to feel her.

Shedding clothes had never been as erotic as this. I couldn't seem to get enough of her pliant, firm skin or her giving, insistent lips. Forcing myself to step back, my eyes raked down her slender body. Beguiling, alluring, tempting, no single word was adequate enough for her perfection.

"You're even more divine than I imagined," she whispered, her eyes taking the same leisurely stroll that mine enjoyed. The gaze warmed my skin. "If I don't touch you soon, I may implode."

"Can I—I need..." Assailing thoughts tangled with alien emotions, making it difficult to speak.

"Do whatever feels good, Jos. Please, just soon." She somehow understood that I needed to touch and explore. She stepped forward, filling the gap between us. As her naked flesh kissed mine for the first time, I gasped, unable to isolate what gave me the most pleasure. Softness like I'd never felt slid against me and my skin erupted in gooseflesh. The responding chill sparked a surprising moan from deep inside me.

My lips sought the sinewy connection between her powerful shoulder and graceful neck. Tasting that part of her, taking in her scent, my eyes squeezed shut to calm the flood of giddiness. I brought my hands to her flat stomach, splaying my fingers up along her ribs. A tremor rippled through her as my hands inched higher, studying every sinuous plane. Reaching the swell of her upturned breasts, my breath hitched and my heart clobbered against my chest cavity.

A rhythmic thumping sped up to a rapid hammering under my hand. Her breathing matched the speed of her heart rate and soft sighs led the way to breathy moans. "I have to touch you, Jos. Please let me."

"Anything, Raven." I tipped my head back, breathless from her urgent tone. "Everything."

Her hands immediately moved up from her sides to my waist. The touch set me ablaze, spurring on my own exploration. I filled my hands with her breasts, testing the buoyant heft, flicking my thumbs over her dark brown nipples. The already hardened peaks grew rigid against my thumb pads.

"God, yes," she moaned, flattening her hands against the small of my back and pushing out over the crest of my rear. She tilted into my body, and I pushed back with equal need. "Lie down," she ordered hoarsely. "I need to feel all of you."

I leaned back, taking her with me onto the bed. We inched backward, mouths connected, hands searching, until we found ourselves somewhere in the middle of the bed. She left my mouth and moved down my throat. Her silky hair caressed my jaw and her lips pulled exquisitely on my neck. I looked down the length of the body covering mine until she sensed my plea and turned her face up to look at me.

"You're beautiful," I whispered as her lips claimed mine again.

When her hands grasped my breasts, I'd found bliss. She knew how to touch perfectly, expertly, giftedly. With fingers, palms, knuckles, even the backs of her hands, she used everything to feel. She wasn't touching for her own gratification as had been the extent of my experience before. No, she touched to give me pleasure, and I knew instinctively that my pleasure would make her feel more.

A leg nudged between my thighs. I spread them willingly. She shifted to lie between them, holding herself above me on her elbows. Slowly, she lowered her weight onto me, and the sensation nearly made me cry out from excitement.

"Okay?" she asked with concern as my eyes must have flashed the clutter of emotions I could no longer hide.

"Yes, yes." Or I would be if I could just get control of my heartbeat, and breathing, and stop trembling.

"You feel so good, so excited." She took an earlobe between her teeth, ramping up the tremble to a full-blown shiver.

I realized the fire I'd been feeling had caused an arousal like I've never known. The moistness of my past sexual encounters didn't begin to describe what felt like the flood now between my legs. *God, what was she doing to me?* The perplexing notion flew out of my mind the second her mouth attached itself to my breast.

"Raven," I groaned, unable to believe that someone could be this talented at pulling pleasure from my body. Sex had never felt this amazing before. If I were being truthful, I'd have to admit that I'd never really understood what all the hype was about. Now, with her soft body over mine, her mouth and hands working me like she knew every secret pleasure zone, I finally got it. The revelation distracted me so much I wasn't entirely aware that her head had settled between my legs. Hot breath blew onto my over sensitized flesh, and the smoothness of her face made my thighs twitch with unrest.

"I'm going to taste you." Raven's eyes locked with mine before she moved forward and ran her tongue along my drenched core.

I bucked at the feeling then groaned when her mouth affixed itself to me. Nothing could have prepared me for this. Oh, I'd experienced oral sex before, but never with such expertise. Her mouth took me in, stroked me, pleasured me, loved me. In that moment, I felt a surge of panic inundate my system as I realized I wouldn't be able to convince her that I'd climaxed. She would know; she'd have to, especially in her position right now. *Oh, hell!* Why hadn't I thought about this before I went to bed with her? Would she be discouraged with my inability to orgasm?

When the panic tightened every muscle in my body, I reached down under her arms and gently tugged. Her mouth left me, eyes searching with question. "Up here," I coaxed.

"Let me make you come first." Her tongue reached forward again, making me hiss.

"Please, Raven," I pleaded. "I need to touch you."

"Oh, honey, anything you want," she assured when my voice cracked with desperation. She crawled up to kiss me with those lips that had given me more pleasure than I'd ever known.

Urgently, I rolled her onto her back, pressing my weight onto her. When I could wait no longer, I tore free of her mouth and slipped down her body, pulling gently on every inch of velvety skin. She was so smooth, soft but firm, so different from anything I'd ever known, but so perfect. Reaching her breast, I lashed my tongue against the pebbled nipple, wanting to tease before I tasted. Her sudden intake of breath told me she enjoyed the teasing. I pulled the nipple into my mouth, flicking and sucking, basking in the moans that escaped her.

I straddled her thigh, nearly biting the tip in my mouth when my engorged clitoris rubbed against the crest of her hip. This heightened reaction was so foreign to me that I didn't know how to deal with it all. My hand felt its way down her abdomen, loving how her silky skin seemed to jump into my fingertips. When neither of us could stand the delay, I delved my fingers through her slick folds.

"Yes, Jos, that feels amazing. I'm so close already. I don't think I'm going to last."

"Don't hold back, lovely," I groaned, my head pounding with ecstasy. My fingers swirled around, mapping the creases and ridges and valleys of her sodden flesh. Teasing and tantalizing until a finger chafed her clit directly.

"Oh God, oh, oh, Jos!" Raven shouted just before her hips bucked against my hand. I felt the orgasm slash through her and watched the flush of her skin under my mouth. A sheen of perspiration beaded everywhere as ripples tensed and relaxed each of her muscles. The pulsations against my fingers felt almost as good as the sight of her head and shoulders jerking against the bedspread. A rush of power crashed into me at the realization that I'd given her such pleasure.

Before she'd fully recovered I resituated my face between her legs to study the twitch of the glistening pink folds. An overwhelming need to taste her tore at my being. I kissed the shiny skin of her inner thigh, heading toward the only taste that would quench my craving.

"Oh, honey," Raven sighed breathlessly as she reached for me. "Let me finish making love to you now."

"You said anything I want, lovely." I was too close to her center to stop now.

Her head dropped back to the bed with a groan. "I like the sound of that."

I grinned wickedly at her. "Letting me do anything?"

"That, too, but I like when you call me that."

"Good, now let me do anything all over you, lovely," I commanded playfully.

With a moan, she complied, inching her legs wider. I

nipped at the tender skin of her thigh, watching her open more for me. Her eagerness and trust squeezed at my heart with exquisite pressure. A muskier version of her scent slammed against me when I lowered my head to her very being. The first gush of flavor sated my tongue like no other taste I've encountered. Her satiny flesh quivered in my mouth as I licked every surface, missing nothing but her clitoris. She'd liked the teasing before, and I felt like I could taste and tease all night.

"God, Jos, please!" she begged.

Before my tongue found her clit, I fastened my lips to her hood, sucking first then let my tongue join in. Her thighs closed around my head, and she pressed harder into my mouth. My hands clutched her firm ass, pulling her closer. This felt so natural I couldn't believe I'd never found it before.

I laved my tongue to her opening and thrust inside, once, twice, and again before her labored breathing and moans told me she was close to the threshold. I moved back up and sucked her extended need into my mouth, lapping at her until she cried out my name and crashed into another orgasm.

"Oh yeah, oh wow! Jos, that was fantastic." She pulled me up to lie on top of her. The friction I felt nearly made me scream with delight. I'd never been this close to the edge with anyone before.

Her lips cherished my face like she had last night. When her mouth fused to mine, she rolled me over, pinning me under her. Her eyes danced with desire while her hands touched my breasts again. I tried to stem the panic I felt, hoping I wouldn't disappoint her with my noncompletion.

She replaced her fingers with her mouth and let her hand drift downward. I seized up, the frenzy of sensations so wild and unfamiliar. A throaty chuckle sounded just before her mouth dipped quickly to my frazzled need. When she sucked me into her mouth, I skittered along the precipice, willing myself to tumble over. Begging and pleading with my body and mind for release. What felt like a tingle of that unattainable swirl flashed through my belly. I'd long ago learned to bury any frustration at never reaching orgasm with a lover. But this time, I wanted it so much—for her.

"Come for me, Joslyn," she ordered softly.

I want to. Oh God, Raven, I want to!

Her tongue explored every part of me, patiently, languidly. A hand glided up my torso to tweak a nipple, sending a new jolt of pleasure through my body. My heart strummed harder than I thought it could handle without causing cardiac arrest.

The faint tingle turned into an insistent churning. *No, it can't be. This doesn't happen to me. I can't be about to climax.* It didn't matter that her mouth felt like it has been pleasuring my body for years, knowing exactly everything I needed. Even I had trouble making myself come. There was no way she was going to make this happen. Only it felt so good, so right, so extraordinary. No, I don't orgasm, not for anyone. Not even as much as I wanted to. Except...*yes, yes, I'm coming!*

"Raven!" I screamed, riding out an orgasm so forceful it made me doubt I'd ever experienced one before. The pulsations continued, relentlessly wracking my body while her lips and tongue eased up on the pressure.

Finally, she crawled up over me, staring down in wonder at my still shuddering body. "Feel good?" All I could do was stare back at her. "Guess so." From anyone else that would have sounded smug. From her, it sounded reverent.

"You—I can't believe—you, you made me come."

"Yes." She fluttered her eyebrows. "I loved making you come." When I didn't respond too astounded by my first orgasm with someone else, her expression grew concerned. "What is it?"

Unexplained tears flooded my eyes. A barrage of emotions assaulted me without relent. God, I'd turned into one of those people. Ruled by emotions, unable to contain their release. And in this beautiful woman's arms, too. I'm such a pathetic schmuck. *Stop crying! Stop it right now!*

"Sweetheart," Raven spoke softly, watching me with concern and understanding in her eyes.

"I'm sorry," I croaked when I gained some control over the roiling sway within me. "I don't cry. This isn't normal for me, I assure you."

"Assurances aren't necessary, Jos. You don't need to withhold what you're feeling right now." Tender fingers wiped away the tears that had fallen. She pressed kisses to my tear-stained cheeks.

I clutched her against me, loving the feel of her weight on top of me. What was happening to me? I'd always wanted to be free of any restrictive heft, to be done with any reminders of the sex I'd had. This was different, she was different and not because she was a woman. Raven was different. "You made me come," I repeated when I'd trudged my way to the top of the emotional mountain.

She cocked her head. "You seem surprised by that. You made me come, too. Twice."

"I don't usually..." I couldn't finish what I'd never told another living soul before.

Her surprise told me she knew what I hadn't said. "Not usually?"

"Actually ... never."

"But, by yourself?" Embarrassed, I nodded once in response to her question. "Oh, sweetheart." Her voice held wonder, and I felt those pesky emotions start to bombard my tightly held control.

Was this what everyone talked about? Falling so quickly and thoroughly and hopelessly? No, I've gone thirty-seven years without falling in love. I must be making more out of this than is there. The orgasm, I'll blame it on the orgasm. The devastating, earth-shattering, inconceivable orgasm. At the hands of someone else. Well, mouth of this incredible woman. Yeah, a good orgasm could wring the sensibility right out of anyone. It was the only explanation for me bursting into tears after climax and clinging to Raven like I didn't want to leave.

"Stay," she said after the slightest shift of my body from beneath hers. It didn't sound like an order or a plea. It was as if she'd slipped inside my mind and knew that I always left but didn't want to tonight. It was an invitation when one wasn't necessary. Like when people say "have a seat" after someone is already in the process of sitting. "Will your dogs be okay for the night?"

I couldn't believe she remembered them let alone thought about them right now. Her concern made me drop the preconceived excuse. "They should be fine."

"Then it's something else." Raven drew her fingertip down my forehead and onto my nose. "You're embarrassed about crying." It wasn't a question, and I couldn't have denied it had she been asking. "Don't be."

"Easy for you to say." I tried for a lighthearted response.

"Don't be," she repeated, a request not a command. Desire and something unidentifiable brightened her brown eyes. "That was the most beautiful thing that's ever happened to me. Please don't be embarrassed, Joslyn."

"I seem to do the most unexpected things around you, Raven. I don't know how to handle that." Or these tumultuous emotions.

"Don't try to handle it." A simple order accompanied by a commanding kiss. "Let me see you, not the person you wear around for the rest of the world. Please stay. I don't want to give up this night yet."

God, she was good at this. So good, I may never want to give up this night.

Chapter 17

"Good morning," I murmured, still drowsy from not enough sleep. Despite not being used to waking up in someone else's bedroom, it took only a fraction of a second to realize where I was and whose hand was making my skin leap. I issued the greeting to the ginger colored window coverings I was facing. Raven's body melded to mine from behind, her arm draped over my middle, hand drawing lazy patterns on my abdomen. I rolled onto my back and suppressed a moan at the sight of a sleep-tousled Raven.

"How are you?" Her eyes, nearly hidden from unkempt bangs, showed a touch of apprehension.

I smiled up at the concerned face leaning over me. Brushing the bangs back from her stunning eyes, I teased, "You're afraid I'm freaking out."

"A little." She shrugged with just the right amount of

insecurity to eliminate arrogance from her personality traits. "Are you?"

Was I? Nearly unprecedented sleepover aside, I was waking up with a woman for the first time in my life after having ravaged her for the better part of the night. I should be, a little, right? But I wasn't. And I stopped my mind from analyzing why, or I might end up contemplating that whole love thing again which this so wasn't, or couldn't be, well, shouldn't be because I barely knew her. Okay, that part freaked me out a little.

"So not," I answered truthfully because my hesitation made her concern grow. When a glint of skepticism crossed her expression, I went with more honesty. "Mmm, looks like I'm going to have to prove it." Lifting my head, I closed my mouth over hers and propelled up and over until she was on her back under me. When I pulled back from the kiss, her now bruised lips spread into a sexy smile. "Convinced?"

"I don't know," she breathed seductively. "Do you have any more proof?"

I laughed at her delight and ran a hand down between our bodies to stroke her plump, slick flesh. "Hours and hours worth."

After I'd convinced her twice more, we lay spent until we could move in an upright position. She offered me the shower but decided to conserve water and join me. Once we'd helped each other wash and dry, I couldn't believe how energized I felt. If I hadn't already made love to her several times over the course of the night and morning, I'd press her against the bathroom counter and have at her again.

While she ran a dryer quickly over her hair, I started pulling on my clothes, thinking I should do something to feed us. My brain was still mush from all of the fantastic, beyond belief, hall of fame sex that it took me a second to figure out I needed to leave the bedroom and find the kitchen for sustenance. I walked out into the hallway, tucking my shirt into my pants and finished with the zipper and button.

Had I been looking where I was going, I would have noticed Raven's niece coming up the stairs. Instead, when I looked up, Ray was practically on top of me, eyes wide with shock. Perhaps it was my years of training at masking surprise with client confessions, or maybe it was because I'd just had the best night and morning of my life, but I managed an unassuming smile. "Hi, Ray."

She blinked and blinked and blinked some more then stammered, "Oh, I, um, well, see we were going, ah, I was supposed to, oh man, horses! That's why I'm here."

"Okay," I accepted calmly yet started to feel the embarrassment of being caught just minutes after having sex with the aunt she idolizes.

"Sweetheart?" Raven's voice flowed out of the bedroom, stopping any reply. "How about omelets? Then we should go check on your—Ray?!" I'd been blocking her view as she surfaced from the bedroom, but I felt her shock when she gripped my waist to get us moving.

"Um, hi, Aunt Raven," the young woman greeted sheepishly. "Remember I asked if Kelly and I could ride your horses today?"

"Oh, yes." Raven slid an apprehensive look my way before stepping around me. "I forgot."

"This is a bad time, obviously." Ray's gaze moved studiously between her aunt and me. "You didn't answer the door, so I figured you were down at the office. I wanted to grab a riding helmet for Kelly."

A meaningful look passed between them before they both glanced at me with apologies and hesitation. The tension was ridiculous, so I joked, "Well, so much for keeping this to ourselves."

"I won't tell anyone!" Ray jumped to promise us.

Raven, who'd been staring at me with a look of

amazement, turned to her niece and laughed softly. "Try, Ray, please? It's my news to share if I choose."

"No one will hear it from me, honest. I'm sorry to bust in on your morning. I'll be out of your hair in a flash."

Raven squeezed her shoulder. "All right, but I moved all the riding gear to the storage closet in the garage. I'm hoping it motivates me to finish the tack room out in the barn."

"Oops! Then I'm really sorry." Ray glanced up with remorseful eyes, two shades darker than Raven's. "Thanks again for letting us ride today. I'll feed them for you when we get done." She flicked her gaze to me. "In case you had other plans."

Don't blush, please don't blush, hold it in! With practiced casualness, I said, "Have fun on your ride, Ray."

She fought back a knowing grin. "Good to see you, Joslyn. Bye, Aunt Raven, thanks." She skipped rhythmically down the stairs and out the front door.

"God, Jos, I'm sorry." Raven approached tentatively, staring at me like she thought I'd be mad or something. Embarrassed, yes, but mad, no.

"So, how many of your relatives have a key to your place?" I asked dryly but let the humor seep through in my smile.

She blew out a relieved breath and launched herself into my arms. "Be glad it wasn't my brother or he'd be interrogating you right now. The witch trials would be considered a cakewalk by comparison."

"Remind me not to run into him again." I laughed and pressed my face into her slightly damp, citrus scented hair. "New plan. We go to my house for that breakfast you were mentioning before Kelly gets here. Then we can spend part of the day paying attention to my neglected dogs."

Before she pulled back, I thought I felt her stiffen. More unidentifiable emotions drifted into her expression until happiness pushed them aside. I wanted to question what brought on the kaleidoscope of expressions, but she asked in that seductive voice that tested the strength of my legs, "And for the rest of the day?"

"Oh, I think we can figure something out, lovely." My fingers slid up from her waist to cup her breasts through her shirt, flicking over her nipples. She gasped when they hardened in response. Her head fell back, and I kissed the exposed offering. "You're going to need to boost your energy for all the rest."

Her hand linked with mine and started us down the staircase. "You've been doing more than your share of the work. It's your energy I'm worried about."

We loaded into the car with silly grins and drove back to my house. The dogs, having not been gated into their sunroom crashed into us the moment the door opened. "Hello, puppies." I dropped to my knees and touched them all until their wiggling bodies calmed down. My silly grin widened to sheer happiness when I looked up and saw Raven had taken the same position a foot away. *She loves my dogs. Now, that's sexy.*

"I feel guilty for keeping you from them."

"If they knew you were the reason they got to sleep all over my furniture last night, they'd want to go home with you."

"Hmm, a stickler for rules, eh?"

"They know their room, and it has plenty of comfy chairs to shed on. It's not like they're deprived."

"I'm still going to make it up to them." She pulled me up with her for an unrelenting kiss. "You play with them. I'll cook."

"They're going to want to keep checking on you, so we'll both cook. Besides, I like being next to you in a kitchen."

Her eyes glowed with my reference to the evening we spent at Amalia's restaurant. "That was a fun night."

"Fun and enlightening for me." I went to the fridge and

started pulling out what we'd need for omelets.

"Amalia's a great teacher." Raven began slicing the green onions and mushrooms while I shredded the cheese.

"That, too, but my enlightenment came in the parking lot later." The knife in her hand stopped slicing as she turned to me. "You see, before that night, I'd never wanted anyone to kiss me as desperately as I wanted you to kiss me."

"Oh, Jos, I wanted to. I almost did."

"Then you tore out of the parking lot so quickly I could smell the burnt rubber. Yeah, that did wonders for my ego." I enjoyed baiting her.

"Stop." Her hand slid up my arm to cup my throat gently. The gesture felt intensely intimate. "I couldn't, not without your permission."

"You have it now." I tilted forward and met her lips, taking everything from this kiss that I'd been denied that night weeks ago. "Food, dogs, orgasm, in that order."

"Orgasms, plural. Yours, specifically." Her eyes sent me promises that I believed for the first time in my sexually active life. She took me into her arms. "We'll go at your pace, sweetheart."

"I don't want you to get frustrated."

"I love giving you pleasure, in whatever form. I won't get frustrated that we can't give you release. Making love isn't about a race to see who makes it to the finish line. It's about giving and getting pleasure; it's about connecting with another beautiful soul."

My heart, which had been thumping heartily since she'd first kissed me out on that ledge, felt like it stopped entirely. She understood me and accepted me without judgment. *Slipping, slipping faster. I still had time to grab onto something before I fell completely, but did I want to?*

Chapter 18

*T*raitors! Ungrateful little turncoats. The minute a beautiful, kind woman comes around, they jump ship and lap at her feet like she was the one to feed them, love them, and walk them for their entire lives. *Hmph!* My furry deserters lounged at Raven's feet and flanked each side of her, throwing whoa-is-me eyes and aren't-I-the-cutest glances at her. Seeking any form of attention, even if it was just a quick pat on the head. Doggie-Hos, every last one of them.

"They have your number." I shook my head as she shifted position to bring her back and shoulder up against me. The dogs took the opportunity to reposition some of their limbs on her lap and stretched out legs.

She chortled, burrowing into me until my arm came around and tucked her in. "This from Ms. Take In Seven More Dogs Than I Wanted? You're just jealous that after only a day, they're ready to go home with me."

"Who wouldn't be?"

She twisted to face me and winked. Charmer. "Speaking of which, can I interest you in coming home with me again tonight?"

My head pitched back. "My place isn't good enough for you and your merry band of defecting dogs?"

Brown eyes widened, giving me both surprise and joy. "Are you inviting me to stay over?"

"It's the only way I'll get to see my dogs tonight," I joked.

A mock huff left her lungs before she swung up and over to straddle my lap. The porch swing rocked with her movement and the two smaller dogs jumped off with the sudden motion. I stared up at her, recognizing the glint in her eyes. My body responded to her seductive glance and the gentle rocking of her hips against my lap.

"Give me a better reason, or the dogs and I go," she ordered with feigned seriousness.

"We had an agreement this morning. So far your guilt has kept us from completing all three." I referred to the fact that since breakfast we'd spent the whole day and evening giving attention to the dogs with walks, throwing retrievable items, and watching them take a swim in the pond on my property. Other than a caress or two before a nap in the late afternoon sunshine out here on the swing, we'd yet to get around to item three on the list.

Her hips undulated against my lap, and I bit back a groan. "Remind me?"

"Hmm, let's see," I drew out. "There was food. Breakfast, lunch, and dinner, check, check, check. Then I believe it was the dogs. All five of them, check to the fifth power. After, I think we agreed to paint the barn/guesthouse/extra building that currently serves no purpose."

The motion of her hips this time was forceful enough to

get us swinging again. "Really? Is that how you remember it?"

My hands fisted against her hips as we swayed to and fro. "Yep."

"I'll only help with painting if you help build a tack room in my barn. I figure you've got some experience with that." Her eyes twinkled at me. "Oh, and if we don't use any of those colors you've already got up over there."

"What?" I looked over at the building with the three blocks of color. True, they'd been up there for months because nothing jumped out at me yet. "Marco can't stand them either. He's refused to send over his painting subcontractor to help me if I'm using one of them."

"Wise, wise man," she heckled.

"Well, you can just try and get him to help you build that tack room, lady."

"Hmm, what's his phone number? Maybe he's free tonight."

Her brazen tone made me laugh. "You'll be occupied. Item number three and all."

"That was what again?" The heat spread from our joined limbs to every part of me. I couldn't take the teasing much longer. On the next swing forward, I planted my feet and lifted off. Raven shrieked, wrapping her legs around my waist and tightening her hold on my neck. "Strong little thing, aren't you?"

"Watch it, now. You've got, what, three inches on me, and if you clear a buck twenty, I'd be amazed." Her legs slid down from my waist and planted on the ground. She nipped my lips twice before kissing me thoroughly. One of her intoxicating moans filled the night air on my porch. "I take it I've convinced you to stay tonight?" I asked when her mouth glided over to nibble along my jaw. She groaned and gripped me tightly against her. "Long enough to let me convince you to play hooky with me tomorrow?"

"What?" She pulled back to stare at me.

"I don't have any meetings until Tuesday, and I'm guessing that you've never taken a day off work in your life."

One look at her face gave me my answer. "You want to spend the day with me tomorrow?"

"Definitely. Well, you and your horses. I'm using you, you know."

"Oh my," Raven breathed with a soft smile. "Normally, I'd be able to think of a comeback, but all I can think to say is, use anything you want of mine."

I sucked in a breath at the honesty that came through with her offer. I immediately regretted having kidded with her. "We need to go inside now because I'm not letting the mosquitoes feast on you before I can."

"Best idea I've heard all day," she agreed, slipping her hand into mine. She was a hand holder, and while I'd never been, I didn't find myself minding at all.

I tugged on our connected hands and brought us in through the sunroom. My dogs plopped onto their favorite beds with a snap of my fingers. I closed the door so they wouldn't be tempted to jump the gate anytime during the night. I wanted Raven to myself.

Clothes got stripped away in between kisses and provocative gropes. Her moans encouraged my own as I sat her on the edge of my bed. Kneeling between her legs, she gave me full access to bring her off swiftly with my mouth, temporarily quenching her need and further igniting mine.

"My God," she panted, her torso rocking forward through the aftershocks of her climax. "That was instantaneous."

I reached my arms around her still trembling body. "That was impressive."

"Com'ere." Raven pulled me up from my knees to stand in front of her. She leaned forward and kissed the swell of my breast.

I gripped her face as her mouth performed arousing

magic on my sensitive, and until this woman, attention-deprived nipples. Her hands skimmed up the backs of my legs, grasped my butt, dipping then gliding up to my back. When they crested my shoulders and moved down to where her mouth attached itself to me, I groaned at the throbbing I now felt between my legs. "Feels so good."

Her fingers slipped down to their starting places, and I waited for them to repeat their path. Instead, I felt them press into the backs of my knees. I didn't immediately relent until she slid back on the bed and the pressing turned into pulling. My right leg knelt onto the bed beside her thigh, and my left followed suit until I was straddling her lap.

"Show me," she whispered, tilting her face up to look at me.

"What?" I swooped down to kiss her masterful mouth.

When the kiss broke, she said, "I want to watch you this time."

My legs contracted in response, straightening to lift me up from her lap. Her hands gripped my shoulders from the back to keep me in place. I realized my eyes were closed, so I opened them, searching her out. This wasn't a request I'd ever complied with in the past.

"You're still anxious about getting to a release, Jos. I can see it," she said softly. While we'd spent hours exploring each others bodies, I'd only climaxed the one time. I couldn't deny that I was concerned it was a fluke and that it would eventually disappoint her. "I told you that I'm happy to give you as much pleasure as you can handle, but I know you want to climax." She held my face in her hands. "Show me how you make yourself come."

I waited for embarrassment to touch me, but her husky plea prodded the flames of my desire. Looking down, I watched her eyes dilate with another wave of arousal. I leaned in and kissed her again, forsaking my usually strict inhibitions. My hand left her shoulder and sought the inside of one straining thigh. Discovering a surprising slickness, I jolted in disbelief at how excited I was.

Raven broke our kiss to look into my eyes. "You're beautiful, Jos, and so damn sexy. Show me, please."

The familiar motion of my fingers brought out unfamiliar responses under the weight of her rapt attention. Her eyes moved from my hand up to my breasts, which swayed close to her mouth, then up to my eyes as I watched her watching me. Her desire pulsed over me in waves that threatened to drown. When her eyes dropped back to my pleasuring motions, her hands slid down to my thighs and gripped tightly. Her stabilizing grip set my other hand in motion, seeking out one of my nipples. Her eyes flipped up to observe the spiking tip in front of her face. When she parted her lips, I groaned involuntarily.

"Raven, please!" I pleaded, feeling both close and miles away from the edge. I wanted her to be the one to push me over. "You, please, you. Take me. Make me come."

She gripped my forearm, keeping my hand in place. Her face tilted up, and I dipped my head to kiss her, needing that contact. When she pulled back, her eyes moved back down to the crest of my thighs. Her hand slid along my arm, fingers linking with mine. After several combined circles of our fingers, she pulled my hand away and placed it on her breast. The slickness on my fingers lubricated her nipple as I teased the hardening tip mercilessly. When her hand returned, she went directly for my aching clit. She'd paid close attention and the expert stimulation propelled me toward climax.

"Give this to me, Joslyn." Desire and something else turned her eyes into potent beacons.

I looked into the beautiful brown, reading every emotion from excitement to rapture. They told me that she considered my orgasm a gift. That was when I felt myself fly apart. "I'm coming for you, Raven!"

The convulsions rocked me against her. I felt her arm

slide around my waist to keep me from toppling backward off the bed. My legs gave out and I dropped to her lap, trapping her hand in place. My breasts brushed against hers with each pitch and roll of my orgasmic wave. All the while I held her gaze to extend my contractions past any conceivable duration.

"You take my breath away," she whispered as the last of my tremors subsided.

"That was..." My brain must have locked up in the throes of my ferocious climax because I couldn't think of anything. I finally settled on, "Indescribable."

Her face broke into a lazy, satisfied grin. "You were stumped there, weren't you, genius?"

"You fried every brain cell I have with that orgasm, sexy thing. Don't make fun while I'm trying to piece together words to express your mastery."

She laughed, shooting another bolt of excitement through me. Just as I was thinking I might never get enough of her, she pulled me tightly against her and fell back to the bed. I laughed with her and kissed the nearest patch of skin under my mouth. Her throaty chuckle stopped with a moan. "Again?"

"And again, and again, and..." I made sure her eyes registered my intent before setting my mouth and hands in motion. This woman made me crave things I never knew I was missing. And the realization hardly terrified me anymore.

Chapter 19

The vibrating ring brought my cell phone to life on the desk and a smile to my face. Raven was such a creature of habit, which worked out well because so was I. She usually waited until after work hours to call me, but if she did call during the day, it was at lunch so she wouldn't disturb any meetings.

"I'm only talking to you if you tell me you're actually breaking for lunch today," I told the open line.

"Don't suppose you're kicking back with a sandwich yourself there, are ya?"

I studied the piles of reports stacked around my workspace, no food items to be found. "I just got back from Amalia's."

"Liar," she accused.

"All right, smart aleck, what's up?"

"You know that quiet dinner I promised to make you

tonight?" Her hesitant tone brought me bolt upright.

"Average-sized wrench or monkey wrench?"

She chortled, shooting a stitch of relief through me. "Definitely of the simian variety."

"That's okay. I think I can spare you for a night, but I will hold you to making me dinner some other time, lovely."

"Actually..." she posed without enough intonation to assure me this wasn't something to worry about. "My brother dropped by today."

"He's your new dinner date?"

"You could say that."

"What else could I say?"

"That I told him about us, and he's invited himself, his wife, and his kids to join us tonight." Her news stunned me into silence. "You still breathing?"

It took me a moment to formulate a response. "Pulse is thready but still breathing."

"Think you can handle a little more?"

"No," I squeaked. If she tells me that we'll be competing in an Iron Chef-like competition with her brother's family as judges, I'm out. Completely. Well, at least for tonight.

"He talked to our parents, and they want to host the dinner."

Gulp. "What exactly was in this conversation with your brother?"

She hesitated so long I wasn't sure she'd answer. "I might have given him the impression that I was a little taken with you."

Not that I hadn't guessed, but hearing her admit it with the slightest trepidation like she was afraid I'd run screaming made my heart swell. "If I'm showing up for this thing, you better be more than a little taken, lovely."

"You don't mind? Really?" Sheer excitement replaced her anxiety.

"Can I make one request?"

"Anything, *tesora*."

I loved when she called me "sweetheart" whether in English or Italian. "I'd be a lot more comfortable if we had the dinner at your place. Do you think your parents would mind?"

"No, they just want to meet you."

"What time should I be there to help you make dinner? And what should I pick up now that our number has ballooned to fifty?"

"Stop," she laughed, a lot of relief coming through in the rhythmic sound. "You don't have to help."

"I want to, and it should provide the necessary excuse to convince your brother that I still need my thumbs."

"God, I lo—you're so great."

I pulled the phone back to see if I'd lost some reception with that hitch, but all the bars showed through. "5:30?"

"Perfect. Thanks, Joslyn, this means a lot to me." She signed off with a heartfelt goodbye.

At the end of the work day, I pulled around to the back of Raven's barn so that my car wouldn't block anyone in. I'd changed three thousand times, thought about taking several over-the-counter anxiety medications, and dropped probably five pounds with all the fretting, but I was on time. That should count for something.

"Have I mentioned that you're incredibly beautiful when you're nervous?" Raven called out from her back deck as I approached. She grabbed my grocery bags which freed up my hands to grasp her waist and kiss her thoroughly before her parents and brother arrived.

"You look stunning."

"Thank you. You didn't have to bring anything, though." She peered into the grocery bags.

"I've got more." I dashed back to my car for the pasta salad, minestrone, and tiramisu that I'd spent the afternoon making. It was either keep busy or panic.

"How's your heart rate, *tesora*?" Raven's eyebrows rose in jest when I came into the kitchen.

"I won't need to go to the gym for the next few days."

"At the risk of making it worse," she started, turning to put the groceries on the counter. Serving dishes stacked up next to the sink and several pots were already going on the stove. It looked like she was making enough to feed an army.

"What? They're all vegans?"

"No, but there may be a few more people here tonight."

"By a few, you mean that Ray's bringing Kelly and your nephews are bringing their girlfriends, even though they're probably too young to have them."

She tilted her head. "You wouldn't mind if Ray brought Kelly?"

"No, why would I mind?" I turned back from inspecting one of the simmering sauces to look at her. "Kelly was always nice to me."

"You seemed like you didn't..." Raven shook her head, confusion still marring her expression.

"Like I didn't what?"

"Nothing, that's ... nothing."

"Raven?"

She expelled a long breath and blurted, "The family wants to come over, too."

"Hold up!" I stepped backward until I stumbled over the area rug in the dining room. "The family, as in your family? Most of whom I've already met and all of who hate me? That family?"

"They don't hate you."

"Other than your brother, your niece, and your uncle, your family would have gladly stuffed me into one of their shipping containers and sent me to Siberia."

"Is Siberia all that bad anymore now that the KGB has stopped using it as banishment for criminals and rebels?" She wiggled her eyebrows.

"I think my twisted sense of humor has rubbed off on you, and not in a good way."

"You can rub anything you want—"

"Raven! This is serious." I seized her hips just as they connected with mine. She couldn't distract me that easily. Okay, maybe she could, but my anxiety pushed through the distraction. "All morning I was looking forward to our dinner after not seeing you for a couple of nights, then I find out your immediate family will be joining us, but now it's the whole lot of them? I don't think you realize just how much your cousins can't stand me. I forced less than desirable changes on their departments. I made both your uncles aware of their deficiencies, enough so that your uncle Nathan isn't all that fond of me now either. You're nuts if you think this is a good idea."

"Honey, I told you how close my family is. We all get together for some reason at least once a month. There's no way to avoid it. So, we can get this over with in one night, or we're looking at a summer filled with invitations to each of their homes."

The only thing keeping me from going ballistic at this ambush is the mention of the summer, which I read as a future with her. Before Raven, that statement would have given me pause and started my passive aggressive tendencies to force the end of a relationship. I sighed dramatically, no reason to make it easy on her. "You know if I wasn't so enchanted with you, I'd be back in my car right now, don't you?"

"Enchanted? Are you saying that I've put a spell on you to make you be with me?"

"Enthralled, bewitched, charmed, entranced, bespelled, ensorcelled, it's got to be something to make me consider staying for this thing tonight."

"Ensorcelled?" she tossed back in an amazed tone. "I don't know whether to be impressed by your intelligence or frightened by your all-encompassing knowledge of witchcraft. I can't decide which."

"Good pun." At her frown, I supplied, "W-h-i-c-h, w-i-t-c-h, get it?" She shook her head and rolled her eyes. "Watch it now, lovely. I'm still thinking I should throttle you for not telling me about everyone being here tonight. But I have to admire that you realized it was the best way to get me to stay."

"Without a whole afternoon of worry," she inserted with an omniscient look. "You should really be thanking me for the concern I have regarding your heart's wellbeing."

"Now, you're just pushing it."

She leaned her forehead against mine and stared into my eyes. "Thank you for this. They're my family, and it's important that they get to know you. I know it's nerve-wracking, but I'll show you how grateful I am once everyone leaves."

"Promises, promises."

"Ensorcelled, where do you come up with these words?" she pondered, releasing me to unload the groceries. "They'll be here in an hour. We've got a lot of work to do."

"I think tunneling from here to your barn where I can get at my car will take longer, don't you?"

"Be nice or I'll make you sit next to Robert at dinner."

"Ooh, put me in between Robert and Nick. Make sure the rest of the boys are nearby as well." If tonight was going to blow up in my face, I might as well take the whole house down with me. Make me spend too much time with all eight of her cousins and no one will be left standing.

Chapter 20

A t the sound of the car outside, I turned to Raven. "How do I look?" I hated the nervousness in my voice and the insecurity I felt.

"You look beautiful, sweetheart. They're going to love you." She took my hand in hers and confidently walked me out front.

The doors of the white Cadillac opened in what seemed like slow motion. A tall, lean man stepped out from behind the driver's seat. His hair streaked with silver but still had a touch of the blond of his youth. He looked like an older version of his son. Raven's mom looked to be in her mid-sixties, very distinguished, much shorter than her husband. She and Raven didn't resemble each other much, except for their eyes.

"Hi, Mom, hi, Dad." Raven went to hug them both. She reached back and pulled me to stand beside her. "Mom,

Dad, this is Joslyn Simonini. Jos, my mother, Anna, and my father, Wyatt."

Since her father stepped forward and held out his hand, I greeted him first. "Nice to meet you, Dr. Paul." I couldn't help feeling like he was testing me with his handshake. Since many corporate executives tried this with me, I simply used a polite amount of force and smiled like his crushing grip didn't bother me. When the vice grip loosened, I turned to Raven's mom. "A great pleasure, Dr. Paul."

"Oh, so formal." She winked at Raven before pulling me into a hug. "My patients call me Dr. Anna, but you'll call me Anna."

"Yes, ma'am," I complied, tongue in cheek.

"I already like her," she proclaimed, keeping an arm around me and sliding Raven into her other arm. Apparently, the Pauls liked making affectionate proclamations.

Wyatt frowned in a discouraging manner at his wife. "My brothers told me everything you did with the company, Joslyn."

A question never actually followed, despite my waiting several awkward seconds. I decided to respond anyway. "Archie asked me to look at everything, sir. I'm afraid my analytical nature makes me a little more thorough than some owners are prepared for."

"She did a great job, Dad," Raven piped up, starting us toward the house. "With her recommendations, the projected five-year numbers are going to be better than any five-year period we've had."

"I'll believe that when I see it," he grumbled.

"Raven tells me you struck out on your own seven years ago?" Anna spoke over her husband's objection. "That's quite young to start your own company."

"It's a service business, so it's not as impressive as it sounds."

"Humble, too?" Anna raised her eyebrows at her daughter.

Before we made it to the house, Daxson's SUV pulled up behind his parent's car. We turned back to greet the younger Paul's family. Daxson's wife was beautiful, which wasn't surprising since Ray was a looker, too. She didn't appear old enough to have a twenty-year-old daughter, but Dax was eight years older than his sister and didn't look it either. The two boys that climbed out of the backseat ran immediately to their aunt for a tag team bear hug. Their white blond heads reached up to her neck.

"You guys are getting so big," Raven cooed at them. They puffed up their chests before grabbing on to their grandmother. "Hey, Tanya, Dax. T, come meet Joslyn."

"The famous Ms. Simonini, or if I listen to my cousins, the infamous Ms. Simonini." Daxson joked, offering his left hand as his right was currently wrangling in one of the boys.

"Good to see you again, Dax, and I thought we decided that I was better at coming up with villainous fodder about me. Why are you wasting time listening to your cousins when you could come straight to the source?"

"Told ya I liked her." Dax tipped his head at his mom.

"It's nice to meet you, Tanya." I shook his wife's hand.

"You're in for an evening, I hope you know." Tanya's long dark hair brushed my shoulder as she whispered her playful warning while everyone's attention was on greeting Dax and the boys. I tilted to smile into the dark eyes that she'd passed on to her daughter.

"My sons, Eric and Steve." Dax gripped the squirming boys' necks, bringing my focus back. "Say hi to Joslyn, guys."

"Are you Aunt Raven's girlfriend?" the one that looked like a Steve asked.

Before I could respond, Raven interjected, "We're going to be without garlic bread tonight if I don't get my two favorite chefs inside right now." They shouted something that got lost in their rush toward the house. Everyone laughed at their eagerness and followed. Raven got them situated with the makings of garlic bread and a salad before joining us in the living room.

Wyatt went to the sidebar and started mixing drinks for everyone. Tanya leaned in with another tip. "Drinking is a good way for a first-timer to make it through one of these things."

I laughed silently, but Wyatt caught us. Tanya bent back upright and went over to join her husband on the sofa. Wyatt barely let her settle in before he asked, "Tell me, Joslyn, where did you go to school?"

This guy was worse than a father of an innocent prom date. "I stayed here for undergrad at U-Dub then off to a couple of different places for grad school."

"How nice," Anna said.

Wyatt spoke over her, "Where exactly for grad school?"

"Dad," Raven used a tone that sounded like a warning. We hadn't spent a lot of time talking about her dad, but there was a dynamic here that I wished I'd learned about.

"Don't tell me you have two graduate degrees?" Dax trampled over the tension that his father was creating.

"She has a MBA and a PhD," Raven boasted.

"That makes you a doctor, too, doesn't it?" Anna shot a told-you-so look at her husband.

"Not the kind that can make you feel better, no." I dismissed the idea in front of these actual doctors.

"What schools?" one-track-mind Wyatt persisted.

"Chicago and Penn."

"Business major?"

"For grad school, yes. I was a history major in undergrad."

"So, when you said Penn, you meant Wharton, didn't you?" Dax shot an impressed look at his mom. "Jeez, she may be smarter than you, Ma."

"Of course she is," Anna was quick to add.

"My father and brother would be the first to say, 'never mistake education for intelligence.'" At their squints of confusion, I added, "They're both master carpenters, no college between them, but they're brilliant in their craft and the way they live."

"That sounds wonderful," Tanya said.

"What about your mother?" Wyatt asked.

I hesitated but felt Raven's arm slip around my shoulders. The show of support quieted my unease. "She used to work for my dad and his business partner in their construction company. Then she moved to New York with my step-dad, had twins, and found it to be a full-time job."

"Amen," Tanya murmured, glancing into the kitchen at her two boys who were just over a year apart. Thankfully, no one stated the obvious about not growing up with my mom. It usually made people uncomfortable. Society was crazy like that.

The doorbell rang and moments later, Archie and his wife let themselves in. Anna and Raven went to greet them as I stood to face the next few hours of scrutiny and judgment. I'd never once willingly met my significant other's family; although, I'd been tricked into meeting them once or twice. To voluntarily subject myself to this kind of torture meant that Raven was more important to me in the short time we'd been together than any person I'd been with for months and months before.

After the entire clan arrived and introductions were made, I stole away to the kitchen to help Raven finish preparing dinner. We loaded the hors d'oeuvres on serving dishes, and she took them around to her guests. I put out the starters and cold dishes then went back to stir the pots and check on the rigatoni and lasagna.

"Shoulda guessed you were a dyke," Robert's voice interrupted my task.

"Why's that, Robert?" I responded with casual disinterest.

"Because you're such a bitch."

"And that has to do with my sexuality, how?" His expression told me he didn't catch that I was making fun of his flawed logic. Big surprise.

"You might have my dad fooled, and you certainly have my cousin fooled, but I saw who you really were when you worked for me."

"A better salesperson and manager than you?" I jabbed because he was starting to tick me off.

"Bite me."

"Professional courtesy ended with my contract. I was willing to give politeness a try because you're Raven's cousin, but since you clearly have no respect for her or me, I won't bother."

His face grew red with what I assumed was anger rather than embarrassment. "I don't usually care who my cousin is screwing, but I plan to tell her all about what a useless bitch you are."

I pulled off the oven mitt and casually tossed it onto the counter. Bullies can't stand when you don't get all riled up over their antics. "Tell me, Robert, what pisses you off more: the fact that, in two weeks of pretend working for you, I was able to close more sales than your entire department combined for the quarter, or the fact that I told your dad that your AA could do your job better than you?"

His eyes stretched so wide I thought they might pop out of his face. Archie must not have mentioned my recommendation to him. Can't say as I blame him, but still, he should have at least talked to Robert about working a little more efficiently. "You goddamn bitch!" He stepped toward me with a vicious spark in his eyes. I'd never liked being crowded and being hit ranked even lower. Not that I believed he had the guts to actually hit me. Before he had a chance to do either, a large hand appeared out of nowhere and grasped his shoulder to swing him around.

"Your dad's looking for you, cuz," Dax drew out the family connection.

"He can wait. Joslyn and I were having a little discussion."

"Yeah, heard some of it. Be glad it was me and not Raven 'cause she'd be kicking your ass for being such a dick to her girlfriend. You do remember Raven's ass kickings from when you were a kid, right, Bobbie?"

"Shut up," Robert muttered but left with a death glare in my direction.

"I'm sorry," Dax and I said together. We both smiled and he gestured for me to continue. "He's never been happy with me, and I'm afraid I provoked him just now."

"He's an idiot, always has been, but usually he's harmless."

"Well, I appreciate your intervention."

"Can I ask you something?"

I took in his earnest look and didn't need him to voice his question. "Listen, Dax, I have a brother, too, so I know what you're going to say. You don't want Raven hurt, neither do I. You want to make sure that Raven has someone worthy of her, so do I. From the moment I met her, I recognized that she was special. Now that I'm involved with her, I know she deserves to be treasured. That's my plan with her."

Dax considered me for a minute before nodding. "Actually, I was going to ask how you stand working with a company where you may find resistance and sometimes hostility. But all that stuff about my sister was good to know. Thanks." I blushed at his ribbing. Brothers, good ones, can be both wonderful and exasperating all at once.

"What's going on in here, bro?" Raven came up and slipped her arms around my waist to hug me from behind. "Not giving poor Jos a hard time, are you? She's been put through the wringer enough tonight."

"I've only just gotten out the water wheel and straps, sis. C'mon, let me have some fun."

"Back off, Dax." She moved around to place herself between me and her brother. If I hadn't witnessed their ribbing nature before, I might be a little nervous that she felt she had to literally protect me. "Go deal with Dad, will you? He's griping about something again."

"Don't let it get to you, Rave. You know you can't change him." He squeezed her shoulder and tipped his head at me before leaving the kitchen.

"He didn't come on too strong, did he?" Concern flickered through her expression.

"He was great, but I should warn you that Robert really, really, really hates me. The gloves came off right before Dax walked in."

She pulled me into her and tilted my chin up to catch my eyes. "Did he do something to upset you? I swear that boy always was a handful."

"Don't worry about it. I handle people like Robert every day. Eventually they stop blaming me for their own inadequacies, but maybe we don't have another family barbeque any time soon?"

"I was just thinking that myself." She pressed her forehead against mine, swaying our bodies gently.

"Something tells me I'm not a favorite of your dad's either?"

"Don't take it personally. He's, well, he still isn't entirely comfortable with my sexuality. He seems to take it as a personal affront that I prefer women."

That definitely never came up in any of our discussions. I hugged her tightly. We hadn't been afforded any personal time tonight, so I took this private moment for all it was worth. "I'm sorry. That must be difficult."

"I'm used to it. I'd hoped meeting you would be different because Uncle Archie thinks so highly of you. He'll come around."

"If there's anything you'd like me to do or say, just name it."

"You're so amazing, Jos," she declared with glistening eyes. "You've handled this night really well. My mom adores you. My brother wants to hire you to shape up his office, and he doesn't let anyone near his business. My sister-in-law has found a co-conspirator in family gatherings. You're even winning over some of those cousins you mentioned. You're doing great, sweetheart, just a couple more hours."

"And then?"

"I seem to remember an item number three from a few weeks ago. That sounds really good right now."

My eyes lit up at the reminder of that first weekend together. "We'd better get these people fed and out of here then."

"You're good at planning. I think you should do all the planning from now on in this relationship."

"I can handle that." I tipped up to catch her lips for a quick kiss. Maybe tonight wasn't a total catastrophe after all. "I can definitely handle that, lovely."

Chapter 21

*W*alking around Marco's latest jobsite, my dad and I mentally ticked off all that still needed to be done. Marco was ahead of schedule, way ahead. I made another mental note to redo his contracts to include a bonus if he finished his jobs ahead of time. It saved the homeowner thousands on mortgage payments or delayed interest for what would have been an unoccupied home.

"The boy gets better and better with each project." Dad said as we looked out of the second story framing. This was the only unenclosed room because the homeowner decided at the last second to add a mother-in-law apartment over the garage and had just acquired the permits to begin building.

The rest of the crew was working on the main house, but Dad wanted to check out the framing and progress of the plumbing before the drywall went up. Marco was using a new plumbing subcontractor, one that hadn't been around when Dad owned the company. The copper piping held nice welds and good spacing, so Dad could stop worrying.

"He's an artist, Dad, just like you taught him to be. Nice design, by the way."

He shot me a surprised glance. "How'd you know?"

"I've been looking at your houses all my life, Pop. You don't think I can spot one of your masterpieces?"

"It is rather dazzling, isn't it?" He wrapped an arm around my shoulders and squeezed me to him. "So, what's new with my best girl?"

My stomach felt like it dropped ten stories as I contemplated how to share my news with him. Normally, I didn't mention the people I was dating unless he specifically asked if I was seeing someone. I never made a big deal out of it because it never was a big deal. I couldn't say the same about this time. Raven was different in so many ways, and I wanted to tell the man who'd always been the most important person in my life.

"Haven't seen much of you lately, so I assume something's going on?" he persisted.

Taking a deep breath, I announced, "I met someone, Dad."

"A special someone?" He spun toward me.

"Very."

"Has he passed Marco's decency scale?" he teased about Marco's constant disapproval of the men I've dated.

"You could say that."

"Really?" His jaw popped open.

"Marco has given his blessing."

"Wow, he must be special if Marco's okay with him. When can I meet him?"

"You already have." My throat suddenly went dry. I crossed my fingers and attempted, "I'm, well, the thing is..."

"Jos? Who is it?"

"Raven," I admitted, watching him closely. He squinted

in confusion then cocked his head. "You met her at the law enforcement gala." When his eyes registered the recognition, I plowed ahead, "I know this is a surprise; it was for me, too, but she's...she's amazing, Dad."

"Raven?" A frown crinkled the expanse of his weather beaten forehead.

"I don't know how to explain it. We clicked right away, and that never happens to me." I checked to see if his expression had changed. It hadn't. "Are you doing okay with this?"

"Okay?" He sounded dazed.

"I don't know what I'd do if you can't handle my being with a woman. You're too important to me not to have you okay with this." I spilled out the whole deck, no card left unused.

"Sweetie." He wrapped his arms around me and held me close. "All I've ever wanted for you is happiness, and I can see how happy you are. She must be a remarkable lady for you to finally let someone in. I'd like to meet her again, just so I can thank her for making you so happy."

"Oh, thank you." I couldn't contain the elation that he'd accept this like it was the best thing to happen to me, which I couldn't deny, it was.

"Don't get me wrong, I'm still going to grill her. Make sure she's gonna do my best girl right, you know. Marco'll want in, too. Better make it a whole weekend so we have time to grill her and see if she can hold her own on a construction site."

"Dad." I chuckled, smacking his shoulder.

He grinned wide enough to almost peel back his face. "Do you love her?"

"Dad!" That was surprising, but only because he'd never asked me that of anyone I've dated in the past. "I haven't, I mean, neither of us, we haven't..."

He waved his hands. "That's okay. You don't need to say anything. I know my daughter. I know the answer already. I'm happy for you, sweetie. You've deserved this for so long."

"Thanks." I leaned in for another hug. Not many dads could compare to mine.

* * *

Malicious little bastard! I should have expected Robert to react this way. So, why did I find this news surprising? As soon as I set down the phone in my home office, I picked it back up and dialed again. I couldn't let Robert get away with such a stupid move.

Although Raven's tone had been exasperated when she told me, she sounded more resigned than upset that her cousin was such an idiot. I would have wanted to kick him from the sales department down to HR to make him reverse his decision. Instead, she'd been told as soon as she found out, which was a week after the fact. By then, nothing could be done. Well, I was going to rectify that.

"Thanks for calling, Jos." Zina greeted me an hour later in the café where we'd agreed to meet. "I could use the distraction."

"Hi, Zina, I'm glad you could make it on short notice."

"I've got nothing better to do with my time right now." Zina referred to the fact that she no longer had a job, thanks to Robert's insecurity.

"I believe I owed you a lunch anyway, right?" On cue, the waiter approached, and we placed our orders.

"So, what's new with you?" Her blasé attitude over losing her job for no apparent reason made me chuckle.

"I'm sorry about your job."

"Oh, I know it's not your fault, Jos. Is that why you asked me here? You thought I got laid off because of your recommended cut in workforce?" She grasped my forearm, concerned for my visible guilt.

"No, I know why you got fired. It wasn't because of my

consultation, but it was because of me." Or because Robert was the most insecure ass alive.

"That's not true. Those layoffs stopped weeks ago."

I steeled myself to tell her the truth. "Yeah, but you were fired because I told Archie that you could do Robert's job better than he could."

Zina's eyes bugged out as she rocked back in her chair. "You said what, woman?"

"I recommended to Archie that he demote Robert to senior sales rep and give you the CSO position. Of course, he thought I was joking."

Her head shook as she worked her way through my news. She'd braided her hair sometime since I last saw her. The tight weaving patterns rounded precisely over her skull and left more of her face to see. "When did you tell him?"

"After the presentation to the sales department."

"If you're so sure that's what got me fired, why'd it take so long?"

"Because, idiot that I am, I told Robert the same thing when I saw him Friday before last. He definitely took me seriously. I'm sorry, I should have known he'd retaliate against you."

Zina's head shake turned into a sinister smile. "I wish I could have been there to hear you tell that jerk that his AA could take his job."

"That's what you've got to say?" I huffed in disbelief, barely noticing the waiter drop our lunches off at the table. "I get you fired and you're only wish is that you'd seen Robert hear me call him incompetent?"

"Sure. That woulda been a riot." She took a bite of her lunch like it was any other day. "Don't worry, Jos. That right there was worth having to update my résumé and begin a job search. I didn't like working for him anyway."

"Well, how about me? Would you work for me?"

She dropped the fry that she'd raised to her mouth and stared at me blankly. The usual rapid retorts stayed locked in her brain. "What?"

"I've always had the luxury of picking my clients carefully, and I've never been rushed to move on to another project. But lately, I can't keep up with the requests. I've been contemplating hiring someone to help out, run the business while I'm out consulting. Train someone on conducting part of the research for me so that I can spend more time on analysis. Would that interest you?"

"Are you serious?"

"Sure, I could take on more clients, focus on the parts of consulting that I like best, and not worry that I'm missing out on other interesting projects because I'm running around trying to tie up all the loose ends." Until I made the offer, I hadn't realized how much I needed someone.

"You didn't work with me for that long. How do you know if I'm qualified?"

"Zina, you're a rarity. I see maybe one employee like you in every twenty companies I analyze." I smiled at the modest look that crossed her face. "I can offer you a thirty percent raise and a car allowance. You'll work hard when we have clients, but you'll get the same breaks that I take in between clients. I can't say that I'll always be a dream to work with, especially when the client is an asshole, but we've always had a good rapport. I think it'll work out great."

"Not that I was worried about that, but the fact that you said 'work with' not 'work for' tells me you would value any employee."

"You game?"

"I'm game, set, and match, sister. Sign me up."

"Great." I sighed with relief. This would work out beautifully. My dad had been bugging me to get some help for years. I couldn't ask for someone better. "Can you start next week? It'll give me time to get you a laptop and set up a network so we can work from our homes until I think of something more permanent."

"Sounds good to me. Thank you, Joslyn. I appreciate the opportunity. I know I'll learn a lot from you."

I imagined I'd be learning just as much from her. This would be a massive change for a normally independent person like me, but I had to attribute my lack of anxiety about it to my relationship with Raven. Being with her had opened up so many experiences I'd never considered before. I felt like there wasn't anything I couldn't undertake, and the knowledge was empowering.

Chapter 22

A whole weekend together. I could hardly wait to see her. The past three nights had been spent at long dinner meetings with potential clients. It was getting ridiculous how much I missed her when we were separated. To make matters worse, my next client was out of town. I'd be leaving Thursday after next for two weeks. This was the first time in my consulting career that I thought about canceling out on a client because I didn't want to be gone for that long.

When I heard the car drive up, I raced to the front door and flung it open. I didn't want to waste one second of this weekend. The sight of my dad's truck, followed by Marco's shocked me. "Hi there, best girl." Dad stepped down from his truck with a big smile.

"Hi, Dad. Was I expecting you tonight?" My brain tried to sift through the conflicting thoughts of surprise, joy, and disappointment.

"You didn't think we'd let you leave town without a traditional sendoff, did you?" True, we often had dinner together whenever I had a long-term contract out of town, but two weeks hardly qualified.

"What? We're not welcome alla sudden?" Marco jabbed when he and his wife caught up with my dad. Phoebe's shoulders nearly touched the short bob of dark blond hair as she shrugged apologetically. She didn't believe in no notice drop-ins but, obviously, she hadn't been able to stop her husband's mission. Her blue eyes tried to convey that she was completely on my side with this one. "If you happen to be spending the evening with a certain someone, well, all the better for us, right, Michael?"

"A certain special someone," Dad pitched in.

I scoffed, caught between enjoying their banter and what I knew would be Raven's anxiety. "You guys, you can't ambush her like this."

"Seems like this might be fair payback for that dinner you had to suffer through," Marco commented about the Paul family get-together. I immediately scolded myself for telling him about it. I should have known he'd find a way to use it against me.

"It wasn't that bad, and her family's different from you guys."

"You're saying she actually likes them?" Marco joked.

"Jeez, what would that be like?" Dad quipped. He grabbed me for a hug and kissed my forehead. "Just a quick meet if she's not up to having us stay, okay? I barely got to speak to her when we first met, and it's a father's prerogative to get to know your special someone."

Well, that was unfair. Like I could deny his request now. "Fine, but let me break it to her when she arrives. Give her a chance to bolt if she's not ready."

"Show me to the grill, Jos. The Q-master has arrived. Phoeb, bring on the steaks," Marco mock ordered his wife, knowing she'd already done all the unloading of groceries. The men in my life never thought I had enough food for them to consume, and they were usually right.

Ten minutes later, Raven arrived. I was at her car before it came to a complete stop. I opened the door for her and pulled her into my arms. "Hi, lovely."

"Hey, sweetheart, I've missed you." She kissed me with so much enthusiasm it practically erased the past three days absence. I wasn't sure how I'd make it two weeks away from her. When she pulled back, she glanced over at the other vehicles in my driveway. "Don't tell me you've traded in your classics for two pickups?"

"Well, actually, we have some company. Surprise company. Uninvited company," I stressed.

"If I'm reading the logos right, seems like the surprise company might be related to you?" She referred to the S&V Construction label painted on the door panels.

"I'm sorry, honey, they just showed up. We usually have dinner together before I go on extended road trips."

I couldn't get a bead on all the emotions that skittered through her expression before she smiled like a trooper. "Do they know I'm coming to dinner?"

"I told them I already had dinner plans, yes. They're a little hard to chase off, but they won't stay long. I promise it won't be that bad." Well, it might just edge out a short stint in a Turkish prison anyway.

"I liked meeting them before. I'm sure this will be fun." She released a long breath and pushed off toward the house, not waiting for me. Determination, one of my favorite of her traits.

When we made it out to the back porch, we found Marco fighting with Dad about how much salt should be added to the marinade. My brother and I were both worried about his high blood pressure, so we took turns nagging him about it.

"Break it up, guys. I'll pull this whole backyard over if

you don't drop the salt and step away now, Dad."

Phoebe and Marco laughed at my threat. The salt shaker stayed suspended in the air until Dad made a grand show of setting it down and stepping partially behind Marco. "I don't remember her being this bossy when she was a kid. Must be your influence," Dad accused Marco.

"I taught her every decent thing she knows," Marco boasted.

I rolled my eyes. "Raven, you remember my dad, Michael, and my brother, Marco?"

"Of course, it's nice to see you both again."

"Damn glad to have a chance to get to know you, Raven." Dad pumped her hand with both of his. He scrutinized her blatantly, only partly because she was so gorgeous.

"Give her arm back, Michael." Marco stepped up to give her a much shorter version of the same handshake.

"And this is my sister-in-law, Phoebe Ventano. Phoebe, this is my girlfriend, Raven Malvolio."

I felt Raven go rigid beside me through the length of her arm touching mine. A short burst of sound came from her mouth as she swiveled her head from me to them and back to me. "You—you told them? A-about us?"

My family looked at me in surprised silence. I found myself just as shocked by her question. "Is that all right? I assumed that, since you told your family, it was okay to tell mine."

Raven's mouth trembled. She nodded her head and buried her face in my hair, clutching me to her. Silent shivers grew to soft sobs, and I could feel her trying to gain control.

I looked over at my family with the same dismay they showed me. Phoebe cracked an understanding smile. "Oh, thank God, another crier." The men chuckled at the idea that Phoebe, who was very sensitive outside of her job, would have a comrade in crying jags.

Raven tipped back, her cheeks flushed pink with embarrassment, eyes still moist from her rush of emotions. She gave me such a look of, well, if I had to guess: love. The realization made me dizzy and hopeful and serene all at once. "I'm sorry, I can't explain that away." She turned to face them. "I wasn't expecting this tonight. I didn't realize that Joslyn had told you. It's such a surprise."

"A good surprise, I hope, young lady?" Dad asked.

"The best, actually."

"Good to hear. My Jos is a tremendous girl. She tells me you're special to her, which makes you special to us." Since Raven looked like she was going to crumble into tears again, Dad wrapped his big arms around her. God, I loved that man.

"And if you keep crying, Marco won't feel so ostracized every time he bursts into tears at a family gathering," Phoebe kidded, making everyone laugh.

"I'm sorry, it's very nice to meet you, Phoebe." Raven pulled back from the hug and shook Phoebe's hand. "I hope I haven't ruined the first impression."

"Don't be silly," Phoebe assured. "We're all so happy for Jos that she has you."

"It doesn't matter that I'm a woman?" Raven asked tentatively.

"You're smarter, kinder, and way better looking than the other people she's dated," Marco joked and got an elbow to the side from his wife.

"As long as Jos is happy, we're happy. From everything she's told us, you seem like a wonderful person. She deserves someone like you," Dad announced, and my own eyes misted up.

"Only one question remains." Marco turned serious enough to garner everyone's attention. "How do you like your steak prepared?"

"All my life I've been dealing with this loon." I jerked a thumb at him.

When I turned my grin to Raven, I saw that look again. This time there was no mistaking the interpretation, and my heart took control of my conscious thoughts. *Oh yeah, no more falling, I'm all the way in now.*

Chapter 23

"I know that was embarrassing." Raven settled in beside me on the couch after we'd said goodnight to my family.

For a moment I wasn't sure what she meant. Then I remembered her teary reaction to the introduction of her as my girlfriend. I turned to face her, bringing a knee up on the couch. One of her hands immediately reached for my thigh, squeezing gently. I took her free hand in mine and brought it to my lips. "I believe you assured me that crying is nothing to be embarrassed about." Brown eyes tracked the path of her hand, closing slowly as I pressed a kiss to the center of her palm. "Everything all right now?"

"You surprised me by telling them."

"Why wouldn't I tell them?"

Raven took what I'd come to recognize as her calming breaths before she spoke. "In grad school I got involved with someone who'd never been with a woman before. She seemed sincere, and I knew there was a risk that she'd consider it a college fling, but the relationship grew deeper than that. The only problem was that she wanted to keep everything completely private. She didn't even want me to tell my friends and certainly not my family." She glanced away, pain tightening her expression.

"Months go by and she's still not telling anyone. That's when I realize she hasn't even admitted it to herself. Coming out is difficult for almost everyone, but what we had should have been worth it." Her hand squeezed mine, but she kept her face turned toward the window. "I let this go on for another couple of months before I confronted her about not admitting that she was a lesbian. She denied being gay, and even worse, she said that what we were doing amounted to foreplay, so she couldn't be gay. She'd told me she'd be embarrassed if people knew that we'd been together. It felt worse than betrayal because she'd rather continue to lie to herself and deny her feelings than accept our relationship and stay with me."

The straight woman that I'd overheard Dax mentioning, the one who'd hurt her. Burned her, more like. No wonder she had such a strong resolve to stay away from the same possibility. "That's horrible, Raven," I whispered, pulling on her chin to face me. "I'm sorry you were hurt so badly like that."

"Thank you. It wasn't an easy time to say the least."

"It couldn't have been." I leaned forward to kiss her cheek then brush her lips. I tilted back and caught her eyes. "What made you think that I'd want to keep us a secret? I mean, we had your family over, and Ray even saw us together that first morning."

"The same morning that you wanted to get out of there before Kelly arrived," she added.

"Oh no! You thought that was because I didn't want anyone to know? Honey, I was thinking about you. You're

Kelly's boss. I thought you might want to maintain some professionalism with her. I figured Ray might tell her eventually, but it wouldn't be the same as if Kelly'd run into us that morning. I was trying to save you from becoming the juiciest piece of office gossip."

She smiled and shook her head in amazement. "I'm sorry, sweetheart. I should have known it wouldn't be like that with you."

"That's why you wouldn't let me answer your nephew's question about me being your girlfriend? You thought I'd be uncomfortable?" She shrugged in response. "I'm honored to be your girlfriend. Every time you call me sweetheart I can't believe how lucky I am."

"I feel the same way, Jos." She brought her hand up to cup my face gently. "Until you introduced me as your girlfriend to your family, I didn't think it was possible to love you even more."

"What was that?" My heart erupted into a high paced clattering inside my chest. I leaned forward with a grin that threatened to spread to every cell in my body.

Raven's hand flew from my face to clamp over her mouth. Clearly, she hadn't meant to say that out loud, but her gorgeous mind worked through it quickly. The delighted expression I wore probably helped a bit. When she dropped her hand, she gave a silent laugh. "I think you heard me."

I wiggled my eyebrows and widened my grin. "You're madly, head over heels, hopelessly, desperately in love with me."

"Desperately may be going a little too far."

"But not by much, right?" I teased and watched her fight a telling smile. "I knew it!"

She laughed out loud this time. "What gave me away?"

"Oh, I don't know, you can't seem to keep your hands off me, you're always staring at me, you're bringing me home to meet your family." I ticked off each item with my fingers. "Or it might be because I recognize in you all the same things I'm feeling myself." Those tempting lips trembled again as she registered what I meant. "I love you, Raven."

"I love you, too, Joslyn. I've wanted to tell you for so long, but I didn't want to scare you away."

"You can't scare me." For the first time in my life, I knew that was true.

"Your last relationship lasted six months and you weren't in love. I didn't want to rush you."

"I already told you, you're not like anyone I've ever known," I assured her. "I must have been waiting for you to come along before I could feel everything that you make me feel. I don't care how long it's been, I know I'm in love with you."

"Desperately?" A sly grin inched her mouth wide.

"Well..." I kidded back.

She gripped my face. "Your eyes are giving you away, *tesora*. I'm willing to bet that you don't know they've been my very own mood ring for you all along."

I cocked my head, confounded by her statement. "Mood ring?"

"Your hazels are so beautiful. I love when they move from amber-gold to silver, but my absolute favorite shade is smoky grey because it doesn't happen very often. The first time I kissed you, when you first asked me to take you to bed, the first time I made you—"

"Okay, I get it," I cut her off, feeling heat burn my cheeks. I'd seen my eyes turn many different shades of amber and grey, but never the color she was describing.

"We need to get you to a mirror right now, sexy. They're smoldering, and you should get a look at your best tell."

"It's a good thing you love me or this knowledge might be something you could sell to my clients and ruin my unforgiving reputation."

"You better not be showing that color to a client!" Her fingers tightened on my jaw. "That's for private moments only."

"Private like when I do this?" I slid my hands under her shirt and inched it upward until I had it over her head. My mouth went dry at the sight of her red lace bra and already flushed skin. I unbuttoned her pants and encouraged her hips up so I could bring them down her toned legs. Matching lace panties started my own heavy breathing. "Private like when I do this?" I leaned over her semi-prone form and took a nipple into my mouth through the satiny lace.

"I'm on fire, Jos," Raven moaned, grasping my head as the smooth material got wetter under my mouth.

"For me?"

"Yes, God, yes. You make me so hot." Her hands forced my head up to look at her. "Get naked, quickly."

I laughed with a seductive throatiness that never existed outside of making love with Raven. I went up to my knees, and she helped me shed my clothes. Her hands immediately grasped my breasts, flicking over my nipples as I'd tantalized hers. Without my having to tell her, she knew how sensitive mine were and how much they liked the attention.

Only her sexy underwear remained. My mind vacillated between the benefit and the hurdle of keeping them on. Before I made a decision, I caught her wicked grin as if she knew exactly what I was thinking. She'd probably worn this enticing set for just that reason.

"This is private for me," I growled, plucking a finger under the front clasp of her bra and the lace popped free. The creamy expanse of her skin crested into two perfectly rounded breasts with light brown areolas and nipples that darkened as they puckered in excitement.

"Only you," she agreed in a voice that seemed to restate her love.

Once I'd slid her panties off, I settled between her thighs and pressed her back against the couch. Her lips beckoned first before I slowly made my way down to her now exposed nipples. "You're so beautiful, Raven."

"So are you. I love you, Jos."

"I love you, too." I rose up to kiss her tempting mouth, savoring her flavor but craving another. I dipped down to taste her as she bucked into my mouth, coating my tongue with her arousal.

"Oh, God, yes, that feels so good."

Her hips undulated fiercely under my clamping hands and mouth. Moans turned to intermittent shrieks, signaling just how close she was. I sucked her engorged clit into my mouth and licked directly until her legs strained with the crest of her orgasm. Just as she was declaring her arrival, I pulled back, taking away all stimulation.

She cried out incomprehensibly at first before actual words formed. "Don't stop! Jos, please. You're killing me."

I kissed her tense stomach, keeping away from her aching need. "Yes, but see, I've been noticing," I kissed into the valley between her breasts, "that you rather enjoy," my mouth reached her neck and sucked on a patch of silky skin, "the buildup."

"Please, please, please." Her body strained to grind against me, but my arms flexed to keep her at bay.

"You like to be teased, lovely. I'm going to make sure that you get everything you like."

She growled in frustration, but her eyes glowed with the ecstasy I knew she felt. "You're evil."

"Thank you." I swelled with delicious pride. When I kissed her mouth, she tugged on my lower lip with a little more pressure than usual. A snicker escaped from me into her mouth. I dropped a hand down to her outer thigh and pressed against her leg. When the pressure became insistent, her mouth popped off mine, and she looked at me questioningly. "Turn over, lovely." I left no room for debate in my request.

Her eyes flared with anticipation. A shiver ran through her whole body before she rolled onto her stomach. The sight of her stretched out beneath me brought on a shiver of my own. I spread my fingers wide and traced a hand down her spine. Her strong, lean back arched into the path of my hand. My leg shifted forward between hers, eliciting a whimper from her. I massaged the supple flesh pressed against my leg as I sank down onto her back and kissed the path that my hand had followed.

"Joslyn," she whispered her plea this time.

Pulling back slightly, I coaxed her up to her knees. Her excitement spread directly to my center, and a flood of arousal trickled onto my thighs. This time, I wasn't surprised by how turned on I was.

I took my time exploring her before stroking and swirling her slick sex. When I couldn't hold back, I plunged two fingers inside of her warm, wet center. She groaned and twisted her head to lock eyes with me. I began a slow thrust, filling and withdrawing. Her hips rocked against mine. My other hand slid around her waist and dipped to stroke her. Grazing lightly over her clit, she jerked back against me and her head dropped to the arm of the couch. With one more swipe of my fingers, she cried out.

"I'm coming, Jos! God, I'm coming so hard." Her body bucked up against mine, her tight sheath squeezing my fingers. When her legs gave out, I dropped to the couch with her. "Oh wow," she managed after she'd regained her breath.

"I'll say," I agreed. The feel of her flushed, damp body beneath mine was almost too much to bear.

Her shoulders shifted, and I pushed up onto my arms to allow her to flip onto her back underneath me. She tipped up to lock her lips over mine, pulling and sliding in a sensuous kiss. "I didn't know teasing could be that good."

"It'll get better with more practice. Lots and lots of practice."

"You're such a perfectionist."

I slid my slick fingers up her abdomen to her breast, coating the nipple before squeezing her firm flesh. "Only in private."

She speared me with a seductive look. I knew she was seeing her favorite color again. "Only with me."

"With you," I agreed, leaning down to kiss her hungry mouth. "Only for you."

Chapter 24

Before we'd cleared the front of my car, Raven stopped us. "You don't have to do this, you know. I know you're not much for large gatherings."

"Wanna bet?" I smiled wryly. "There's a reason your friends picked this bar on this night to meet me. This is a test, lovely. See how the former straight girl does with all these lesbians."

She waved her hands defensively before they landed on my shoulders. "No, they wouldn't do that."

"It's okay. I know what I'm facing tonight, and I want to meet your friends. Now's as good a time as any." I squeezed her waist and tipped up to brush my lips against hers. When I pulled back, she reached down and grabbed my hand, tugging us toward the bar.

After paying cover for this monthly event, I scanned the layout. Pool tables would help, not crazy about the dance floor, but I could make due. Before we'd gotten halfway to the bar, the tall brunette from the basketball game stopped us with a shriek. "Finally! We've been waiting hours," she said. "Hi, remember me? I'm Nora, we met at the game."

"Of course, nice to see you again." I went to shake her hand, but she grabbed me for a kiss on the cheek. Friendly little thing.

Before I could share a look with Raven, Nora was dragging me toward a back corner table that overflowed with women, all ecstatic to see Raven. They tossed out names and greetings giving little regard for the fact that I'd never remember them. That wasn't the point. I wondered how long it would be before the inquisition began.

I didn't have to wait long. Five seconds after Raven left to get us drinks, a curvy blonde asked, "So, how did you meet our Raven?"

Our Raven. Point taken. "Her uncles hired me to consult for their company."

When I didn't offer anything else, a thin, pretty Asian piped up, "How long have you been together?"

I let out a brief laugh. "A while."

"And you're in love?" a heavyset brunette with a farmer's tan asked in a mocking tone.

Raven's friend Elise, who'd taken the seat next to mine and looked about as comfortable in this bar as I did, stiffened beside me. She leaned forward with a menacing look, but I jumped in before she put herself out there. "That's between Raven and me." A round of ooh's circled the table. Half of them seemed to like my smack down, the other half were a mix of suspicion and disbelief. Perhaps no one had dared cross this woman before.

"Hey," a voice interrupted any retort by Farmer Tan. I twisted to look up at the person who'd interrupted. Her brown eyes locked on mine. She had short dark hair and wore a white t-shirt with rolled sleeves and dark jeans with doubled up cuffs, making her look like she'd stepped out of a 50's diner. "You're a new face and a gorgeous one at that. Great body, too." She leaned down and placed her hands on the table and the back of my chair, trapping me in place. "I'd like to lick every bit of it."

Sharp gasps, groans, and nervous giggles sounded from the observers at the table. Elise's partner, Austy, scoffed, "Jesus, Ruth."

I didn't know if this was part of the test, but I couldn't let it faze me. "Wouldn't we all live a charmed life if we got everything we wanted? Too bad only one of us gets that privilege tonight." Confusion knitted her brow as my gaze moved past her shoulder and focused on a stunned Raven who'd just returned from the bar with our drinks. "Hi, honey, I was just making a new friend."

The woman stood bolt upright and swung around to face Raven with her hands up. "Oh, hey, I didn't know she was taken."

Raven advanced and set the drinks in front of us, glancing curiously at her friends before addressing our newcomer. "I'm Raven."

"Ruth," she inserted nervously.

"I see you've met my girlfriend, Joslyn. Having a nice conversation, sweetheart?" The wicked grin she wore cranked up my internal thermometer.

"I was just telling Ruth how rare it is to lead a charmed life. Since I'm new at it, I still appreciate what it was like not living one."

"Listen," Ruth began, bouncing her gaze between Raven and me. "I didn't mean, um, I just saw, anyway, nice meeting you." She glanced beside me to address the three women she apparently knew. "Aust, Elise, Cheryl, good seeing you."

"Well done," Elise commented in a low voice as laughter chased Ruth away.

Raven slipped into the seat next to me, resting her arm on the back of my chair. I turned a grateful look at my unintentional hero. "Hi, lovely," I whispered. "Glad you're back."

"Slyn?" Trinity's voice cut in. "I didn't know you'd be here."

I looked over and found Trinity and Kayla coming to a rest beside our table. Trinity gave me a fist pound and Kayla leaned down for a quick squeeze. "Yeah, Raven's friends invited us out." We took a moment for introductions and dragged a couple of seats over for them.

"Little different from the last time we came, right, Slyn?" Trinity motioned to the bar.

"What?" at least four people asked at once. They didn't bother to hide the shock. Even Raven turned an interested stare my way. "You've been here before?"

"Yeah, I dragged her out with me a few times when I was getting over my last breakup," Trinity supplied for me. "My psycho ex turned all our friends against me. Slyn was the only one who stayed on my side."

"I can't believe you didn't mention that." Raven poked my shoulder with two fingers.

"Told you I knew what I was getting into tonight." I winked at her.

After Trinity's declaration, the mood at the table lightened tremendously. They all began interacting the way they normally would if I weren't there. It was nice to see Raven had a handful of really great friends. No one quite as unique as my friend Stuart, but they were fun to be around.

An hour later, dancing seemed to be the activity of the moment as most of the table left for the dance floor. I was warming up to the idea when I noticed that Elise and Austy stayed seated. "You don't dance?"

Red touched Austy's cheeks, but it was Elise who responded. "We're not big on it."

"Oh?" I turned a questioning gaze to Raven. She seemed to understand what I was asking and nodded. "I'm not either, but Raven likes it. Any chance you'd step in for me, Elise? If Austy doesn't mind keeping me company, that is. I've been on my feet with presentations all week; I'd rather sit it out."

Elise looked guilty but hopeful; Austy looked grateful. "Perfect solution." She squeezed her partner's hand before Elise and Raven made their way to the dance floor together. "Thank you for suggesting that."

I shifted chairs to sit next to the woman who had been quiet all night. I could tell some of the group thought she was aloof, but I figured she was ultra shy. "It keeps me from making a fool of myself on the dance floor. I get the impression the bar scene isn't for you?" She smiled and blushed again. "Me, neither. I've enjoyed getting to know you both, though. Seeing as Raven and Elise are good friends, maybe a dinner for the four of us would be more comfortable next time?"

"That would be nice, thank you. Would you like another drink? I'm in need of a refill." She hopped up at my nod and pushed her way through the throng of people to the bar. The mass swallowed her pixie-like form within seconds.

"So, you got Raven?" an accusatory claim sounded from behind me. I turned to see a tall, well built, androgynous looking woman. Powerful and confidently intimidating. She was one of the original three I'd met at the Storm game with Raven. Hilary, I think her name was. Before I could reply to what I assumed was a teasing taunt, she continued, "And you're straight."

I glanced behind her to spot Raven still on the dance floor with Elise. All of her friends were in the same area, some dancing in a group, others coupled up. Looks like it would be me and the Xena wannabe alone. I gestured to a chair, but her glare told me she wasn't about to acknowledge my politeness. "What's your point?"

"Huh?" She squinted in confusion, clearly thinking I would have said something else. An immediate denial, a plea for friendship, a rush to make her like me.

"Well, you've approached me when none of your friends are here, you don't sound pleased that Raven and I are together, and you're trying to provoke a specific response from me." My own accusations caused a storm of emotions to roll through her expressive face. I wondered if she knew how telling her face was. "Let's skip the long discussion where you'll undoubtedly get more annoyed and frustrated with me. Just tell me what you want me to say so that you feel satisfied with the outcome."

"Christ!' she breathed out slowly, shaking her head but maintaining the accusatory stare. "You're not even gonna try to kiss my ass?"

"Why should I? You've made up your mind about me already. You had even before you'd met me when you heard my last relationship was with a man. No amount of effort on my part is going to change that. So in the end, anything I tried would only frustrate me. I like it better when others are frustrated."

A short snort of amusement escaped her lips before she went back to stony intimidation. "Let me give you a tip, dykes don't like being used by straight women."

"No one likes to be used, so I guess that's a universal concept."

That didn't sit well with her. "Then, you admit you're straight?"

"I didn't, and I don't." I wouldn't give her the satisfaction of a complete explanation. Without being willing to get specific about my feelings, she could never understand my view on this subject. My relationship with Raven made me a lesbian. If something happened to break us up in the future, would I only consider dating women? Since I couldn't imagine ever feeling about someone else the way I felt about Raven, as evidenced by the thirty-seven Raven-free years, I didn't really have an answer.

"That's it?" she asked incredulously.

"That's it for me, but it looks like you're still angling for something. What do you want to hear?"

"Damn! How does Raven stand you?" she barked at me.

"Raven likes me, you don't. News flash: I don't care. It would be nice to have all of Raven's friends like me, but that's a tall order. It only matters that Raven likes me. It's all that should matter to you as well."

"It isn't."

I cut her off before she could continue on the same circle of our conversation. "I can see that. Let me guess why. You either used to go out with Raven and want her back, or you've always wanted to go out with Raven, but she's only ever thought of you as a friend." The immediate crimson shade that came over her face told me my guess would have won me a stuffed animal at the carnival. I relented a bit on my cavalier tone. "That sucks, Hilary, really. I'm sorry that it's not worked out for you, but I'm not the reason why."

"That may be true, but I know that being straight is only going to hurt her in the end. And that, that…"

I stood up, not making much of a dent in the height difference between us, but I wanted to be on the same level as her. "That what? I'm not good enough for her?" I'd really expected more than the typical formulaic argument. I saw Austy approach cautiously as she took in our stances. "Second news flash: if you knew Raven like I do, you'd know that absolutely no one is good enough for her. I'm doing everything I can to keep her from regretting her decision to bless me with her love. It's all I'm capable of." Using the shocked silence I'd evoked as cover, I reached for the drink that Austy was offering. "Thanks, but I suddenly feel like dancing with my girlfriend." Austy gave me an encouraging nod as I left to find the woman who's made everything so clear for me.

Chapter 25

The letters exploded off the page like little landmines trying to take out my eyesight. Alone, each letter was harmless, but string them together and *ka-boom!* I stared at the document, willing the letters to rearrange themselves on the page. No doubt there were enough of them to make up other words. Other words that wouldn't hurt someone I loved.

Nicholas Paul. Saul Cholinos, Chip Anolusal, Palino Lausch, the combination of letters could easily be found in other names. So why didn't they? Why was I staring at a corporate charter document that listed Nicholas Paul as the CEO? And why did the charter list the business type as a bank? And for the love of Pete, why did the bank have a DBA name that matched the one on the loan documents in front of me? The same name on that loan document that I'd questioned at Paul Industries.

This was not good. So not good that I actually hesitated trying to figure out the right thing to do. Of course, I knew the right thing to do. I just didn't know if it was right for everyone involved. In the end, only one option remained. With dread weighing down my limbs, I gathered the strength and resolve to do what had to be done.

"Hello, Ms. Simonini, back for more?" the receptionist at Paul Industries greeted me a few hours later.

On the drive over, I'd managed to calm myself, rationalize away the awful feelings, knowing I was doing the right thing. I'd rehearsed what I was going to say for an hour before calling to make an appointment. This had to be done delicately.

"Just a standard follow up visit, Yvonne. Archie should be expecting me." She handed me a visitor badge, notified his EA, and told me to head on back.

Despite my relationship with Raven, this was the first time I'd been back to this building. I wanted time to let all the changes that I'd recommended settle in before offering my mug as an object of hatred again. Too bad the papers in my briefcase screwed that up for me.

Walking down the hall toward Archie's office, I scarcely remembered the supply room encounter on that weird day. I didn't know if that kiss truly helped open me up to the relationship I had with Raven, or if it was simply a harmless kiss. All I knew was that I glanced at the room with fondness as I passed by.

Only I didn't get far. A dragging force pulled me into the dark room, igniting an eerie sense of déjà vu. Breath rushed out of me in a silent exclamation of surprise as I was pressed up against a wall so quickly I barely had time to think. "I'm not Raven!" I protested, saying the first thing that came to mind.

A low, throaty chuckle filled the small room. A sound I knew so well. A sound I loved hearing. "I'd say so." Raven pressed her familiar body up against me. I wished I could see the satisfied grin I knew she was wearing right now, but when her lips descended on mine, I didn't think about anything other than how her tongue swept delicately into my mouth, tantalizing and coaxing mine into hers. *Now, this was a kiss.* I might have been provoked by Kelly's, but this kiss enlivened and electrified. Raven's kiss was love.

"You're so bad," I croaked when she pulled away. "You can't kiss me like that and expect me to go on with my day."

"How do you think I feel?" Her breath was heavy against my temple where she'd buried her head. "I'm innocently going about my day, and I see the sexiest, most alluring woman I've ever met walking down the hall toward me. What was I supposed to do?"

"Wait, you saw yourself walking down the hall?"

Her palms pressed against my shoulders, pushing playfully at me. She flipped on the light and that sexy grin of hers made my legs tremble. "You're too good to be true. Now, tell me why I got to enjoy this secret fantasy today?"

"This was a secret fantasy of yours?"

"Ever since I heard my own damn AA got to kiss you in this very spot."

The trace of jealousy in her tone delighted me. "She didn't kiss me like that. In fact, compared to your kiss, she didn't kiss me at all."

"Good answer," she practically growled and brought her mouth to mine again. She wasn't just claiming me with her mouth this time. Her heart took hold, too. "Tell me you came to convince me to play hooky again? I no longer care about all these meetings today. Not with you on a flight tonight."

Oh, how I wish I could tell her that. I wish I could tell her anything, but I couldn't. I needed to inform the CEO first. It didn't matter how much my heart screamed at me; I couldn't make myself feel better at the expense of professional propriety. I would tell her afterward.

"I wish, lovely. No, I've got a meeting with Archie. I did push my flight to the red-eye, so we'd have a few more hours tonight. Can you slip out early?" *We're going to need to talk.* Only I didn't voice that. In a relationship, no one liked to hear those words. Not that I meant them the same way others in relationships did. We'd need to talk about my meeting with Archie. She'd be upset, rightly so, but we could work through that, and I wanted those extra hours to make love with her before I had to leave for two weeks.

"I'll leave as soon as my last meeting is over. I can write up the notes tomorrow." Raven winked conspiratorially. "A few hours extra, ooh, I can't wait." She kissed me chastely this time otherwise we'd never get out of this room. "You leave first. I don't want to cause a scene. Not that they won't see that you were well kissed as you walk away."

I laughed at her feigned cockiness. Everything about her made me crackle. I'd never felt this alive in my life, probably because, before I'd met her, I was merely existing. "I can't get over how much I'm in love with you, Raven."

Her eyes misted, and she touched her forehead to mine. "Do me a favor and don't try to get over it, Jos. I love you just as much."

I bit back the responding moan, but a breathy sigh escaped. "Archie's going to wonder if I got lost."

"Go, *tesora*. I'll be going insane all day waiting to get to your place later."

I cupped her neck, feeling her pulse thump under my palm. She matched my intimate gesture. I couldn't stand that I might bring hurt to her with this meeting, but I had a job to do. I turned and left the room, not wanting to look back and see Raven slip out after me.

"Well, Joslyn, what brings you back down?" Archie greeted me at the door to his office. It was the first time I'd seen him since the dinner at Raven's house. While that night had been daunting, it didn't compare to how I felt facing him now.

I closed the door behind us and asked to take a seat. "I'm afraid I've got some bad news, Archie. I hate to be the one to bring it to you, but I really have no choice."

"This sounds serious."

"It's grave, and I'm not one for dramatics." I pulled out the loan document and charter papers from my briefcase and placed them on the desk. "These documents show that your nephew Nicholas has been embezzling money from your company under the guise of repayment of a loan." Archie rocked back against his chair without focusing on the proof in front of him. "If you'll notice here," I pointed to the charter documents, "Nick established a corporation several years ago. Please note the name in the DBA line matches the name of the bank which granted your 'loan' for a manufacturing warehouse you already owned. A few years ago, you sold the warehouse, but continued to pay on the fictitious loan."

"Nicky's always been an enterprising lad. I'm sure there are thousands of businesses out there with this same name."

"You're probably right, Archie. Unfortunately, the checks your AP division has been sending match up to the address of Nick's company."

"That doesn't mean it was Nicky." Archie's face hardened. I hadn't expected it to go easily, but his look of disbelief was a little disconcerting.

Glad that I'd gotten further proof, I pulled out the canceled checks. "These are the checks your company has issued as payment of principal and interest on the loan. You'll note Nick's endorsement on the back. You can also see the account number into which they've been cashed. Having looked over your payroll records, I know that Nick's paychecks are directly deposited to the same account."

"You're accusing him of stealing from me? From the company? From Nathan, his own father?"

"I have proof that he's been stealing from you, sir. I'm sorry to have to give it to you." I hoped he could recognize the regret in my tone.

"What if I told you that I authorized a loan to Nick?"

"I'd like to believe that, Archie, even if the means by which you would have provided that loan isn't exactly on the level. Unfortunately, I know it's not true."

"You can't know that," he spat at me.

I sighed heavily. "I understand this must be hard for you to hear."

"I'm telling you it's a damn loan to my nephew!" Archie roared, standing up to lean over the desk.

"I have his bank and credit card statements," I came back calmly even though my pulse raced at his intimidating stance. "Nick uses his credit and debit cards at various casinos, Emerald Downs race track, and one well known betting house. He's obviously been paying off gambling debts for several years. If you'd known and wanted to help him, you would have given him money, Archie. Setting up a payment stream on a fabricated loan would have risked exposure by your auditors."

"This is a family matter," Archie said gruffly. "We'll handle it internally."

"The amounts have escalated significantly to just shy of 300 thousand over the past five years, Archie. He's responsible for fifteen percent of the losses your company has suffered in recent years." That didn't seem to sink in either. "It's not just internal, and you know it. You have silent partners and a board of directors that aren't related to this family. Nick has perpetrated a fraud on them, too. If they find out, they can press charges."

"Are you threatening me?"

I sighed again, baffled that he was acting like a mama bear protecting her cubs. Nick didn't deserve that kind of unconditional devotion, not with the proof I had. "No, sir. I don't plan to tell them."

He sat back down and laced his fingers behind his head. "That's more like it."

"You can cover for Nick internally if you really believe that will do him any good. To do so, you'd need to pay back the money for him so that your silent partners aren't cheated out of their share of the current and back dividends."

"It's about time you showed some loyalty to this family." A hand unlocked from behind his head, tapping a finger in the air at me. "I like that you're placing your relationship with my niece ahead of your sense of duty. There's no reason this has to leave this room."

"Ethics is the reason it should leave this room." I paused to let that sink in. "But I'm in love with your niece, and that's the only reason I'd even consider letting you make reparations for your corrupt nephew."

"That's good to hear. I'm sure Raven would appreciate it if she ever found out, which she won't."

I shook my head, dread filling every inch of me. "Obligation, sir."

"Pardon?"

"Legal obligation is the reason it will leave this room."

He stopped the rocking of his chair. "You're only legally obligated if the firm wants to press charges. Since I own this company and I plan to make restitution, no one outside the family will have reason to press charges."

"That would be true if Nick hadn't pulled the same scam at his previous employer."

Archie's head fell into his hands as he took in the magnitude of his nephew's predicament. I took out the copies of the loan documents he'd drawn up with his former company. The one that had just hired my consulting services, which is how I'd come across Nick's embezzlement scheme. The amounts were much smaller, but theft is theft, and Nick was in deep trouble. "I'll pay that back, too," Archie offered.

"Do you really believe that would help him, Archie? He's committed two felonies. If you bail him out, he may commit more."

"Don't tell me you know what's best for MY nephew!" Archie stood again and grabbed up the phone in a vicious swipe. "I helped raise that boy. If you're going to tattle on him, you better be sure you let that company know that I'll pay them back. I'll have my lawyer over there so fast they'll beat you to the door. But not before I throw your ungrateful ass out of this building. You are no longer welcome here, and you are no longer welcome in my family." He barked orders into the phone, but I was already grabbing my briefcase to leave. This went far worse than I expected, and I hadn't expected much.

Security intercepted me when I was ten feet from his office. They made a grand show of flanking me until I'd gotten into my car and driven away. How would I explain all this to Raven? She adored her uncle. If he hated me now, could she forgive me in time to make it up to her tonight before I got on the plane?

* * *

Gravel and dust soared when Raven's car skidded to a halt in my driveway. The door flew open and her voice preceded her body out of the car. "How could you not tell me?"

The accusation sounded so unfamiliar coming from her. Hard, serious, indicting. I hated the sound. "I get how you might be upset, Raven."

"Might be upset?" Her usually loving brown eyes blazed. I felt like stepping to the side in case they shot flames into their path. "Two hours ago you're in my arms, kissing me, acting like nothing is wrong. All the while you're planning to drop this bombshell on my family."

"I needed to notify the CEO first and would have asked permission to tell you had he not had me escorted out."

She started pacing from the front of her car to the back, her door still open, keys left in the ignition. That annoying dinging sound kept time with her steps. "He asked you to leave after you hung a member of my family out to dry."

"You make it sound like I deliberately intended to cause Nick harm."

"Are you saying that you haven't yet turned over your evidence to the police?" Her pacing stopped so she could turn a hopeful look in my direction. .

"I didn't have a choice," I replied, chasing the remnant of hope from her expression. My newest client made that decision for me. They weren't satisfied with Archie's offer to pay back what Nick had stolen. I couldn't blame them, despite my hope that they'd let greed rule their decision.

"There are always options. If you'd come to me as my girlfriend, we could have evaluated the choices together."

"Raven!" I was shocked as much by my admonishing tone as her belief that any other outcome could have been reached. "I'm actually disturbed that you believe there are other choices here. I knew you'd be upset, but I can't let my personal life shape my ethics. Your cousin stole from your company, your silent investors, and, in turn, your entire family. How can you think I did the wrong thing?"

"Because you're putting my cousin in prison when he should be in a rehab program dealing with his gambling problem. I grew up with him. I love him. I can't stand by and watch him go to prison. Had we discussed this, had you respected me enough to include me in this, we could have come to a reasonable solution."

I chose to ignore her deliberate jibe about not respecting her. No need to add more fuel to this incendiary situation. "I'm shocked that you believe I should have kept this under wraps just because of our relationship."

"He needs help. He needs our compassion. My lover should have recognized that, but you let your usual professional detachment rule your decisions. You made this a black and white situation like almost everything else in your life."

What did that mean? My muscles clenched with worry that I'd been misreading her reactions in our relationship all along. I tried to stay calm, but I felt my defenses rising. "I agree that he needs help. Every criminal needs help, but most have to suffer some repercussions first. Unfortunately, it's up to the courts to decide that before we can get him the help he needs for his problem."

"We?" she spat harshly. "That's laughable. Without regard for my feelings, for my family's feelings—my family, who have been so good to you and mean so much to me—you strip us of a member and hand him over to the police. You honestly think you'll be helping us to resolve this?"

"I don't know what your uncle showed you." I reached for her arm to stop her from pacing, but she twisted away just as my fingertips grazed her skin. The rejection stung almost as much as her words. How could she think I could keep this from the company that had hired me? I had an obligation to them, and she wanted me to ignore it? "But if you saw all the evidence and you're still feeling this way, then you're not the kind of person I thought you were."

She went still and looked me dead in the eye. "Neither are you, and it breaks my heart."

My hand curled into a fist and slammed against my leg, praying that this was just a bad nightmare. When the stinging pain shot through my leg and into my hip, I knew this was real. I was standing in front of my very angry and hurt girlfriend, who now seemed to consider me a heartless bitch. "No matter what your uncle is telling you, I had no choice." I tried for rational, but her agitated state didn't guarantee that anything was getting through. "Well, I guess

I did. Either I turn him in, or if someone found out that I didn't, I could be jailed for withholding evidence. Is that what you want, Raven? Should I have sacrificed my freedom for the man who methodically stole over 300 grand?"

"I don't believe it would have come to that, Joslyn. We could have handled everything and gotten Nick the help he needs. My family knows what you mean to me. They'd protect you through this." She raked a shaking hand through the long layers of her stylish shag. Before I'd always marveled at how the layers would slide back perfectly into place. Now the anger with which she performed the gesture made me queasy. "Instead, you shunned their acceptance, ignored my feelings, and left us with no choices. That's not the kind of woman that cares for me so much that she'd sacrifice some guilt to her conscience to allow me some peace."

The queasiness ratcheted up to full blown nausea. "I'm sorry you feel that way, but you're out of your mind if you think I'd sacrifice what we have to assuage some guilt."

She pivoted swiftly, eyes clashing with mine as breath pumped rapidly through her frame. "I must be out of my mind to think that we had something special, something that I thought might last."

"It will last, Raven," I said definitively, feeling my throat tighten in response to the finality in her tone. "You're upset right now, but when things settle down, we'll be able to move past this together." When she had enough time to step back from the hurt, she'd see I had no choice. She was too smart not to.

"I wish I could believe you," Raven whispered hoarsely, tears threatening. She stared a moment longer. Her expression had moved beyond hurt and into betrayed. Those tears sprang free and splashed onto her deathly pale cheeks. When her voice sounded again, it was heavy with anguish. "Goodbye, Joslyn." She slid into the car and got it moving as quickly as any race car driver.

And there goes the love of my life because I'm too damn good at my job. I could now officially count myself among the masses of people who hated me.

Chapter 26

*W*hat's so great about falling in love anyway? People dedicated songs, poems, plays, sonnets, entire novels to the subject. Apparently, everyone on the planet falls in love at some point, and often, more than once. For thirty-seven years, I'd been shielded from what I'd considered an unnecessary emotion. Now that I'd experienced it for the first time, I considered it a devastatingly cruel sentiment that must be avoided at all costs.

Truly, why would anyone willingly fall in love when a broken heart feels worse than any pain someone can endure and still remain living? Not that I was living. Working on autopilot more like. I'd even stayed an extra week on the out of town consultation just so I wouldn't have to return to Seattle and be reminded of all the places Raven and I had gone together.

No more excuses, though. I had several client consultations in town this week. I could put them off, but then I'd have more time to let the pain in my chest metastasize. If I could only get back to being numb. I could handle numb just so I wouldn't have to feel like bursting into tears every time I turned my head and saw Raven. While we were together, I had no idea she had that many clones out there. She was everywhere until I got to within reaching distance. Then, of course, she'd dematerialize and someone who looked absolutely nothing like her stood before me instead.

Why weren't there more songs about how much a broken heart destroys every part of you? I'd even take a simple haiku at this point. Anything that would have served as a sufficient warning. I contemplated writing one myself as I turned the corner in my driveway and spotted my dad sitting on the porch swing. I didn't expect he'd still be here. He usually cleared out from his dog sitting duties before I got home. Yet here he sat patiently, expectantly, almost as if he knew I didn't want to be alone.

"Hi, sweetie, how was your trip?" He headed to the trunk to grab my suitcase before I'd even gotten my door closed.

"Fine, Dad. It's good to see you." I hoped my voice didn't sound as dead to him as it did to me.

He dropped the suitcase and embraced me tightly. His spicy scent gave me the first calm I'd felt in weeks. He'd done this for me my whole life, and I felt the tears start again. I willed them back because I never cried. Well, not until the heap of emotions I'd experienced since knowing Raven. Now, I was a puddle waiting to splash on everyone.

"Everything go okay with the dogs?" I floundered for any subject that didn't involve another flash flood of tears.

"They're all doing great, Jos. Damn good company. I'm thinking about getting one myself."

"You should. We could head over to the shelter this

weekend and pick one out for you." Not only would it be fun to pick out another dog, it would provide a much needed distraction on my now free weekend.

"I'll think about it, hon." He curled his arm around my waist, picked up my suitcase, and brought me inside.

The dogs went ballistic having me home. It felt good to let go and feel their love. This was the kind of love I could handle. "I missed them."

"They missed you. I might have cheated and let them sleep with me a couple of nights." He looked suitably guilty.

"Great, breaking that habit won't be hard at all," I groaned. He didn't have trouble sleeping. Having five dogs shifting about on the bed wouldn't bother him at all. Even in the calm of my hotel room for the past three weeks, I'd barely slept. No chance I would try sleeping with the dogs in the room.

"What happened, Jos?" My gaze snapped up at his question. His sad and serious expression reminded me of the day he told me that my mom wouldn't be living with us anymore. At the time, the sadness that I saw in him kept me from asking any questions. It was the only relief I could give him. This look gave me the same feeling of doom.

"My trip went well, Dad. I stayed an extra week because they wanted me to train the sales staff on corporate clients."

"I'm talking about Raven, sweetie."

"Did something happen to her?" Panic pushed past every morsel of the sadness and pain I'd felt in the past few weeks.

"No." Dad put a stop to my sure seizure. "What happened with Raven? Why aren't you together anymore?"

"How...?"

"At the barbeque before you left, we got to talking about how much she liked your house and what she hoped to do with her property. So, I thought I'd draw up some rough plans for her. I gave her a call thinking she might be a little lonely with you out of town and asked her to lunch to show her the plans."

Great, kill me know. No matter how rough a draft, he would have poured a lot of time into designing a house for her. "I'm sorry you went to all that trouble. I should have said something."

"It was no trouble, Jos."

"Yes, it was and very thoughtful of you. What did she tell you?" I didn't want to know, but my dad had to sit through it, so I owed it to him.

"She thanked me for the effort. She couldn't have been more gracious, but she said that you weren't seeing each other anymore." He bent down to catch my gaze. "When I asked her what happened, she told me that I should talk to you."

"There's nothing to talk about." Or at least according to Raven there wasn't.

"Was it your choice?"

"No! I still want her in my life, but it's not up to me. I didn't measure up."

"Surely, that's not it. Maybe if you tried to see her. She sounded as sad as you do right now."

"Unfortunately, it doesn't seem to be just the two of us making decisions about our relationship."

"When have you ever met an obstacle that you can't get around?" he encouraged. "You were the most resilient kid I'd ever seen. I thought having your mom leave would devastate you, but you worked through it. You became my inspiration for getting on with living my life."

Tears sprang forth without regret this time. I hugged him fiercely, hoping the constriction would be enough to stem the tears. "I love you, Dad."

"I love you, too, hon, and I know you love her. Don't let whatever came between you become insurmountable. You can scale anything."

"I appreciate your encouragement. I really do."

"Think about it at least? Seeing you in love made me happier than I've ever been in my life aside from your birth. Even more than watching you graduate from all three colleges. I wished for the kind of love that Raven gave you from the first moment you announced you were going out on a date." And, did he ever panic. To this day, I believe he assigned Marco as my tail that night. They both denied it and still do, but you don't just run into your brother at the burger joint across town and again at the movie theater farthest from the burger place specifically to avoid seeing him.

"Don't worry about me. I got all that resiliency from you. Things will work out."

"I hope so," he murmured.

Of course, he didn't realize that I meant that things would go back to normal for me in a few weeks when I got over the stabbing pain in my chest cavity. If it took a few months, what did it matter? A few years might get to me, but my biggest fear was that it might take a few decades to get over her.

* * *

"This is meeting 220 this week, isn't it, Jos?" Zina looked up from her desk as I passed through the reception slash conference room slash Zina's office area until Marco or my dad had a spare weekend to help me enclose part of it for her.

I'd finally found a use for the extra building on my property. And settled on a color, or lack there of since Marco convinced me to shingle it and stain the cedar instead of painting. He was right, as usual, not that I told him. Converting the building into an office allowed Zina and me a place to work together. Our previous arrangement, working out of separate homes, wasn't conducive to getting her trained. Dad and I renovated the interior, but we still needed to work on getting Zina an office with walls and a door.

"219," I shot back with a smile.

"Really, girl, you're going to work yourself to exhaustion like that herding dog of yours."

"We could all learn a thing or two about work from Eras, my dear. Did you work up a cheat sheet for me on this one?" I patted my briefcase, asking for the one page summary of the corporate officers, financial ratios, org chart and other miscellaneous data that I might need in an initial consultation.

"Right here." She thrust a page into my hand. "I was hoping to talk some sense into you about all these potential clients. Even with my brilliant self around to triple your efficiency, I'm not good enough to make this kind of work load manageable."

"It's not that much work." The lie rolled off so easily I should be worried.

"Something is seriously wrong with you. We will talk about it tomorrow morning." She made a mark on her desktop calendar.

"Tomorrow's Saturday; you're not working," I ordered in my best boss voice. "On Monday morning, we'll be talking about the training schedule for next week. I'd like you to start shadowing me at the next client. Some of these clients are going to be yours."

"You'll do anything to avoid thinking about your personal life."

"Not open for discussion." I could hear my voice throw up a roadblock.

"You don't talk about it, you don't think about it, and you certainly don't live it."

"Zina," I started to protest, not knowing how to deal with it. The worst thing I could do right now was burst into the tears that threatened to fall. Other than telling her I was seeing Raven when we started working together and admitting that we were no longer together on one of the phone calls while I was out of town, we'd not had a discussion like this.

"You did the right thing, Jos. What else could you do?" While it was nice having Zina on my side, she hadn't liked Nick much more than Robert. She wasn't exactly unbiased. "You should call her again. Raven's practical. At some point, she'll realize that her cousin is an ass and doesn't deserve her loyalty."

"Please, let's not get into this." It wouldn't do any good to start thinking about Raven right before a client consult. Nor would it do any good to start thinking about Raven period. The situation had been impossible, and her reaction was completely understandable. I'd hoped that with a few days to think it over, she'd see things from my point of view. But after the sixth unreturned phone call while I was out of town, I'd given up hope that she'd forgive my actions and give us another chance.

"I haven't known you very long, Jos, but I know deliriously happy when I see it. You two are good together. Give her a call. If she needs more time, give her more time, because deliriously happy is worth it."

"I'll keep that in mind. I'm going to be late." I rushed out of the office before the tightening in my throat and stinging in my eyes turned to the crashing, unstoppable waterfall I expected.

A cool blast of unnecessary A/C hit me when I walked into my potential client's extravagant lobby. Recommendation number one: lose the A/C when it's seventy-three degrees outside. While I waited at the reception desk for my dinner meeting attendees, I took in all the ornate decorations, panels, and art work in an area where people spend less than one minute each visit. As much as I wanted to keep busy, I didn't think I could deal with the carelessness I saw everywhere in this organization.

I'd listen to them over dinner then send a summary report and rejection next week.

The elevator doors opened, and the cool air got sucked out of the room. Chase McCovey strode toward me with a slick smile and an expensive suit. "Hello, Joslyn. It's good to see you." He pulled me into a hug that trapped the use of my arms. Before I knew what was happening, he dragged me away from the reception desk. "I wanted to say that I'm sorry how things ended between us. I wish I could take back that night. I've missed you."

"Chase?" I finally managed to unlock my tongue.

"You look really hot. What have you been doing with yourself? At least you didn't get into a bon-bon eating contest of depression after we broke up."

I ignored everything but what I wanted to know. "What are you doing here?"

"Huh? Oh, I switched companies last month and recommended they hire you to turn them around." He grabbed my hands and squeezed as if trying to get my attention. "That's okay, isn't it, Jos? I mean I know we're not a couple anymore, but you're the best at what you do. I want to make a good impression here, and I know you're just the person to help me do that. C'mon, babe, for old time's sake? Maybe I can even convince you to give me another chance."

Surprise twisted my tongue again. Had I really ever felt like this man could make me happy? Knowing how amazing a relationship filled with love, respect, generosity, and caring was, I didn't know how I could have kidded myself that anything less would be satisfying. He was a nice enough guy, had consideration for others, wasn't too selfish, but he wasn't Raven. No one was. Crap, I'm doomed. "I don't think this is a good idea, Chase. I'm glad to see you, and I wasn't happy how we left things either, but we don't belong together. I'm not sure I should be working with your company."

"C'mon, Jos, please, I need to look good in front of my new boss. Listen to the guys at dinner. It's an interesting case for you. I know you'll be convinced after you hear these guys out." He looked over at the elevators. "Here they are now. Let me introduce you."

Four men came off the elevator toward me. All tall, all wearing dark suits that cost more than the riding mower making tracks over the football field of a lawn out back. Their pasty white skin told me that they took summers in Seattle for granted; that alone was a crime. I hadn't thought this would work out before; now, I was utterly convinced. The least I could do, however, was go to dinner with them.

Or so I thought.

When we pulled into a familiar parking lot, one wish ran through my mind while stepping out of their massive SUV. *Please, let us be eating at the Mexican place across the street.* No such luck. Chase hustled ahead and opened the door of Amalia's restaurant, and I wanted to scream and run in the other direction. I couldn't do this. I didn't have the strength to sit through a meal in this place that means so much to Raven and came to mean so much to me. Those glorious people would be in there, and I feared I wouldn't be able to stop the tears. Well, at least I wouldn't have to worry about needing to decline this business. They wouldn't want me after seeing me cry through every course.

Since I had no choice, I walked inside and willed myself not to let the familiar smells and sights wreak havoc on my barely controlled resolve.

Chapter 27

"*Buona sera, amici. Sei per la cena?*" Giovanni greeted.

Before he could translate his question of six for dinner, I stepped around Chase. "*Buona sera, Giovanni. Come stai?*"

"Joslyn!" He threw his arms around me and dragged me to him. Several mouths in my party dropped as I dove into the hug. His scent a welcome respite to the heartache I'd been feeling. Raven must not have told him to hate me, not that I expected she would. I just assumed that he'd feel some resentment toward me for hurting her.

"Guess they know each other," Chase muttered.

"These are some potential clients of mine, Giovanni. I haven't had a chance to tell them what a mouthwatering treat they are in for yet."

"My Amalia is like no other." He gestured for everyone

to follow him to an open table, keeping an arm around me the whole time. "You sit, please. I take Joslyn back to see Amalia. I will return her soon."

Chase beamed and his colleagues chuckled as Giovanni shuffled me with him. We went through the kitchen doors, and the staff made way so he could get to Amalia quickly. She was doing a mean whirling dervish impression, so adept at keeping that kitchen running.

"*Amore mio, ho una sorpresa,*" he announced that he had a surprise for Amalia. I only hoped she'd find me the good kind of surprise.

"My goodness, Joslyn. You have finally come to see us. We missed you." Her arms wrapped around me, and I realized how much I missed these hugs. Amalia's hugs were even better than her cooking.

"I've missed you both, too."

"Why have you not come for visit? It has been so long."

"I didn't think you'd want to see me for a while." I couldn't meet their eyes.

"That is crazy. We adore you. We would like you to be with our Raven, yes, but we want to see you even if you are not."

"To talk you into being with Raven again," Giovanni inserted.

"It's not up to me," I reported dejectedly.

"But Raven is so sad." Amalia's already wrinkled forehead crinkled further. "Your eyes, you are sad, too."

"You talk to her," Giovanni ordered kindly.

"I've tried."

"You try again." Giovanni must subscribe to the try-and-try-again course of action.

"I'll try again," I agreed just so we could drop the subject of Raven. Talking about her was even worse than thinking about her.

"You are here for meeting?" Giovanni finally took the hint and let up on the pressure.

"A consultation over dinner. Thank you for accommodating us."

"Any special your friends want, they can have. I will bring ravioli to the table for *antipasti*. On the house."

"Thank you, Giovanni. Amalia, it was so good to see you both."

"You come see us again soon," Amalia insisted with another quick hug.

"I definitely will." I jumped at my chance to escape, and I did it without looking at the sink where Raven and I had stood side by side doing dishes, talking, laughing, and finding excuses to brush arms or hands together. I couldn't start thinking about that, or I'd never make it through the meal.

Back at the table, the men had torn into the bread and olive oil. They were talking loudly and with great camaraderie. Chase tried to keep up, but it was clear he was the newbie in the group. "You had that man twisted around your finger. Are you related or something?" the CEO asked.

I chuckled but didn't bother to answer. It would be a dream to be related to them. "I've been told that you can order off the menu if you like. Any Italian dish you can think of Amalia can make."

"Wow, you must have some pull," the CFO commented.

Giovanni materialized and took everyone's order, complimenting each for their choices and suggesting wine or side dishes to go along with their orders. He was really good at the soft sell. My clients could learn a thing or two from him.

During dinner, the CEO and COO took turns going through what they felt was lacking in the company, why they'd decided to bring in a turnaround specialist, and what they hoped they could get out of it. If I hadn't already decided not to take the job, everything they said convinced me more. That they wouldn't take responsibility for any troubles in the company told me that they could never accept any recommendations for improvement.

Only coffee remained to get through then I'd be free to head back to the office and send them a rejection letter. Usually, I'd sum up what I felt were the high level problems and recommend another firm. I wasn't sure I'd bother to do even that with this obnoxious client.

"Isn't that a friend of yours, babe?" Chase asked from right beside me. He'd been inching closer and closer all dinner, trying to convince his new boss that we had the kind of relationship that would influence my decision.

I shot a glare at him and noticed that his arm rested on the back of my chair. He was really pushing it. His possessiveness perturbed me enough that I didn't register what he'd asked. As I turned my head back to the others, I caught sight of a swoosh of black hair on a trim body that I could recognize in any crowd. "Raven?"

She froze, stopping what looked like an escape then spun back to face us. "I didn't want to interrupt." The bite in her tone sounded like she wasn't over the anger. Nearly a month and she hadn't relented. Nearly a month and she looked as gorgeous as ever. Nearly a month and seeing her made my heart crack against my ribcage to the point of sure damage.

"Hi, Raven. Good to see you again." Chase stood and offered his hand.

Raven's icy stare flicked down to his hand before she gripped it briefly. "Nice to see you, too, Chase. If you'll excuse me, I need to find Giovanni."

"Wait, Raven," I started, watching in disbelief as she ignored my request and practically ran to the kitchen. I turned to my tablemates. They were so wrapped up in their little land of egocentric denial that they didn't notice anything odd. I decided to seize this opportunity. "Well, gentleman, I've enjoyed meeting with you all. Your company poses some significant challenges, and I'd like to get a jump start on the initial analysis right away. If you'll excuse me, I'm going to head into the kitchen to thank my friends again. I'll let you know about my decision by next week Friday, if that's acceptable."

"You don't need a ride back, babe?" Chase tried for casual, but I could see confusion and dejection swim through his expression.

"It's not too far, and the walk will do me good after a big dinner." I said goodbye to each of the executives and let Chase hug me because I had to store up all my fight for pleading with Raven.

The kitchen doors swung open just as I reached them. Giovanni yelped, set down the tray of dinner plates, and scooted me into the kitchen. What I saw there made me want to twirl back around and hit the exit. Double time. Amalia had her arms around Raven, stroking her back soothingly as Raven buried her face in the older woman's hair.

I swallowed the jawbreaker-sized lump in my throat at the sight and resisted punching my thigh to distract me from the dread in my stomach. This wasn't going to work. She would never forgive me. "Raven," my mouth spoke before my mind could get a grip on it.

She jerked in Amalia's arms, but Amalia used her leverage to turn Raven around. Giovanni shoved me toward them. I got close enough to be assaulted by Raven's familiar scent. "They didn't tell me I'd be interrupting a dinner date," she managed in a rough voice.

I shot a questioning look at Giovanni, who gave me a shrug and left to retrieve the dinner plates he'd abandoned. Amalia smiled sweetly and pulled Raven toward the back office. She looked over her shoulder at me and nodded for me to follow. Once inside, she disappeared as convincingly as if she were a character in the Harry Potter series.

"Giovanni called and asked me over." She could barely

meet my gaze. "I'm sorry, I didn't mean to break into your meeting."

"We were done, and I'm glad to see you." Understatement of the year.

"I wanted to ... I called your ... he told me you'd come in for dinner with some clients. I didn't realize that Chase would be here or that you'd gotten back together with him."

"I haven't!" I denied so vehemently that she jolted in place. "I'm not with Chase, not at all. I had no idea he'd be in this meeting until I showed up for the client consult. He changed companies and recommended me, but I didn't know a thing about it."

"Oh, okay." Her frown told me she didn't entirely believe me or she was confused about something else.

"Did you come over here to see me? It wasn't just Giovanni trying to put us in the same room together?"

"I wanted to talk to you, but when I called your house, I found out you were still out of town. I didn't know you were back until he called. I wanted the chance to apologize for my behavior. For my lack of faith in you. For my unfair judgment of you. I believed my uncles who lied to me." She glanced away in shame. "Even if they didn't tell me about Nick embezzling from another company, I shouldn't have doubted you. You did everything you should have done, whether it was just my family's company or another company, and I didn't stand by you. I don't know if you'll ever forgive me, but I wanted the chance to apologize."

I felt a glorious absence where the pain in my chest used to be, replaced now by a pounding that increased tenfold and made me a little breathless. "Are you under the impression that I'm angry with you?" I moved closer so that barely a breath stood between us.

"I was awful to you, Joslyn. I said horrible things to you. I'm so sorry. I understand not wanting to return my call and for avoiding me by not going to the last basketball game."

What? "First, I never knew you called."

She jumped in before I could say anything else. "Someone answered your home phone, told me you were still out of town on business, and took my message to call back when you returned."

My mind flickered through the possible explanations and landed on the most likely. "That was probably Antonio. He likes to keep my dad company on dog-sitting duties. He's eighty-five and has a hard time remembering to hang up the phone much less relay a message. I should have wondered why I only had two messages on my machine when I got home."

"So, you not getting back to me wasn't on purpose?" she asked tentatively.

"Of course not."

"But you didn't go to the Storm game."

"Stuart wanted to impress his new girlfriend and her kids, so Trin and I gave up our tickets. We sat behind the bench instead."

Her whole face opened up. "You weren't avoiding me?"

"Raven, I'm not angry with you. Your uncles helped raise you. Of course you're going to believe them. Your loyalty is one of your best traits. I completely understand." I reached out to draw my fingertips down her cheek. "I wish that I'd never taken on that client. If I could have let your uncles handle it, I would have because of how much you mean to me. But I had no choice, and I'm so sorry it hurt your family and tore us apart."

"You forgive me?" Her eyes grew wide.

"I knew you'd be upset. I should have told you when I saw you at work before my meeting." I kicked myself daily for that stupid move. "I shouldn't have let anything stop me from sharing that with you right then. That was my mistake."

Her head shook in disbelief. "You're not upset? You're

not thinking I have no right to be asking for your forgiveness? You're not going to storm out of here and never let me see you again?"

My heart's gaping wounds miraculously sealed up and the muscle pumped joyfully for the first time in a month. "Why is it that the person who'd never once been in love, the person who had to be convinced that love even existed is the one in this duo who fully grasps just how amazing our love is?"

A truncated sob leapt from her mouth as tears shimmered in her eyes. She tilted toward me, and I slid my arms around her. Her body shook while the tears kept coming. I'd learned that it was best just to let her cry. She didn't do this often, but when she tried to stop it, the hiccups began and it would be another ten minutes before she composed herself. "You still love me?"

"Raven," I sighed contentedly, pulling back so that she'd look into my eyes. "What do you see?"

A sharp intake of breath told me she recognized what I hoped she would. "Smoky grey," she breathed in wonder.

"You know what that means. I love you. Madly, head over heels, hopelessly, but most of all, desperately."

"I like desperately." She smiled, eyes still shiny with tears. "Desperately suits us both. I love you, Joslyn, desperately. And I love when your eyes are smoky grey. I'm going to do everything I can to keep them that color."

"I know how we can start," I told her suggestively.

"Home, right now," she ordered. "I don't care if you're not done with your meeting. I have a month to make up for."

"I'm done, and I need a ride."

"That's the second best thing I've heard all day."

"And the first?" She shot a surprised look at me before I teased, "Wait, let me guess. Could it have something to do with how much I love you?"

"No more lost time, sweetheart. I love you. Come home with me."

Chapter 28

The only thing making this evening worthwhile was knowing that I'd have Raven to myself in less than an hour. Back together for three weeks, and I couldn't get enough of her. I wasn't sure I'd ever get enough of her.

Tanya's snarky comments also helped. I was really starting to like Dax's wife. She had a unique outlook on the Paul family dynamic and had no problem sharing it with me. Basically, she knew that Raven and Dax were different from their cousins and, because of that, all of the cousin's wives took great pleasure in making her feel like she didn't belong. Thanks to my actions, she was now considered an angel compared to me. When she realized this, she sidled up next to me and stayed nearby all night.

At least, it was only Raven's immediate family tonight. Even though both Archie and Nathan found out that I'd asked the district attorney, a former client of mine, to be lenient with Nick, they'd only managed a grudging thank you by phone. The DA had struck a great deal with Nick, two year suspended sentence and sixty days in rehab. Of course, he'd struck an even better deal with me for my pro bono consultation with the county prosecutor's office. When it came time for re-election, he'd be sitting pretty.

I never anticipated that any of the Pauls would find out, but Raven had some connection down at the courthouse through Elise. The day she found out, I didn't think she'd let me out of her arms for a minute. What I loved was that she'd already taken me back before she found out that I'd tried to help Nick. Even her father seemed impressed by how I'd handled the dreadful situation.

"Ten minutes, *tesora*, and you're mine," Raven whispered as she passed through from the kitchen after clearing the coffee cups. I sucked in my breath when she flashed me a private sexy grin. She shuttered it closed before facing her parents again.

"I absolutely love not being in your shoes anymore," Tanya joked from beside me. "I would have encouraged Raven to bring someone home to meet the family years ago if I'd known they'd redirect the heat from me."

"Glad I could help," I said with a snicker.

"Let me return the favor." She cleared her throat and looked pointedly at her husband. "It's getting late, honey. We should get home and relieve the sitter."

"Do we have to?" Dax whined from his settled position on the couch. "Can't we leave them with her?"

"You're the one that wanted boys, Dax. I'm the only one other than your mom who's managed to bring a darling little girl into the family."

"She's an angel," Anna spoke up about Ray.

"That was all me. Dax is responsible for the boys. Speaking of which, let's go spend some time with them. We should all get out of Raven and Joslyn's hair before they make us do the dishes."

Everyone laughed and took the hint to leave thanks to Tanya's set up. Now I really, really liked her. We walked them out to their cars and watched them drive off. One more family night down. That I hadn't been shot on sight meant that at least her immediate family understood my predicament with reporting Nick.

"I love you." Raven breathed a sigh into my ear. Her arms wrapped around me from behind as we watched her brother and parents drive away. "I'm in love with the bravest person in the world."

"Really? I didn't realize you knew any lion tamers."

"You're definitely a lion tamer, sweetheart."

"That should come in handy when I get you inside, lovely." I spun around and pushed her into motion toward the house. I'd waited too long for this tonight. "We're ignoring the dishes."

"Dishes? What dishes?" She flashed that surely illegal grin and led the way to the bedroom.

Lying back on her bed, Raven's naked body covering mine, her mouth and hands creating new erogenous zones, I realized I'd found my heart after years of disregard. She wasn't just the best lover I'd ever had, the only real lover I'd ever had, she was now the sole possessor of my heart. I no longer had ownership rights.

"God, you're sexy, Jos. I'll never get enough of you," she moaned against my neck.

"That suits me just fine, lovely," I managed when her mouth latched onto my breast. "You're beautiful, and sexy, and talented, and—"

"And I'm going to make you come first tonight," she growled her promise. "I'll go as long as you need."

In response to her generous offer, I shut down the anxiety before it could take hold. Instead, I slid my feet back toward my hips and spread my knees, offering myself completely. "I love that about you."

She took in a long breath, looking down at my trusting

posture and absorbing my words. "And I love when you give yourself to me."

She kissed a path down my abdomen, swirling her fingers and palms along my overheated skin. Each touch sent me higher and higher until I could barely stand the barrage of sensations. Her mouth nipped and kissed and licked, bringing responding moans from me. If I let her, I had no doubt she'd do this for hours without complaint or bother. The realization nearly brought about my release.

I reached under her arms and pulled her up, stifling her protest with a kiss. "Together, Raven. Please make this happen," I pleaded, needing to have her with me when I fell.

"Together, Joslyn. I want to be inside you when you come. We'll make this happen, together." She leaned down to capture my mouth and moved a hand to where our hips connected. I let go of one of her breasts and mimicked her movement. Feeling her wetness revved up my own arousal. I stroked her creases, trying to give her the teasing that she liked, but I knew her ministrations were already taking me close to the edge.

Her fingers circled my clit with the expertise only she possessed then dipped lower, poised to penetrate. She pulled her mouth from me to watch my eyes as she slid two fingers inside. My head tilted back against the pillow with the sensation of being filled by her. She thrust against me with her hips, her fingers reaching parts of me that had never been touched by anyone but her.

"You feel so good inside me," I whispered, tipping up to draw her mouth back to mine.

Recognizing the once elusive orgasm was within reach, I swirled her entrance then plunged into her without pause. My mouth swallowed her responding cry. I thrust back at her, curling my fingers to find that spot that made her crazy. But before I reached it, I let her ride me to the precipice first, pulling back from her kiss so she could see my eyes.

"I'm there," I breathed out before the explosion wracked my body.

"Come, Jos," she commanded, holding on for another second before I thrust into her once more. "I'm right with you!" Her body convulsed against mine as we went through the violent shudders of our simultaneous orgasms. I'd never felt anything more intense.

"That was amazing," I admitted when my body had stopped its seemingly endless pulsations. I felt a strong surge of emotions that no longer frightened nor seemed so foreign anymore. "That's never happened to me before. Thank you."

A soft smile touched her talented mouth. "I love you, Joslyn. I loved sharing that with you." When her head dropped into the crook of my neck, she slid her hands underneath me and wrapped her legs around mine. As she settled contentedly against me, I realized that I hoped this was only one of many things we'd get to share in the future.

Epilogue

Seven months later

T he construction crew was in the process of packing
it in for the day when I stepped outside. In two
minutes there'd be no sign of them in Raven's driveway.
No dillydallying on Saturday evenings, not for Marco's
crew. They get one day off a week when they had a project
and liked to get a head start on it most weekends.

Waving to several of them on their way out, I made my
way over to the barn to take one last look at the newly
completed tack room before Raven got here. Hearing
voices coming from inside bothered me. No one was
supposed to be in that room, not until we'd presented it to
her as a birthday gift.

"...all my idea," Marco was saying as I went through
the barn doors.

"Now, wait a minute, son," my dad's voice interjected.

"Can't I trust you two for a—" My scolding died on my lips when I walked through the door and saw Raven standing between them.

"You're here!" we both exclaimed and rushed into each other's arms. Her kiss set my body on fire, lips caressing mine like she couldn't get enough. Not our usual hello kiss, but only because I'd been out of town on a consultation. I didn't even care that we had an audience. Not when I'd waited five days for this.

"Whew!" Marco muttered. "Wish my wife would greet me that way when I got home."

We broke apart laughing at Marco's comment. A hint of pink crested Raven's cheeks, impossibly adding more beauty to her gorgeous face. "I didn't see your car when I drove up, and these guys didn't say a word about you being here already." She jerked her thumbs at the smug looking men.

"I parked around back. I was using your shower after I'd spent all afternoon with Dad and Marco on this room. A room that we agreed would be unveiled at the party later, am I right, guys?"

The wide-eyed innocent look from Dad didn't fool me one bit. "Raven wondered why the horses were out in the corral and started over here before Marco and I could stop her."

"I really can't leave you two alone, can I?"

"She loves it, sweetie, don't you, Raven?"

"I love it," she agreed. "Thank you so much. I've been dying to move all the saddles and equipment out of the garage. It turned out even better than I imagined. How did you find the time to build this with everything else you're working on out here?"

"Dad and Marco wanted to get you something special for your birthday, lovely." I gripped her waist, knowing how overwhelming this would be for her. "They could have put this up with their eyes closed; add my help, and they could have done it with one hand tied behind their backs."

"You're all too good to me. Thank you, this is the best present I've ever been given." Tears shimmered in her eyes. Dad and Marco beamed before they pulled her into a group hug.

"Since the reveal is done, you guys need to get home and get dressed for Raven's party tonight. You've got less than an hour," I ordered, staring at their work clothes.

"Not everyone can pull off construction chic," Marco taunted.

"Not even you, Marco. Get outta here."

"You just think you're so pretty all dressed up with your gorgeous girlfriend at your side." He pressed a finger to my sternum, forcing me to look down before he flicked it up at my chin. He and Dad broke into laughter while I simmered. He always got me with that move.

"Out! Now!" I repeated. Both men kissed Raven's cheeks and took off for their trucks.

"You do look beautiful, *tesora.*" Raven stepped around me, checking out my new dress. I didn't feel at all uncomfortable in the dress or with her scrutiny. Something about loving Raven made everything comfortable for me. "I've missed you. I didn't think I'd make it last night when you told me you had to stay an extra day."

"Tell me about it. I missed you, too." I grabbed her on the second pass around and pulled her to me for another kiss. This one private and filled with promises to make up for the past five-day absence. When I tore myself away, we were both breathing heavily. "You should come with a warning label, lovely."

"What would it say?" She nibbled her way down my neck and my already racing heartbeat kicked into overdrive.

"May cause extreme temperature fluctuations, dizziness, heart palpitations, uncontrollable lust, and enduring love."

"Should I get that tattooed on me someplace?" Raven rose up from her slow torture of my neck and fluttered her eyebrows at me.

"Don't you dare tarnish your flawless skin!" I knew she was kidding, but just the idea pushed me into panic mode. "Besides, I already know the warning by heart. No one else is going to get the opportunity to learn the side effects to loving you."

"No one else, eh?" She beamed and stopped my teasing reply with a searing kiss. When she left my mouth quivering in her wake, she glanced around the room once more. "I can't believe your dad and brother did this for me. I know they consider it a gift, but can you talk to them about letting me pay for the materials at least?"

"No." She'd just have to let her independent nature suffer with this one.

"Jos!"

"Rave!" I came back. "They love you. This is something they can give you, let them."

She sighed, and I knew I'd convinced her. "Well, I love them, too. They treat me like I'm part of your family."

"As they should. Although, it is kind of bugging me that your new house is going to be built better than mine, done faster than mine, and will look more beautiful than mine. They so like you better than me."

Where I expected a brilliant smile at my tease, I saw a flicker of uncertainty flood her striking brown eyes. She glanced away and took a shaky breath before returning her gaze. "Maybe they were hoping like I was that, once it's done, you'd consider sharing it with me."

My heartbeat, which had been galloping already, surged into a race worthy clip at her suggestion. "Share?"

She tightened her grip on my waist to pull me closer. "I know we haven't officially talked about it, but we keep making plans into the future. At this point, I can't imagine my life without you in it. I don't want to rush you, Jos, so I thought I'd give you a few months to think about living together."

A smile crept across my face. I couldn't have stopped it

if I'd tried. "That sounds like you want me around for a while. A long while."

"I love you so much. I miss you every time I go even a day without seeing you." Her earnest expression nearly did me in. "I don't want to scare you off. If you're not ready, nothing has to change."

"Well, I'm finding it nearly impossible to sleep when you're not in my bed," I admitted, taking her hands in mine. "I wanted tonight to be special. Show you this room we built, tell you that Marco was ahead of schedule, let you know that you'll be in your new house, which we all love more than our own houses now, in a few months."

"And I've pushed by asking you to move in with me?" Unfamiliar insecurity tightened her expression.

"No," I rushed to reassure her. "You've surprised me, but you haven't pushed."

"A good surprise?"

"Very good," I confirmed, but it did nothing to stop my racing heart. She wanted me to move in with her. I'd hoped but hadn't expected it. "You're the one that's supposed to be surprised on her birthday. Can I give you your present before people start showing up for your party?"

"You've been hinting all week long. I can't wait to see what you came up with."

"It's out in the car. C'mon, lovely." I yanked on her hand to lead her out of the barn and past her soon-to-be demolished house. The new one was being constructed just beyond it.

Once we took the corner around her new house, she stopped dead in her tracks and gasped loudly. "Oh my God! Joslyn! What did you do?" She stared from me to the car I'd parked in a spot hidden from view of the driveway. Her dream car, a classic 1957 Ford Thunderbird in tuxedo black. Raven black.

"Happy birthday, Raven."

"Sweetheart! How? Where? This is too much."

"It's why I was gone the extra day. It belonged to a former client of mine who recently had to move into an assisted living facility. I'd asked him to let me know if he ever wanted to sell the car, and when he called, I thought of you." I waited until she refocused on me. "I know you think it's extravagant, but it needs a lot of work. He was the original owner and hasn't done any restoration. He wanted it to go somewhere it would be loved, so I got it for a steal. Even if it weren't your dream car, I would have snapped it up. Since you're driving my Vette around any chance you get, I'll trade you for your own."

She looked at me with conflicting emotions in her eyes. "Oh, Jos, it's too much."

"You only have a birthday once every four years, lovely." I brought up the fact that she was a leap year baby and only celebrated when the day came around. "Let's call it your stored up for the next three years' birthday gifts." When she didn't immediately relent, I reached desperately for something that might persuade her. "Okay, your next three birthdays and throw in Christmas this year, too?"

"Christmas is ten months away."

"Yes, but you'll be around to remind me, won't you?"

Her eyes glowed at the deliberate promise of my gift. "I love you so much. Forget the tack room and the car, you're the best gift I've ever been given."

"Thank you, Raven. I love you, too. Now, go check out your classic." I shoved her toward the gleaming black vehicle.

She circled it three times before she dared open the driver side door. When she floated into the seat, her blissful smile turned into pure joy. As expected, she reached out with her hands and touched every surface.

Nervousness almost kept me from joining her in the passenger seat. Only one place left to explore, and while I now had some assurances, I still had some apprehension. She popped open the glove compartment and spotted the black velvet box sitting on top of the owner's manual. Her head snapped up to lock eyes. "What's this?"

"The car's your birthday present. This," I reached in and grabbed the small jewelry box, holding it in the palm of my now trembling hand. "Well, I never imagined I'd fall in love. Now, I can't imagine my life without the joy of being in love with you. You're definitely not rushing by asking me to move in." I managed to open the box with my shaking hands. "This is your engagement present. You're the love of my life, and I don't want to spend it without you. Will you marry me, Raven?"

Her mouth parted and her eyes flicked from the ring to my face and back. "Oh, Jos!" Rapid breaths kept her from speaking above a whisper. "I love you. I love you. I love you," she repeated until she crushed herself against me and kissed me deeply.

I had a vague awareness that the ring was smashed in between us, but I didn't feel anything other than her soft lips and searching tongue and the thunder of her heart against mine. After a few minutes, she leaned back to stare at the now closed jewelry box. I opened it to reveal the two carat, round cut amethyst set onto a platinum band.

"Amethyst," she breathed, fingering the gemstone.

"I noticed you only wear your birthstone." She nodded absently, still focused on the ring. "You actually have to accept this present. If you want to, that is," I added, heart pounding with the possibility that she might not. We hadn't specifically discussed marriage, but every serious talk we had included plans for a limitless future.

Her eyes snapped back to mine and widened. "Wait!" She reached back and opened her door, springing out of the car and sprinting toward her house.

I was so shocked by her sudden disappearance that I didn't immediately react. It took a few moments before I eased out of the car, baffled and panic stricken. The last thing you wanted to have happen when you propose is for the object of your proposal to flee the area.

Raven came hurtling back around the side of the new house, pulling up a step away from me. Her face was split wide with a smile, glee making her body tremble.

"Raven?" I questioned because I couldn't stand the silence anymore.

She produced a larger jewelry box of her own. Inside were two platinum wedding bands with intricate patterns inset in each. "I picked these out a month ago and have been hoping for the chance to ask you to spend your life with me. I didn't know if it would ever come because of what you've told me about your other relationships."

I placed my hands on her shoulders and leaned my forehead against hers. "You changed my nature, Raven. I want to spend every moment reveling in this new life you've made possible for me." I barely had to move before my lips pressed against hers for a kiss. "So, I guess that's a yes?"

"You're showing me smoky grey again. It looks like that's a yes for both of us."

"We're going to have to build a bigger garage now."

She pressed me back against the car. "Thank God I asked you to marry me before Marco's crew left."

"I asked you!" I interjected with conviction.

"You're just marrying me for my car."

"I'm marrying you to get my own car back. Don't think I didn't notice that my Vette was gone when I got home today."

"It'll be our car now, sweetheart." She tipped her head with a wicked smile and winked. I loved when she did that.

I took the amethyst ring out of the box and slipped it onto her finger. A perfect fit for a perfect mate. "Let's save your rings for the day we move into your new house. We can start our new life together then."

"My, you're good at planning things." She kissed me again, tearing the breath from my lungs with her passion.

Maybe it was fate or luck or paid dues, or maybe it was the fact that I'd never known this kind of joy in thirty-seven years. Something intervened to allow me to find such a remarkable partner and to fall so deeply. Whatever the reason, those solitary years would ensure that I'd never take this elation for granted.

Don't miss the next in Lynn
Galli's Virginia friends
series, BLESSED TWICE,
due out in October 2008.

There were about a million other things I could be doing right now. Playing tennis, reading a mystery, calling my son at summer camp, working out, rollerblading, base jumping, banging my head against a low hanging beam, and all would be more pleasant than my sixth first date. Cripes, my friend Caroline knew a lot of women. A lot of women who were so wrong for me.

This one's name was Polly, and she worked as a court clerk. After her third cup of coffee—I'd learned never to commit to anything that would last several courses—I could sum up Polly's personality with one word: drama. Or, issues. Or, get me the hell out of here, please!

"And then I was, like, 'what do you think you're doing with my stuff, bitch?' I mean, like, can you believe she was walking out on me and expected to take the one and only gift she, like, bought me in the entire two months we'd been together? I was, like, 'you didn't even pay me rent for two months, you're not taking my Maroon 5 with you.'" Her pretty green eyes stared expectantly at me, asking me to agree.

Still stuck on some of the other intimate details she'd shared prior to talking about a massive blowout over a piece of plastic that costs twelve dollars, I merely nodded then shook my head. I didn't know if she expected me to say, "Yes, I completely agree, even though you're a loon," or, "No, that's just awful, especially since there's no way you could ever replace such a priceless item. Unless, of course, you walked into any music store, or better yet, downloaded the songs so no one can walk out of your life with her love and your CDs."

"You're so easy to talk to," she jabbered on after I'd

apparently given the appropriate response. "I can't believe Caroline never introduced us before. I'm having so much fun." Yeah, because drinking coffee is a riot a minute. "So, like, what's your story?"

Well, I've never used the word "like" as a verbal pause, I've never moved in with someone after one night together, and I've never considered a CD worth the effort of an argument. Oh, and I now deem dating a soul draining experience.

"Briony?"

I looked up and felt my stomach plunge as swiftly as if I'd been pushed out of an airplane. M was standing by my table, iced coffee in hand on her way out. She was in casual clothes, showing a hint of midriff, envious calves, and just the barest promise of cleavage. "Hey there, M." I hoped she caught the relief in my tone. Wow, she looked good. No makeup today and her hair was a little more chaotically styled but wickedly attractive. Beyond, actually, more like hot. Yes, hot suited her just fine. Why wasn't I on a date with her? Oh, crap, Polly. "This is Polly. Polly, my friend and colleague, M."

Polly must have picked up on my blatant interest in M, because the next thing I knew, she was telling her, "We'd invite you to join us, but we're on a date."

I didn't know who cringed more, me at the idea that this could really be counted as a date or M at the rude dismissal. My eyes snapped up to hers in apology. Before I realized what I was doing, I made the ASL sign for "help." It was one of a few words I'd learned for when my son spent time with his hearing impaired best friend. This was the first time I'd ever used it, and I never imagined I'd be using it for evil instead of good.

"Pardon the intrusion, but I thought we said two o'clock?" M asked me with the perfect amount of urgency and innocence. "I grabbed a table up front and left all the lecture notes and business plans there. It's a few hours of work, and I've got plans tonight, but if you need a little more time, I understand."

"Is it two o'clock already?" I brought my wrist up to check the time on my watch. "Gosh, I'm sorry, Polly. I didn't mention this work thing because I never thought we'd still be here. You just made the time fly by." Two hours that I'll never, ever get back.

She beamed at my compliment but disappointment showed through. "Caroline said you were a workaholic, but we can work on that." She reached for a hug, which I made lightening quick, and finally, the sixth date on my path through hell was over. Polly banged through the coffeehouse doors with all the drama she'd expressed during her diatribe.

"Thank you for saving me."

"Think nothing of it." M said it like she believed it when I was considering erecting a life-sized shrine and lighting a candle every night. Her eyes darted to the door as her customary introversion returned. "Nice running into you, Briony. Enjoy the rest of your weekend."

"Tell me about those plans you mentioned," I blurted before she could disappear.

"I lied," she admitted with a shy smile. "I figured if I didn't give a limited window of time, she might think she could get us to postpone our work meeting."

Strangely, I felt more relief hearing this than getting out of my date with Polly. "So, you've got nothing going?" She shook her head. I smiled and stepped toward her. "You do now."

I couldn't think of a better way to spend my Saturday than with this beautiful, enticing woman. Not really a date, but far better than anything my friends could set up for me.

ALSO BY LYNN GALLI

WASTED HEART

Austy Nunziata has spent two years pining for her married best friend and about the same amount of time berating herself for it. In fact, she's so adept at trying to stamp out her feelings that she could probably write a How-To guide on the subject. One, move 3,000 miles away from your best friend. Two, get a time-consuming job so you don't have time to think about your best friend. Three, hang out with new friends who aren't anywhere as enchanting as your best friend. Four, get involved with a striking woman who is smart, sexy, caring and, most importantly, available, unlike your best friend. Five, hope the new love interest doesn't find out about your pathetic best friend obsession before you have time to replace it with actual life-altering love.

Even following her own step-by-step process, Austy may not be able to redirect all of her misguided feelings. Becoming involved with Elise Bridie helps her realize how pointless her pining has been. But when Elise suspects that she harbors feelings for someone else, will their new found love survive the unrequited infatuation of Austy's fantasies?

Learn more at:
www.outskirtspress.com/<u>lynngalli</u>

ALSO BY LYNN GALLI

IMAGINING REALITY

Considered Charlottesville's most eligible lesbian, Jessie Ximena has recently grown tired of that status and has stopped dating entirely. She'd rather focus on the important things in life like her family, her friends, and her job. There will always be plenty of time for relationships when she feels like jumping back into the fray. If she finds someone to hold her interest, that is.

Lauren Aleric has been searching for Ms. Right since she began dating, but no one has yet filled the role. Her friends think that she's too much of a romantic mush to settle. She wishes she could be more like her good friend Jessie, who seems perfectly happy dating casually. But mostly, she wishes she could be like her best friend, Austy, who's just found her forever love.

Imagining Reality is the story of these two friends and how they discover that what they're both looking for isn't as far apart as they might think.

Learn more at:
www.outskirtspress.com/imaginingreality

Breinigsville, PA USA
21 December 2009
229629BV00001B/35/A